Chapter 1

Riley

No one wanted to come with me!

It's 9:30 pm on a Friday and I'm watching Fifty Shades of 'fucked up' on my own - what a blast!. I'd been waiting for what had seemed like forever to go and see it, so yep; on my own and horny as fuck right now.

Leaving the cinema, the air was warmish and the Friday night picture goers were moving swiftly along the sidewalk, perhaps hurrying home to make out because of what they had witnessed during the two hours of the film; I wouldn't blame them at all!!

Unconsciously, my mind started to wonder as I walked with the crowds. Reliving the sexual scenes from the movie, putting myself in that woman's place and not really paying too much attention to what was happening in front of me – if I had, I wouldn't have walked into the guy in front.

'Shit - I'm so sorry I wasn't looking where I was going' blasted from my mouth as the guy began to turn around.

He was tall, well it's not hard to be when compared to my somewhat diminutive five/five in height, he must have been at least six feet. I moved my eyes upwards and began to recite my apology when BAM!!! those eyes.... holy shit, those eyes!

They were like jet black diamonds surrounded by a gorgeous face, dark brown hair which was just the right of mmmm in length.

'I'm so-so sorry I wasn't looking where I was going. My lame apology spurted from my mouth.

There was no response, just a look. But fuck, a look that could unlock many a woman's knickers I bet.

The guy's eyebrows raised as though he could hear my thoughts. Instantly I prayed 'Fuck - please no! don't embarrass yourself even more. Just wish for the ground to open up and swallow you.

As I moved to the side to get away, his hand brushed against mine, sending the most electrifying feeling throughout my entire body. My breath caught as I again looked into his eyes. For a split second, I sensed more then saw the briefest of reactions as his eyes locked with mine. Did he feel something as well?

The moment passed, and I was walking away. I just couldn't help it, I looked back to check him out. He was still standing there but this time he was staring at me, right at me. I smiled as I turned to continue to walk. Why did I just smile at a stranger who I'd just bumped into – weird!

When I got home, I was still going over the feeling I'd had when I touched that guy's hand. God, he had the

Too Good to be True

Patricia Jelbert

Dedicated to
My Mum's generation of romance readers
Welcome to the 21st century

MAPLE
PUBLISHERS

Too Good to be True

Author: Patricia Jelbert

Copyright © Patricia Jelbert (2022)

The right of Patricia Jelbert to be identified as author of this work has been asserted by the author in accordance with section 77 and 78 of the Copyright, Designs and Patents Act 1988.

First Published in 2022

ISBN 978-1-915164-18-6 (Paperback)
      978-1-915164-17-9 (Ebook)

Published by:
      Maple Publishers
      1 Brunel Way,
      Slough,
      SL1 1FQ, UK
      www.maplepublishers.com

Book Layout by:
      White Magic Studios
      www.whitemagicstudios.co.uk

most amazing eyes I had ever seen. The kind of eyes you could get lost in for a long long time. I started to wonder what else he has going on as I pretty much didn't take notice of anything else other than his eyes.. and oh his mouth, yes that mouth what it would be to taste him, kiss him. God, I was a dog in heat. Why??

The night was filled with images of this guy in the compromising positions from the film I had watched. Unconsciously, my hands began trailing my body andmy thoughts drifted while my imagination ran riot imagining him doing things to me I'd only dreamed of and had yet todiscover.

My hands worked their magic over my body, with those eyes that were constantly there in front of me. I was good at experimenting with my body and pretty much knew what I liked, even though I wasn't a fully-fledged woman yet. No man had ever got me into bed even though I'd had a few that had tried and tried hard.

My hands moved to my wetness that was over the top for any woman, but holy smoke it was a delicious feeling as I touched myself thinking it was him. My fingers moved slowly over my clit igniting that feeling deep inside that was all too normal for me. I was so worked up from the film, that it didn't take long before I was beginning to feel that build up right there, where I was enticing with my imagination and my fingers.

It was not long after my orgasm of imagination that as I lay on my bed, I started to think it was about time I experienced my sexuality for real and not just with my fingers and a few toys.

Saturdays are for lay-ins but not when you have friends like mine. We tend to meet for lunch and fill our bellies ready for the night ahead, so this weekend was like pretty much the rest.

Still reeling from the amazing orgasm I had given myself the night before based on some random guy's eyes was like I had reached new heights. Nothing prior to that climax had come close, but to be honest, I hadn't done pretty much anything with anyone before; all theory, no practice, as they say.

Quite strange for a woman in her early twenties Well I guess I'm strange like that. Always have been, and I guess I always will.

Growing up as an only child, I kind of grew to like my own company even though I never got downtime for long. My parents had me taking self-defence classes, dance classes and many other activities that kept me busy so, I guess they didn't have to spend too much time with me. Sad, I know, but I never knew anything different.

My parents died eighteen months ago in a car accident, and I was left kind of all alone apart from my few friends and the Estate Executors who had this hold over me until I was old enough to financially go it alone. My parents were from 'old money' and had set up a Trust Fund for me which would materialise when I turned twenty-five. According to them, by that age, I should be responsible enough to decide what my goals were and the trust funding would help me. My apartment was taken care of through the fund and as I loved the outside and photography was a passion of mine, my goal was to start my own business and be self-sufficient from everyone by the age of thirty because right now, I was under what I could only perceive, as a lock and key.

6pm came, and I knew I had to get my arse into gear and get ready as the girls were due round at about 8'ish. Our drinking sessions were a laugh, and we kind of all had the same wavelength of how we planned the night to go. Robin and Emma were my long-standing friends. If you could call them that, I met them in college and we'd become firm friends from there. They were a great support for me when my parents died and we have hung out pretty much every weekend since.

Standing in front of my mirror, I was away in space looking at the black lace underwear I had chosen for the night. I drifted off again to those eyes from last night and felt myself again touching my breasts and running my hand down my side to the front of the panties,

Something startled me and I quickly returned to the here and now - bloody neighbours and their bloody noise I thought.

Dress on and looking good!

I was curvy in all the right places, thanks to the wonderful genes of my parents, my skin had a natural tan, fantastic boobs, just the right side of sexy, and, well thanks to my lucky stars my bum was the epitome of perfection. To me my bum did look good in this dress, but then again, my bum looked great in everything.

I had been growing my hair out for the last four years as my mum had said that having shorter hair wouldn't get me a boyfriend and that I was a beautiful girl and long hair was the done thing. She was my mum so I grew it for her. My hair curled and hung down my back like a goddess and I'm sure my mum would have been pleased.

Now ready and with one final check out in the mirror I headed out of the bedroom and down the stairs just as, like clockwork, the doorbell goes and I hear giggling from the other side. As I opened the door my two girlfriends fell into my apartment in a very good mood.

'Looking hot ladies,' I exclaimed. 'Feeling hot,' was Robin's reply.

She was always eager for a good compliment and was happy to take what she could. Robin was five seven and had a body of perfection in my eyes with her long blonde hair, natural of course and a smile that would send men wild. Emma was a tad taller than me and again a beautiful girl with really long legs, dark brown hair and milky white skin, I was what I called the curvy one. However, we complimented each other well.

The prosecco was flowing, no flutes in my place so wine glasses it was. The music was blaring, getting us into the mood for the night ahead.

Three bottles down and I was feeling the buzz. So glad I had eaten loads that afternoon 'cause I would have been blind drunk and in my bed by now.

Snacking is allowed while drinking, right?

We pulled up outside the club and began to make our way in. This was the kinda place that 'rich folk' would go and act like wankers because they could. The

VIP areas are like gold dust to hire, so normal folk would have to cram to the bar and hope for the best.

The music was pumping, and we were feeling the vibes. Robin shouted over the musical din which was fun because she had a big gob.

'Drinks, shots on me' - Oh shit! I thought this was gonna get messy.

Two rounds of shots later and the earlier buzz was now all over my body. I was feeling bloody fantastic and ready to take on the world.

The dance floor was alive with bodies and a mixed smell of aftershave, perfume and sweat wafted across the room. The music was so good that my body just wanted to stay there and be one with it. We were having a great time and then some arsehole put his hands on my waist. I froze and grabbed the hands, spun around and said 'no thanks'.

He was drunk, reeked of alcohol and didn't take the hint so I had to use a hand restraint I had learnt from my defence classes to re-enforce the 'piss off' advice – he rapidly took a step back and left.

'What a dick move' Emma shouted,

My eyebrows raised at her words, 'dick, lol'

'I'm off for the loo, anyone, wanna go?'. I yelled at them both.

Neither wanted to go so I went looking for the ladies toilets alone. Moving out of the heaving mass of bodies I passed the VIP area, and that's when I saw him,

'Shit, shit, shit!', too loud I thought as I stared at him for longer than I should have but thankfully he didn't notice me and I swiftly moved on in my search for sanctuary in the ladies room.

Minutes later I was holding onto the sink staring at myself in the mirror for what seemed like forever, my mind racing at the thought of seeing him again. OMG!

Bad thoughts erupted in my brain and that oh so familiar certain moist feeling downstairs started to well up in me like a bitch in heat.

Jesus, why was it that at times like this my vagina grew a mind of its own and was beyond my control.

I left the ladies staggering a little due to the combination of stupidly high heels and alcohol; not a good mixture. I wasn't paying attention to the route back to the dancefloor when I was stopped by two feet, two legs in trousers, a crisp white shirt and then.....OMG, *HIM!*

His eyes were still like the diamonds I remembered when I saw him for the first time outside the cinema but this time and even through my alcohol-infused state I felt a shiver go down my spine as I drank in the beauty of his face.

I moved to the side to go past him and he moved as well, I moved back and he did the same, not taking his eyes off me.

'Excuse me please', I managed to whisper, fluttering my eyelashes in a sort of cute girlish way. With my heels, I was taller now and he did not seem to tower over me as he did at our first meeting, but I still had to look up.

He lowered his mouth to my ear to be heard above the pounding throb of the music. 'You have to stop bumping into me,' he said in a low and sultry voice that made the hairs on my forearms sit up and take notice. I felt his warm breath on my neck as he spoke and thought he'd leaned into me a little too much in spite of the music.

The feeling of his breath on my skin was enough to melt ice and I lost my step as I again tried to sidestep him and began to fall, tripping over my own bloody feet. He caught me in his arms and held me there for what seemed like an eternity.

His hands on my body was like electricity, that same feeling when we had touched the night before.

My breath caught as I looked up at him and his eyes were wide like saucers staring at me - drilling deep into my brain.

'Thanks' I muttered, feeling small and helpless.

He leant down again to my ear this time he whispered slowly and seductively, 'I want to taste you.'

'What?' was my only reply. Did I hear him right?

'I want to taste you, all of you,' he said with a smile that made my vagina scream at me.

'I'm not sleeping with you, I'm sorry, but I'm not that kind of girl,' I responded and swiftly moved to the side and began to walk away. Oh, I knew he was watching me so I sashayed a little more than normal emphasising my beautiful bum. Before I turned the corner I looked back at him, smiled and finger waved as I disappeared.

Fuck!, my heart was racing like a Formula One car on full throttle.

What had just happened? I wasn't sure but there was a great feeling welling up inside my body, and my vagina was alive and ready to get involved.

When I finally found the girls on the dancefloor, they were dancing like queens with a couple of guys so I wandered off to the bar and ordered another round of shots. Probably not a good idea, but what the hell – I was buzzing and still a little wet with what had just happened.

Trying to coax my girlfriends over for shots was easier than I thought. Both downed the smooth liquid in one and returned to the dance floor where the guys were waiting for them with their tongues hanging out. I was on my own again. Sod this! dance floor here I come.

The music had got to the stage of classic grind music. Bodies were gyrating all over the place and I felt lost in the rhythms. This was my type of music, letting the body decide where it wants to go and how it wants to move.

I smelt him a split second before he touched me. It was a distinct smell from all the others around me. Then I felt his hands move to my hips.

I stiffened for a moment as this wasn't the kind of action I liked. He pulled in closer to me and leaned down to whisper.

'I still need to taste you'.

His words were like velvet and pretty much the most fucking awesome turn on that I had ever experienced. But again, I'd not had much experience in this department at all but he didn't know that.

'I told you I'm not sleeping with you '. Then I went to move.

He tightened his grip on my waist and pulled me in against his broad chest. The music was slow, but I don't remember what was playing. All I knew was that I was in the moment. Wrapping his arms around me and nuzzling my hair as we moved together, I could feel his erection pushing into me while we danced. I eased myself back onto him acknowledging his desires a little bit more.

What was I doing? Was this dangerous? I could feel him begin to turn me around.

'Shit', the words left my mouth in time because as he finished turning me his lips met mine. Soft and delicious just like I had imagined in my dream.

I parted my lips so he could have full access to my mouth. When our tongues met there an instant spark flew through me. My hands went to his neck to deepen the kiss more and we became lost in the moment. After what seemed an age we both pulled back panting, gasping for air. His eyes had darkened with desire. He kissed me again, this time slowly holding my face in his hands. As he pulled back, he held onto my lower lip with the gentlest of touches from his teeth.

A moan left my lips before I even knew it, his eyes flashed at me, and he raised his eyebrows and kissed me again. His hands were roaming my body from the small of my back to the side of my thigh and then to the finish line of my dress, I felt his hand reaching inside and under my dress to my hot bare flesh.

My hands made their way to his chest and gently pushed him away from me as I was getting so close to ripping off his clothes there and then.

He looked at me, then grabbed my hand and guided me away from the dance floor and passed the VIP area to one of the darkened corridors at the back of the building.

He kissed me again harder this time and pushed me against the wall for support. His hungry hands quickly explored my body like he was mapping every inch of me and committing it to memory. He reached down and slowly pulled my dress up until I felt his hands between my legs. I parted them; I don't know why, but this was a feeling I did not want to end before it had to. While he was kissing me his hands swept across the front of my panties causing me to catch my breath, He moved them aside and then there was the feeling that I always craved. His fingers slowly entered me and began exploring my clit like he knew what I wanted, did he?

Fuck!, he growled when he felt my wetness. Probing me in the most intimate way and in a way I had never been explored before he circled my clit faster and then slipped a finger inside me. I moaned as it was a feeling so great, my body responding to each touch by him. He began to speed up, and I could feel myself beginning to reach my potential. He moved his kissing to my neck and thrust another finger inside me, I was quickly getting to where I knew I wanted to go, stuck in the tidal waves of emotional feelings and surrendering to his magic fingers. I was coming hard and fast.

'I'm coming,' I whimpered.

He smiled before he moved in with the kissing again and took me over the edge. I had the hardest orgasm I had had in a while and I loved it. Bracing myself with my hands on his shoulders.

After I came down from the most amazing feeling and he again whispered:

'I want to taste you, all of you'. I was quivering and would have happily had him taste me all night long.

I steadied myself and felt flushed, he was looking at me with want in his eyes and I fucking loved it. I couldn't believe what had happened and needed to get out of this before it went too far.

As I walked away, he called out to me, 'What's your name?'

'Riley' I said

'Just Riley ', he replied

'Yeah, just Riley.'

'You?' I asked with a smile on my face

'Jacob,' he responded with a slight grin in return.

'Just Jacob,' I teased a little with my voice.

'Yeah,' he laughed, 'Just Jacob.'

'What about letting me taste you,' he said as I was almost out of the corridor.

'If you find me again, then maybe you will,'

He looked at me and laughed.

'Is that a challenge?' he questioned.

'Maybe' I replied, 'or maybe just fate, who knows.' I left him there.

Now I needed to get home before I got myself into danger because I was happy to go there right this minute.

The girls were ready, We made our way home and I was feeling fucking fabulous and kinda slutty too, knowing that I've just been finger fucked by a total bloody gorgeous stranger.

Chapter 2

Jacob

Walking on the sidewalk amongst the crowds was annoying as per usual for a Friday night. I was following at the speed of everyone else when my phone buzzed in my pocket. I stopped still to answer it and felt a thud from behind. I was ready to verbally abuse whoever walked into me and then I saw her. Her eyes were beautiful like stars shining on a dark night. She was so apologetic saying 'sorry' twice. I had no words and just stared at her. Fuck! She was beautiful, her lips were sensuous and I don't know why but I reached out my hand to touch her and there was an electric feeling pulsating through me. I looked at her and still, no words left my mouth. She was perfect, natural and I wasn't sure what she looked like under her coat as it was loose but I wanted to see more.

After what was considered too long she walked to the side of me and walked away, I was still staring at her when she turned around and she smiled at me, 'Christ', that smile made my cock twinge.

Then she was gone.

I didn't even get her name or get the fucking chance to speak to her. Why not Jacob? Come on man you're supposed to be good at this shit.

She was on my mind for the remainder of the evening and into the night. I began imagining the feeling of her soft skin under me, on top of me and many other places. Shit, this was gonna be a hard long night.

After releasing myself for the third time in less than twelve hours plus another shower to cool me down I called my friend Harry to organise a training session to release the tension.

Harry was always getting the better of me when we trained but today I was gonna put him on his arse for sure. The session went great. Harry went down three times and I was free from the tension of that street meeting with the girl and I felt great.

Saturday night was lads' night and I needed a drink for sure. The club was busy and we were having a good time up in the VIP Area; why because we could and money was no object to my friends or me. The drinks were flowing and the music was just on point. The dance floor was full of women moving their bodies to the music and clearly having fun while doing it. Then there she was!

I wasn't sure it was her for a moment as I only saw her face in the shadows of the nightclub. But when she moved into the light of the stage it was her. She was fucking beautiful like a goddess, her body was something I wanted to devour and my cock twitched in time with my thoughts. I needed to see her again and find out if there was a connection from last night's brief encounter in the street when she walked into me.

She was on the dance floor having a good time and I couldn't stop myself from staring at her and her friends. Her body was moving to the music and beginning to make my cock swell by just watching her. Some guy moved in and touched her.

Anger coursed through me, my body stiffened and my fists were ready. I wanted to storm over to her and protect her but I didn't.

I just watched as she took care of some guy using with what I can only describe as a defensive move and he quickly backed off. Shit me, that was a hot move, I couldn't help but continue to just look at her. I wanted to approach her then but wasn't sure how I would go about it, considering she may subject me to the same rebuff as the hapless sod a minute ago and I would probably end up on my arse.

For the first time, I felt vulnerable, why?

I watched as she moved through the dance floor closer to where we were sitting so I sat next to my mate and joined the conversation he was having and tried to look like I was engrossed. I saw her approach us and then she looked at me. I could see her from the corner of my eye but did not make contact. She stared for longer than maybe she should have which really made me want to turn to look at her then she left towards the ladies.

I figured my chance to catch her again was as she left the ladies. I waited for her for what seemed like an age and when she did reappear she wasn't walking right and moved in a way that so many of us do when the booze gets the upper hand.

I stood there and waited for her to come to me. When she stopped and raised her head, her face and expression was all I needed to see.

She moved to the side, I moved to the side, she moved back and so did I. The childish things we do just to get a reaction.

'Excuse me please,' she said

Fluttering her eyelashes at me she seemed a little taller than at first glance which no doubt was due to her three-inch heels. Fuck I love these sort of shoes women wear especially when they're over my shoulder as I pound into them.

'You have to stop bumping into me' I said in my best voice, lowering my mouth to within an inch or so of her ear so she could hear me over the music, even though the music wasn't that loud where we were standing. I just wanted to be near her to touch her.

I'm sure the feeling of my breath on her skin was enough to make her quiver. She then lost her step and began to fall, tripping over her own feet. I caught her in my arms and held her there for what seemed like an eternity. Thank god for those stupid shoes.

My hands on her body were like electricity, that same feeling I had when I'd touched her hand the night before.

Her breath caught and I looked down into her eyes. I could sense she was wild with lust.

'Thanks' she muttered quietly and meekly.

I leant down again to her ear this time I whispered slowly and seductively, 'I want to taste you,' I don't know why I said it but it just came out. 'What?' was her only reply

'I want to taste you, all of you,' I said with a smile that made my cock ignite a fire deep inside.

'I'm not sleeping with you, I'm sorry but I'm not that kind of girl,' she responded, her eyes wide and noncommittal. She swiftly moved to the side and began to walk away.

I knew she knew I was watching her so she sashayed a little more emphasising her beautiful arse, Before she turned the corner she looked my way, smiled and finger waved as she disappeared.

What the fuck just happened, I mulled in my head, she was teasing me with her words and her body. God, I wanted her so bad.

I couldn't let this be the only moment with her and I wanted to taste her so fucking bad, like a drug that you can't get enough of.

Walking back to my friends I downed the rest of my drink and felt the need to hunt her down as I wasn't finished with her.

The dance floor was heaving now and I began to scan the dancefloor to find her as I knew she was gonna be there with the friends she came with. I spotted her and she seemed lost in a world of her own totally immersed in the moment of the music. I knew that this was the time as I set my sights on her.

I moved in behind her and felt her stiffen as my hands touched her hips. She went to move but stopped and in a split second, I felt her relax at my touch.

'I still need to taste you,' I whispered into her ear.

Her body continued to move with ease to the music and I moved closer into her, as my hands grabbed her more tightly and I pulled her close to my groin. I felt her pushing herself back onto me and I felt the blood rushing to my cock as it hardened more thanever.

God, I wanted to fuck her right there in front of everyone this was torture beyond anything.

I wanted her to face me and began to turn her around,

'Shit', the words left her mouth just as I finished turning her and my lips met hers, soft and delicious. She parted her lips so I could have full access to her mouth and I accepted her invitation without a moment's pause. As I eased my tongue into her warm mouth I could hear a soft moan escape her lips.

After what seemed like an eternity our lips parted with both of us gasping for air. I kissed her again, but this time slowly holding her face in my hands. I wanted to possess her and didn't know how to. As I pulled back, I held on to her lower lip with the gentlest of touches between my teeth, her face still cupped in my trembling hands.

My eyes widened and my eyebrows raised as I looked down at her beautiful face then I kissed her again as if it was the most natural thing in the world to do. This time I couldn't help it. My hands moved slowly down and began roaming her body from the small of her back to the side of her thigh and then to the bottom of her dress. I wanted to feel her, to touch her there.

She put her hands on my chest and pushed me gently away from her, the look on her face was telling me differently. Hold me, touch me, feel me!

I looked down at her then. I don't know why but I grabbed her hand and took her away from the dance floor and passed the VIP area to one of the corridors. It was darker than the others due to the lights, not all working which was perfect for what I had planned, well at least part of it.

My mouth was hungry for hers and I kissed her again, harder this time and pushed her against the wall for support. I needed her, I needed to explore her, I needed to touch her.

I reached down to the bottom of her dress and pulled it up slightly and then swiftly moved my hands to her sex. I felt her leg's part to give me easy access which was a sign that she wanted this as much as me.

I moved her panties to the side and then gently rubbed my fingers over her clit. She was wet, wet for me and I fucking loved it!

'Fuck,' I growled.

I began to explore her like I had a new toy to play with. I circled her clit faster and then slipped a finger inside her. She moaned as I felt the pleasure rise through her body as it began to stiffen under my touch. I guessed she loved it as much as I did.

Her chest pressed into me and I could feel her hardened nipples beneath the thin material of her dress. I could feel her body changing as I continued to bring her towards the moment of magic and the quickening of her breath on my neck. She was close to coming. I made her like this. I was gonna make her come so hard. I could hear she was close and I started to feather kiss down her neck tasting her sweat as I inserted another finger inside her.

'Shit'she moaned.

Wow, she was wet, so wet and tight. Oh, how I wished my cock was there instead of my fingers.

'I'm coming' she whimpered close to my ear.

I smiled before I moved in with the kissing again and took her over the edge feeling her orgasm, hard and long. Her rigid body arched with pleasure as I continued to work with my fingers. She put her hands on my shoulders for support. God, I could have slipped my cock inside her, I wanted her.

After a short while, she relaxed against me. I noticed the thin layer of sweat had formed across her upper lip and her eyes were closed.

I leant down and told her again. 'I want to taste you, all of you'

She steadied herself and looked a little flushed, well I did just finger fuck her right there.

I wanted her and I knew she wanted it by the look in her eyes.

After her breathing had returned to something near normal she took a step back, did that sort of 'wiggle' that women do to straighten her dress and headed back down the corridor.

As she walked away called out to her, 'What's your name?'

'Riley' She said cheekily 'Just Riley?' I replied 'Yeah, just Riley.'

'You?' she asked with a smile on her face

'Jacob,' I responded with a smile in return, I couldn't help but smile at her. 'Just Jacob?' she said playfully.

'Yeah,' I laughed, 'Just Jacob.'

'What about letting me taste you,' I said as she was almost out of the corridor. 'If you find me again then maybe you will.'

'Is that a challenge?'

'Maybe' she replied and curved the corner and left me there.

'Fuck! - what the fuck just happened, that was mind-blowing and I've never done that before.

I returned to the VIP area desperate to catch a glimpse of her with her friends but no matter how much my eyes scanned the crowd I couldn't find her. I ordered a drink and each time I raised the glass to my lips I could smell her on my fingers and taste her scent. I wanted more! so much more!

The game was on, and I was going to get her, even if it was the last thing I did.

Chapter 3

Riley

Sunday morning hangovers are the worst, especially after shots so yep it was pretty much the same every weekend. Why can't I be good and stick to wine and not mix my drinks?

Sitting up in bed rubbing my head, the fog that was there then decided right at that moment go and bang!! - I remembered the things that went on last night.

OH MY FUCKING GOD !!!

What did I do? What the fuck! shit, oh no. I'm a slut! No, I didn't screw him but oh my god I wanted to. For the first time ever I wanted to go home with that man and let him fuck my brains out.

Flashbacks came to me all morning while having my first coffee through to my third. It was sending shivers down me just reliving it.

'Jacob' I said aloud 'Just Jacob' and smiled. He was a specimen like no other and well I knew that I wouldn't see him again. It was one of those first and last encounters. I could accept that, but my body wanted more of him, so much more.

The day rolled into the night and I pretty much did nothing. The girls were messaging me about the guy from last night and I was hesitant to tell them at first but when I did, they were just screaming and texting me, it made me laugh and blush at the same time.

Who was this guy and why did I let him do those things to me?

Monday morning at work was as per usual boring but I liked what I was doing. Rowthorne Inc was a reasonable company in advertising and digital media.

Nothing like the larger companies in the city, which were massive; the largest of them all being The Sylvesters; They kinda run the city's media and in many other places as well. The amount of money they must have made in a short time was

bewildering, but hey this was a great company too and I was pretty much left to my own devices most of the time.

I was good at my job and never brought attention to myself even though the men would always stare as I walked by. The joys of a woman's figure I guess, but I must be honest, I did little to discourage the looks.

Half way through the morning a news intranet message popped up onto my screen informing us all that there would be a takeover of the company. The Board of Directors had accepted a merger which would take place within weeks. This could be an exciting opportunity for our company and maybe staff too – bigger ladder, more to climb and very much more to gain.

The announcement went on to say our jobs were secure and that the CEO's of the both companies would be along later this week to check out our setup and meet the staff.

Wow, this could be interesting as I had been thinking about my future and career prospects over the last month or so. I had already decided that I had to get rid of the boredom and set my sights higher while embracing new challenges.

Lunch time came around and Greta from accounts popped her head into my area, 'You wanna come for some lunch, Riley?'

'Yes please,' I was starving for the first time I could remember.

We went to a cafe local to our building and chatted about the forthcoming merger and what we had done over the weekend.

Greta wasn't one of my outside friends. She was a work friend and she liked to keep it that way even though I had asked her to come to many of our girls' nights out; she likes to keep things tight if you know what I mean. I didn't tell her about the guy I met just about the drinks and dancing oh and that maggot who had put his hands on me.

'Ew,' she responded, 'what a creep.'

'Yeah tell me about it, I sorted him out though thanks to my defense classes'. I smiled at the thought that I could look after myself and was a tiny ninja.

The afternoon dragged for me as I was deep in thought about the weekend and that guy. I couldn't shake him out of my mind as much as I tried, or did I?

Leaving work at five was a treat as I usually stayed late to finish whatever I was doing but today I seemed to have completed my work so left with the rest of the crowd. This was gonna be a long week for sure.

Tuesday slipped by in what seemed a blur. At four thirty we had another intranet message explaining that our new partners would be paying us a visit on Thursday and all staff had to attend a presentation meeting at ten in the conference hall.

More stress to deal with and we had deadlines to keep to. God, I was so work orientated today.

'Ha' I laughed out loud which made the guys near me look up from their screens. I smiled and they returned to their work.

Roll on Thursday.

Thursday arrived and I was early to the office as I knew I had to keep ahead of my targets and the meeting would probably take forever, what with all the schmoozing that would be going on from my bosses.

At nine forty five, the people around me were beginning to head off for the conference room and I was just about to leave myself when the phone rang. 'Shit, I don't need this right now' I let out.

It was a client who I had worked with on a project and they wanted some detailing work done for a private function coming up. I was polite and we spent the next fifteen minutes talking about her requirements. During the conversation she had emailed me her thoughts, her designs and we were discussing the pros and cons of it all and variations that I knew she would like. I glanced at my watch and it was five past ten! Oh god I'm late and gonna get it for sure as I needed to finalise a couple of additional points with my client.

Finally, at ten fifteen we finished and I was racing from my desk to theconference hall. There was clapping going on and some cheers so I tried to sneak in and not be seen but, as it turned out, it was the wrong moment.

As I pushed against the door the clapping stopped and the creak of the door sounded like thunder in the deafening silence. 'Shit' I murmured under my breath as all heads immediately turned my way,

'Sorry' I whispered and positioned myself at the back of the room.

I looked up and at the other end of the room I saw him. For fucks sake what the hell was Jacob doing here?

He was dressed in a crisp dark blue suit, white shirt and a matching tie. His hair hung loose in a way that was just right for him. He was clean shaven but there were hints of a stubble I'm sure of it. His eyes were just as amazing as I remembered.

It was then he made eye contact with me and my vagina just woke the fuck up and began to sing. Traitor vagina!

I had missed part of the presentation and I wasn't at all too bothered because my eyes were focused on him and I noticed he kept looking my way at every opportunity. My body was reacting to him by him just being in the room. My mind went into panic overdrive when I suddenly realised I was getting wet down below. Could anyone tell?

I told myself to stop fidgeting and stand still. What was going on here? This was new territory when it came to men for me.

The meeting lasted for about an hour and our big boss Mr. Rogers announced that Mr. Sylvester would be speaking with staff throughout the day and that he would be coming round to have a look at all the departments. I needed to leave the conference hall as I felt like I was going to combust but as I turned towards the door Mr. Rogers called out my name;

Riley, come here I want you to meet Mr. Sylvester and his son. SHIT!.

I clenched my thighs together, breathed in, straightened my shoulders and made my way through the crowd.

'Riley, this is Mr. John Sylvester of Sylvester Media and his son Jacob.'

I held out my hand and shook Sylvester Seniors hand and smiled. He was a tall man with flashes of grey throughout his hair and dark eyes like Jacobs; he smiled at me warmly and was confident.

'Pleasure to meet you Riley,' he said. 'Let me introduce you to my son, Jacob, he will be the new CEO in a few weeks as I'm taking some time out'.

When he mentioned Jacob I wanted to tell him we had met before and when we had he'd explored my vagina with his skilled hands. I managed not to blush and then made eye contact with Jacob. God, he was close, oh so close and I swear I could smell his delicious scent again. I raised my hand to his and there it was again, that spark, that electricity, oh my god I needed new underwear for sure right now.

'Nice to meet you Mr. Sylvester' I said all professional 'Call me Jacob,' he said with a smile

'Just Jacob?' I said wryly back at him

He smirked and laughed and said, 'Yes Just Jacob.'

It was a playful moment which I wanted to last for a little while longer but in the present company of his father and my boss I let it go.

Mr. Rogers asked me to take Jacob around the different departments so he could get a feel of the place while he spent time with Sylvester Senior.

Jesus, my head was dizzy just by being around him let alone spending the day showing him round the building..

'Sure thing Mr. Rogers' I responded and I turned to Jacob, 'Are you ready Mr. Sylvester?'

'Jacob please Riley,' he said with a smile.

Mr. Rogers was a sweetheart, a father figure and someone whom I looked up to. He kind of took me under his wing when my parents died and has been looking out for me ever since; a kind and gentle man just like a dad should be.

We left the conference hall and approached the lifts,

'We may as well start with the upper floors and work our way down', I said in a playful way. What was

I doing, this guy was gonna be my boss's boss. Stop it Riley or you'll be in deep shit and that's something you don't need right now.

Jacob followed me into the elevator and moved in close as we started up to the top floor.

'I guess I found you then,' he said with a wry smile

I blushed a little at the thought of his words and our last conversation. 'I guess you did,' I said looking up at him.

'So where do you want to go and let me taste you, then?' he said quite confidently.

'Oh, um I don't think that's a good idea, do you?' I was shit scared and turned on both at the same time.

'You can't back out now, that was the deal. I find you and I get to taste you. Unless you want to do something different' he left the question hanging in the air and again that smile.

This seemed like the longest ride to the top floor of a building ever! I wished for all that is holy that the doors would open 'cause I was drowning in here right now beside him trying my hardest to control myself.

Before I even had time to register my thoughts, I blurted out at him,

'Oh I'm sure you could,' shit my hands raised to my mouth and I saw his eyes darken, oh god what have I done.

He drew himself in closer to me and leaned down and I froze. I couldn't move, he pressed his lips against mine and I let out a moan of want and desire. His hands went to the small of my back and to behind my neck pulling me in closer as he deepened the kiss. I responded with my mouth opening for him and he was just as good a kisser as I remembered. We were startled by the announcer in the lift that we had reached our floor. He moved away from me leaving the air of his kiss, 'Wow,!!' I mustered a little voice. 'You sure know how to kiss. Again, why did those words come out at that time?

'My mouth can do all kinds of things if you let me,' he said, with a low voice. I really needed to get out of there before I let my body take over.

Thankfully the doors opened and it was like fresh air to my lungs, I breathed in so deep my chest felt like it was going to explode.

'This way please Mr. Sylvester,' I said with my sweetest smile.

I knew he was watching me, so I accentuated my walk so my bum smoothly moved from side to side without making it too obvious

He coughed so I knew I had him like he had me.

We made our way through the upper floors and he spoke with many staff and their roles within the company. Each time we made our way back to the elevator my insides knotted at the thought of kissing him again. We were accompanied by some other staff on the way down which I think was a god send.

We checked out the rest of the floors and Jacob spent roughly two hours speaking to people and getting to know what they did and listening to ideas and opinions.

'So tell me Riley, what do you do here apart from being the eye candy?' he said frankly.

I kept my reply professional and to the point, 'I'm not eye candy Mr. Sylvester, far from it. I work in the digital media area on specific projects. I have a passion for photography and this is important in the field of digital work and with my skills set.'

'I bet you do have skills, Riley,' he said with a grin.

The last elevator ride was only a short one but again he was close, so close I couldn't help but look at him. He was looking at me too.

'What?' I said looking him in the eye, shit those eyes are gonna be the death of me right now.

'I'd like to see you, let's have dinner and perhaps get to know each other,' he said.

'Really?' I was confused. Here was a man who could clearly have had any woman he wanted and it seemed that it was me. I'm nothing, a nobody not even slim like the rest of the population, I really couldn't understand his attraction to me unless he just wanted to fuck me.

'Yes, let's have dinner,' I said, smiling.

'Great, how about tonight, no time like the present' he announced and pulled out his card. He pressed the card into my hand, 'Call me on this number and I'll pick you up at seven'

We returned to the conference hall and met with his father and my boss. 'All good Mr. Sylvester?' my boss asked

'Yes very pleased to be here,' he said looking at me His father raised an eyebrow but said nothing.

I excused myself and left, I looked back to see Jacob staring at me and I smiled at him as I left the room.

The rest of the afternoon went by in a blur. What am I going to wear? I thought dinner, probably somewhere posh, I can do posh right?

I left work dead on five and raced home. I messaged the girls about what had happened during the day and they were as excited as I was.

I sent Jacob a message with my address details and included a line about looking forward to dinner. Actually, that was mainly because I'd missed lunch due to the tour and all the kissing. My hand automatically reached up to my mouth as I remembered his taste and his soft lips on mine.

The phone pinged back almost instantly. 'I'm looking forward to spending time over dinner with you' it said, 'Maybe I can taste you too' and there was a kiss at the end of the message.

This is going to be dangerous. I thought I needed to be a good girl, a really good girl.

I showered and chose to put on one of my black cocktail dresses. I owned like six of them, but this was the one to die for. Figure hugging but not too tight while showing off my breasts in the best possible taste, there but not too 'showy' and best of all it made my bum look as good as it was.

The doorbell went at seven precisely and I jumped as I was nervous at seeing him in this way. I opened the door and he looked like heaven.

He was wearing black boots cowboy style and dark denim jeans, a perfectly fitting crisp white shirt and a blazer. His face had just the right amount of stubble which I wanted to immediately rake my fingers over. I wasn't aware but I bit my lip in a pleasurable way.

'We won't be going anywhere if you keep doing that,' he said, drawing me out of my thoughts.

'Sorry, you look good,' I said.

Before I knew it he was on me like a rabid beast. His lips found mine and he kissed me deeply forcing my mouth to open. His hands were on me pulling me in tighter. Before he could squeeze the life out of me, I raised my hands to his neck and pulled him down so the pressure of his chest eased on my nipples.

He pulled away from me panting.

'I'm sorry I just couldn't help myself,' he said, releasing me in the doorway. 'Well that was a good introduction to the evening.' I smiled at him.

'Shall we go before we don't go,' he said 'Yes, let's.' I nodded and grabbed my bag.

When we got to the front of my building there was a beautiful black car waiting for us complete with a driver.

'Wow that's a lush car' I said, not knowing what the hell the make was, it just looked nice. I was later informed it was a Bentley but as I'm not very good with identifying cars I let it go but I bet it was very expensive.

The driver opened the door for me and I got in, Jacob swung round to the other side and got in beside me. His hand touched mine and boom there it was again.

He looked at me as our hands touched and smiled. Did he feel it too?

The restaurant was beautifully decorated old style with wooden beams and cosy table décor. It reminded me of something from the past with just a hint of the present. Tasteful, classy but somehow understated.

The menu was plentiful with food I loved, I just could not decide for the life of me what I wanted, I truly could have eaten most of it as I was starving.

'The steak here is great,' he said while watching me look at the menu. 'Mmm, yes I love steak too' I mumbled in agreement.

'OK then, steak for me,' I said affirmatively. 'Great,' he said, 'that makes two of us'.

The waiter took our order and brought wine. It was delicious and the best wine I had had in a while.

'Perfect' I said as I placed the crystal glass next to my placemat and closed my eyes to savor the taste.

'If you carry on like this I will take you to the back and fuck you hard and fast' he said with a low sultry voice.

'What?' I choked out before I coughed 'You heard me,' he glared over to me.

'I told you I'm not that kind of girl, did you forget?'

'No, I remember but you have challenged me and I tend to win,' he smiled and swallowed his wine.

I could not believe he was so upfront with me, but I was drunk the time we were together at the club and well that really doesn't count.

'I'm afraid you took advantage of me in the club while I was under the influence' I riled playfully at him.

'Oh I did, did I?' he mustered back at me.

'Do you think I would have allowed you to touch me if I was sober?' I questioned him.

'Well maybe we'll have to wait and see' he smiled back at me.

Chapter 4

Jacob

Sunday morning came and I had been dreaming about her, about Riley.

Her mouth was so sensuous I could still feel her passion on my own lips. God the way her body felt under my touch was enough for my arousal to keep me going back into the shower again. The water fell onto my skin as my mind wandered to the night before. I had never been that enticed by a woman like I had less than 12 hours earlier and I'm sure she was gagging for it just as much as I was but never put out.

'I'm not that kind of girl' I remember her saying to me as she left me there in the dimly lit corridor wanting her more than any other woman I'd had before. She clearly enjoyed the way my hands moved over her and my fingers inside her.

My cock was aching at the thought of her hands on my body. My thoughts were of her and I imagined her hands holding me, touching me and taking me to the

edge. Her lips riding up and down the length of my cock until I exploded into her mouth. FUCK!!

I want her and I need to find her as I explode over the shower wall.

This was ridiculous fantasising over a woman. I'm a grown ass man who could have any woman I wanted but I wanted her and I needed to find her again.

Monday morning came fast and the normal routine of meetings with my father who was currently the CEO of Sylvester Media Inc, the largest well at least in the top 2% of the media giants. He was as always enthused by new upcoming blood being introduced into the company and growth opportunities for everyone was one of the things I loved and admired about him along with his desire to succeed. He was a generous man and a hard worker and I wanted to be like him so I always paid attention.

Today was not one of those days where I was focused. I was all over the place and dad seemed to notice as he stood in front of my desk speaking to me.

'I have a new venture to attend to this week Jacob and I want you to come with me,' his voice was loud enough to bring me back from my thoughts and pay attention.

'Yes of course dad, I'll make sure my diary is clear.' I mustered with a laugh.

He sat down and continued. 'It's a Media Company that we are bringing in under our wing. They are a great company with prospects that we could use to our advantage in the long run. They make good profits and seem to have a good number of staff who have incredible talent.'

His eyes were like a child's when given a new toy. He loved the chase and the excitement of a successful takeover more than anything else in his business life. 'Dad, I'm on board, when are we going?' I asked eagerly.

'I thought we could go there, Thursday of this week. Meet with the owners and familiarise ourselves with the place.'

'Yep sounds good,' I said as he got up and headed for the door. New business was good business and I knew my father was incredibly good at finding the right ones for our own expansion.

I'd been thinking about Riley non stop pretty much most of Monday through to Wednesday, even a session in the boxing ring with Harry and the lads didn't help much.

Thursday came and I needed to be on my game so I dressed to impress even though I felt I didn't need to impress as my father was the one doing the schmoozing, not me.

We left our building to go to the company we planned to take over. Well that's how I saw it anyways. The drive was not long so no time for small talk as my father was busy on his phone anyway. We arrived and were escorted to a conference hall to do the presentation and the meet and greet. These things were always the downside to the business takeovers and I hated being sucked up to by those with money who were pretentious arseholes.

The presentation was going well and all were happy until we were interrupted by an annoying noise of a door being pulled open. Most people, including myself, looked round to see the guilty culprit.

OMG! There she was. It was Riley in the flesh, my cock twitched just at the sight of her. Her hair was tied back in a bun with tendrils around her face. Her eyes were alive and alluring.

I loved her eyes. She met my gaze and there it was that connection again. Just by her look and her body reaction I could tell how shocked she was to see me. I loved that I made her feel that way. I will have her, I thought and I will get to taste all of her.

The presentation went on but I couldn't stop looking at her and she too was looking at me. God, I wanted to go over there and kiss her so deeply.

My thoughts were running wild inside me and then as the meeting ended she headed for the door with all the others.

No I thought; please no, I needed to see her, to touch her maybe just a little.

My panic at losing her rose in my chest but Mr. Rogers, the company's boss called out to Riley to come over.

When Riley arrived he asked her to take me round and show me the departments and get a feel of the place. Yes, there was something I wanted to get the feel of - and it wasn't this place for sure. Riley seemed keen to show me around but played it perfectly as she was more than aware my father and her boss were standing within feet of the two of us.

'I guess I found you then,' I said with the intent of getting as close to her as I could.

She blushed so I knew she was thinking that too.

'I guess you did,' she said, looking me straight in the eyes.

'So where do you want to go and let me taste you?' I said with confidence. 'Oh, um I don't think that's a good idea, do you?' She seemed a little scared.

'You can't back out now, that was the deal. I find you and I get to taste you. Unless you want to do something different, I'm sure I can accommodate you.' I gave her my sweetest biggest smile.

'Oh I'm sure you could, she blurted out raising her hands to her mouth with her outburst.

I followed her out of the room to the lifts. I glanced down at her about to say something when the 'swoosh' of the lifts broke my concentration. The door opened and I followed her in.

I couldn't help myself. In the lift I drew closer to her than necessary. She froze as my lips found hers, she moaned as I kissed her making me more eager to take it further.

My hands went to her back and to the top of her neck and pulled her in closer, god I wanted to devour her right there and then. Her response was instant and she parted her lips so I could taste her deep inside. She was a great kisser and the memories of our kiss from Saturday came flooding back, but I wanted more from her, so much more.

We were disturbed by the annoying automated voice of the lift telling us we had arrived on the top floor. I moved away from her, leaving our kiss in the air and I hoped wanting more.

'Wow, !!' she said with a small voice, 'You sure know how to kiss.'

'My mouth can do all kinds of things if you let me,' I said, with a low voice.

She ignored my comment. 'This way please Mr. Sylvester,' she said, 'follow me'. She knew I was watching her so she accentuated her walk and swayed that delicious arse as I fell in behind her. I couldn't help but cough, fuck I was hooked.

The rest of the tour to the departments was a distraction for sure because I wanted to find somewhere to take her and concentrate on other things, but I couldn't see anywhere remotely secluded. Oh for the luck of a dimly lit corridor!

The elevator ride was my only hope. I needed to kiss her again, maybe touch her a little more, I was like a dog in heat and she was my prey for sure.

Clearly there wasn't any hope of getting her alone on the ride down as some other staff joined us in the limited space of the lift. This annoyed me greatly. Just because the sign in the lift says 'capacity for 15 people' doesn't mean 15 fucking people need to be in a lift all the time! They spend most of the day sitting on their backsides in front of a computer screen. You'd think a walk up and down the stairs would do them good. *Take the bloody stairs people!!*

We checked out the rest of the floors and spent roughly two hours speaking to people and getting to know what the company does.

'So, tell me Riley, what do you do here apart from being the eye candy,' I said to her straight up.

She looked directly at me.

'I'm not eye candy Mr. Sylvester far from it, I work in the digital media area on specific projects. I have a passion for photography which compliments my work and skill sets'

'I bet you do have skills Riley,' I returned with a grin.

I could see she was flustered just by being near me and it excited me so much.

The last elevator ride was short but she was close to me. So close I couldn't help but look down at her beautiful face and the lips I could happily die for. She returned my look.

'What?' she said, looking me straight in the eyes.

I repeated, 'I'd like to see you, have dinner perhaps, get to know you,' 'Really?' she quizzed back at me.

She had a non-descriptive look on her face and I wondered if she was teasing me or she genuinely didn't hear my question the first time. I really wanted to know what she was thinking right now.

'Yes, let's have dinner,' she said, smiling, a devil's smile for sure.

'Great, how about tonight, no time like the present,' I said, handing her my business card.

'Text me your address on this number and I'll pick you up at seven' I said, making sure she took the card. I really wanted to spend time with her.

We returned to the conference hall and met with my father and her boss. 'All good Mr. Sylvester,' Rogers asked.

'Yes, very pleased to be here and impressed with what I have seen so far' I replied looking down at Riley

I saw my father raise his eyebrow but he said nothing.

Riley excused herself and left. I was staring at her as she walked away when she turned to look at me then she smiled. Caught hook, line and sinker my friend.

The afternoon went quicker than expected. My father and I discussed some of the 'ins and outs' of the business we were taking under our wing. My mind was elsewhere however but if I'm right, that's what my father was speaking about business but I was thinking about another sort of 'in and out'.

My phone buzzed and I didn't recognise the number so I opened it to find Riley's address.

I replied instantly, with a smile on my face,

Looking forward to spending time with you - maybe taste you too!! X

I saved her number on my mobile and left for home. A short drive later I was back at my apartment, quickly showered and dressed followed by a quick check in the mirror and off we go. I didn't want to be late.

I was dressed smart, casual as the place I was taking her to; Ruffalo's was a classy joint but let you get away with smart jeans, well they did me anyway.

I arrived at Riley's apartment on time and knocked hoping that she would answer the door naked so I could devour her there and then. No such luck.

She opened the door in a stunning and it was a black dress that did total justice to her figure. To be truthful, I was hoping she was eye fucking me as much as I was her.

Her lip was in between her teeth and you know she was thinking dirty thoughts.

'We won't be going anywhere if you keep looking at me like that,' I said to her, bringing her back to the here and now.

'Sorry, you look good,' she said.

That for me was my chance to kiss her and I did like a hungry alpha, I forced her lips apart and probed her with my tongue. She didn't resist, she just reached up and pulled me in closer. Oh baby I thought, this is going to be a night to remember.

She moaned into my mouth which I wanted so badly. I had to pull away from her otherwise it was gonna get dirty real soon. I was panting and looking at her swollen lips from my touch.

'I'm sorry I just couldn't help myself,' I said to her as I let go so she could adjust herself. God, I was a greedy bastard!

'Well, that was a good introduction to the evening,' she said to me, grinning widely.

'Shall we go before we don't go,'

'Yes,' she said, nodding and grabbing her purse.

'Wow, that's a lush car,' she said, looking at my wheels with awe. I'm guessing she didn't know cars; I would inform her later that it was a Bentley.

Edward, my driver opened the door for her and she got in, I didn't wait for him to open my door, I just scooted around to climb in beside her and to be near her again.

I touched her hand as I sat beside her and boom!! - there it was again, I looked at her, then down to our hands and smiled. She must have felt the same….didn't she?.

Ruffalo's was beautifully decorated in an old style with wooden beams and cosy table decor. I loved this place and had been coming here for years. Sophisticated but homely and boasted one of the best menus in town overseen by a chef that most places would die for.

After ordering drinks we sat quietly looking at the menu. I could see she wasn't sure what to go for.

'The steak here is great,' I said.

'Mmm, I love steak' she mumbled back to me, not really paying attention. After a few long minutes which seemed like an age she closed the menu and looked up at me.

'OK, steak for me'

'Great,' I replied, 'that makes two of us.'

Our glasses were empty, so I ordered the wine.

The wine and meal arrived and as she put the glass to her lips I watched in awe as she ran her tongue round the rim of the glass.

'If you carry on like this I will take you to the back and fuck you hard and fast' I said low and in a tone I wanted her to feel the heat between us.

'What?' she choked out and then coughed into her napkin. 'You heard me,' I glared at her.

'I told you I'm not that kind of girl, did you forget?'

'No, I remember but you have challenged me and I intend to win.' I smiled and swallowed my wine.

Her eyes went as wide as the sun for a split second.

'Well I was drunk the last time we were together and well that really doesn't count. I'm afraid. You took advantage of me in that state.' She seemed to be playful with her words. I too can be playful, I thought.

'Oh, I did, did I?'

'Do you think I would have allowed you to touch me if I was sober?'

'Well maybe we will have to put that to the test a little later' I smiled at her before taking another drink.

Chapter 5

Riley

Dinner was a series of flirtatious eye contact, followed by slowly eating the steak that was in front of me, taking my time as I drew it to my lips, clearly making Jacob squirm in his seat.

It was a fun game, but I could sense his desire just by his look. Was I teasing him just a little too much? Right now I would have let him take me on the table.

We were in our own world when I was drawn from my bubble by a woman's voice calling out to Jacob from behind.

'Jacob Sylvester, well I never, so good to see you, how's your delectable father doing?'

Her voice was a drawl. She was an older lady who at first glance reminded me of a Grandma figure but with more sophistication. Ahh old money!

'Audrey Whitmore, always a pleasure to see you.' Jacob replied, swallowing his steak.

WHITMORE, OH SHIT! my thoughts were running wild. Coincidence I'm sure but there weren't that many Whitmore's in this state with money and I knew she had money for sure.

'Who is your friend Jacob please do tell.' She requested. 'This is Riley, Riley-

'Shure,' I said, 'Riley Shure'. Holding out my hand there was no way I was going

to announce that I was a Whitmore too.

She smiled at me for longer than she should and I got the feeling she was almost studying me.

'Have we met before young lady?' she asked.

'Nope I don't think so, I'm sure I would have remembered you,' I smiled and dropped my eyes back to the food on my plate.

'How's things at the Estate?' Jacob asked.

'Oh, you know with the loss of Marcus and his wife Felicity it's been a tough two years almost' She drew her hand to her eye like she was holding back tears.

Did my ears just hear what I was hearing? This woman knew my parents, why had I never met her before. If I'd had I would have clearly remembered her. 'I'm sorry for your loss.' I said quietly like a mouse who was about to be squashed.

'Thank you my dear,' she replied clearly upset at the thought. I couldn't help myself. I needed to know more.

'Did they have any children?' I asked more confidently this time.

Jacob was slightly agitated, but I needed to press her even if it seemed a little disrespectful.

'Oh they had a daughter, but she passed away when she was ten I believe. I never got to see her really only when she was about five, then I guess life takes hold and well you know' She waved it as if it was old news.

I never responded as I was quite shocked.

Why did she fall out with my parents? Why did they say I died, what was going on here?

'We're having our annual ball soon Jacob, maybe bring your friend, Riley was it? 'Audrey you are too kind' Jacob said 'I will do just that'.

She then left.

I was so confused and felt a sort of weird feeling in the pit of my stomach which pulled me right out of the deliriously happy place I had been in just a few minutes before.

'Is everything alright?' Jacob asked, looking at me with concern.

'Um yes thanks.' I never made eye contact with him. He pushed me further.

'She can be quite intimidating,' he said with an ease about him. 'Don't let her put you off.'

He was concerned and I heard it in his voice.

The dinner wasn't going to plan that's for sure, but Jacob seemed to be doing his best to distract me with questions.

'Didn't you lose your parents a while back?' He hadn't yet put two and two together.

'Yes I did,' I replied, 'in an accident' 'So what did your family do?' he asked 'To be honest Jacob I don't know.'

This was the truth. My parents were secretive about almost everything and I'm now guessing about me too.

'I was put into a boarding school when I was quite young and then I went to college. University followed so being around my parents wasn't a sure thing I'm afraid.

'Oh right, god that must have been lonely' he said

'It wasn't all bad. I had good friends to keep me afloat. Even after my parents passed away I had backup, you know the kind of friends.

'Yeah, I like friends like that,' he said.

I felt as though I was drowning. The dinner conversation was making me shift in my space and I felt a little nauseous.

'Jacob, I'm sorry I don't feel very well, I think I need to go home.' The look on his face was pure shock.

'Riley, are you OK?'

'I'm sorry I have to go. Thank you for dinner but I have to cut it short.'

I got up to leave and Jacob held my hand. That spark was just what I needed to feel right now although it wasn't giving me the pleasure that I needed, I just needed to go home and try to process the conversation with Audrey Whitmore. 'Riley, are you sure there's nothing I can do, will you be OK?' He pushed

'I will be,' I replied again, not making eye contact. 'Let me take you home, please'

'I'm good Jacob, I'll get a taxi.' My words were faint in their response, but he didn't push me.

I left Jacob at the table staring after me as I made my way to the door picking up my coat on the way.

Right now I needed to be alone.

I changed into my pj's and scrambled onto my couch with a glass of wine. Not like the one we had in the restaurant but it was still good. Thoughts of Audrey and her comments about my parents and me spun like a whirlwind in my mind.

So many questions and no one to answer them except my trustees. Surely they would know. Sleep was rapidly creeping up on me so I finished the bottle of wine and retreated to my safe place.

Chapter 6

Jacob

D inner started off the way I was hoping it would. The two of us flirting with words and she was tempting me with her mouth and her food. It was like a game of who could pull it off better. She was alive and I could see the agreeable spark in her eyes with what we were doing. I was going for the short game tonight and wanted to seduce her to the point that she was going to give herself to me.

Then for some reason it all just went downhill. I couldn't really put my finger on when or how but from good beginnings we crashed and burned in a matter of a minute or two. The unexpected but pleasant visit to our table by Audrey Whitmore seemed to pop into my head as the turning point but I wasn't sure why. After introducing Riley to Audrey and having a quick chat Riley seemeddifferent, almost withdrawn from our evening.

I left the restaurant and headed to a local bar, texting the lads on the way. The beer was cold and I was thirsty but was it only for her?

The lads arrived. Aaron and Harry were the only ones who came back to me so at least I had company.

The three of us spent the next few hours drinking and talking shit about everything. The subject of women came up, but I avoided that like the plague and didn't tell them how my eagerly awaited dinner date with Riley had gone south. I had a nagging feeling in the back of my mind that bedding the woman of my dreams was now going to be a long game strategy.

Chapter 7

Riley

I woke up with an eerie feeling inside. Something told me I needed to find out some more details on Audrey Whitmore.

I decided to call in sick for the day; something I'd avoided doing no matter how bad a hangover I'd given myself the night before. As it was a Friday and I was up to date with my work I wasn't too bothered about the repercussions of my absence.

I called Mr. Quinn at the Trustees Foundation where all my finances were taken care of and arranged to meet him later in the day at his office uptown. The morning dragged by slowly and I thought about messaging Jacob, but I just couldn't bring myself to do it. I'd most likely have blown it with him anyway and besides, I needed to remain focused on the task ahead.

Mr. Quinn's office was about half an hour away by car. Friday traffic was always a nightmare in the city so I decided on taking the train.

Mr. Quinn's secretary greeted me with a smile

'Miss Whitmore, lovely to see you again,' she said so bubbly. 'It's Miss Shure now, remember?' I reminded her

'Oh, yes I'm sorry, Mr. Quinn won't be too long, please take a seat. Can I get you coffee or tea?'

'I'm good thanks', I was nervous and hyped all at once. Coffee would have been a push too far with my emotions.

I sat waiting for Quinn and it seemed like whatever he was doing was taking forever, but to be fair I was early though so I had to be patient.

Quinn came from his office and was talking to a woman.

'Thank you for your help Roger, I will see you at the Gala won't I?' The woman was still speaking as they crossed the room towards me. I recognised the woman as Audrey Whitmore and I hid my face in the magazine I had quickly picked up.

She air kissed Quinn and left the office. I hadn't realised I was holding my breath until I let it all out a little too loudly. Quinn's secretary looked my way.

'Riley,' Quinn spoke.

I lowered the magazine and stood up to greet him. 'Thank you for seeing me at such short notice Mr. Quinn' 'Please call me Roger,' he said with asmile.

'What seems to be the problem. Come, come into my office and tell me about it'. I followed Quinn down the hall to his office and sat down on his comfy chair

He took the one opposite me and waited for me to speak. 'That woman who was just here,' I said quite nervously. 'Oh you mean Audrey Whitmore' he said

'Yes, is she, is she my-

'Your grandmother, yes she is Riley.' My hands went to my mouth in horror. 'Why does she think I'm dead?' I asked

'It was a request from your parents Riley. It's a very complicated story which I hoped I wouldn't have to tell you.'

'Well the cat is out of the bag Mr. Quinn so spill.'

Over the next two hours Quinn ran through my life and my family history of which the majority of what he said was news to me. It was like listening to my life being re-written from top to bottom.

They say 'money is the root of all evil' and it seems my Grandmother was the devil herself, particularly when it came to my parents.

It turned out that my Mum and Dad deliberately hid me from her to protect me from the path I was to follow according to my grandma's demands. I guess they wanted me to choose my own way and make my own life choices when I was old enough. Such was the interference levels by my grandma that my parents deemed it necessary to change my name in an effort to protect me from her and her influences.

The Whitmore's came from old money and through my parents I would be set up for life. What I didn't know was that I would inherit a lot of shares in many

companies across the city when I turned Twenty-Five. For some reason my grandmother was trying to get her hands on my inheritance but for what reason I do not know. It could not have been just for the money as she was already quite wealthy in her own right.

Quinn had been explaining to her only that afternoon that all information as to who held the shares and in what was confidential and he wasn't able to disclose anything about my family's money, where it went and to whom.

I told Quinn about the encounter with her from the previous evening and her words about not seeing my father since I was five.

'Why was there a falling out?' I was concerned as to why the family was so secret.

'I'm not sure but I think it was to do with your father investing in several smaller companies instead of just one'

He went on to say, 'these smaller companies are now doing well and the financial returns are beyond your wildest dreams Riley.'

'Even the day your parents died, your father had invested heavily in a couple of media companies. One is the company you work for; Rowthorne Media and the was another was Sylvester Media, who are now one of the largest in the city. 'Off hand, I'm not sure what percentage he went for but all the details will be on

our system and I can look it up for you as this is now your estate and you have the legal right to access the file.'

'Thanks Mr Quinn, I appreciate your help.'

As I left Quinn's office my legs were shaking and I felt a bead of sweat run down my spine to the small of my back. So I'm mega rich! Well I will be but that would mean disclosing my real name when the time comes and this will undoubtedly create some problems for me down the line.

I sat in a cafe near Mr. Quinn's office enjoying a coffee and going over in my mind the information he had just given me when my phone broke my concentration.

It was Jacob – texting me.

Hey you, are you OK? I hesitated before replying, Not bad, thanks.

You called in sick today.

Are you spying on me Mr. Sylvester?

No, I came to the company to see you and they told me you were off sick, I was concerned.

Thanks, that's kind. Why did you want to see me?

I wanted to make sure you were OK from last night, you kinda left before dessert and in a bit of a hurry!

I smiled at the last message.

Are you flirting with me Mr. Sylvester? Maybe, is it working?

You need to work harder than that.

How about I come to your apartment and make you feel better.

I'm really not in good company right now, as much as I would like for you to make me feel better, now is not the right time.

How about tomorrow?

Let me see.

I'll call you tomorrow, Riley Thanks Jacob.

I put my phone away and continued my coffee. I sat for a while longer then made my way home.

The girls wanted me to go out with them tonight but I just wasn't up for it. A night with a film and some popcorn was good enough for me.

I was engrossed in my film when the doorbell went, it was late about ten pm. My friends would be partying hard right now so it couldn't be them.

I walked to the door and looked through the peephole and saw Jacob there. Shit! Why is he here?

I opened the door to Jacob and didn't realise I was in my tiny shorts and crop top. Immediately his eyes were roaming over my body. He looked so good in loose jeans and a tight tee that showed off his muscles.

'Are you going to let me in?' he asked practically drooling 'Yes of course, come in'

He sat down on my sofa and made himself at home. 'Comfy?' I asked

'I would be if you were sitting on me,' he replied

I blushed at the thought then my vagina responded with thaturge. 'Drink?' I asked, trying to swerve the desires building inside me. 'Yes, what do youhave?'

'Wine, I have wine, white OK for you?' 'Yes thanks' he said with a smile.

I walked into the kitchen area and placed two glasses on the counter. Before I could turn he was behind me, kissing my neck and as he held my waist his kisses were moving slowly down my shoulder.

I put the glasses back on the side because I would have dropped them. His hands moved to my top and he slid them under and began to caress my breasts.

It felt so good to be touched by him. He was gently teasing my nipples with his hands while massaging them. I moaned out loud and pushed my head into his chest to enjoy this feeling.

He continued to caress my breast with one hand while the other moved down to the shorts I was wearing. His hand slipped in the front of them and to my sex, oh she was singing his tune I knew it. He moved his finger to my clit and his response when I was already wet for him was what I wanted to hear right now. 'Your so wet for me Riley'

He danced his fingers in a circular movement which made me feel oh so great. I could feel his erection from behind and reached round to place my hand on his crotch.

'Oh Riley, fuck' he groaned out loud, so I squeezed him a little more and he pushed himself further into my back.

He released his hands from my clit and turned me round to face him and then he kissed me as if his life depended on it. I was happy to take his kisses and reached behind his neck to pull him closer to me. We were kissing so deeply that I almost forgot to breathe. He broke away from me for only a second then he lifted me up and I wrapped my legs around his waist.

'Where's your bedroom,' he asked 'To the left' I replied

Then he walked to my room holding me in his arms and kissing my neck. I closed my eyes and let the feelings take over me.

He laid me down on the bed gently and kissed me again while laying on top of me. My god this was good so good.

His hands were all over my body touching me, squeezing me. He moved his kissing down my body to my thighs and began kissing the inside.

My breathing quickened as each kiss got closer to my sex.

He pulled my shorts down and planted kisses up my legs and then that's when I felt him. His tongue met my sex and I was like fuck this is better than I had imagined. He teased my clit with his tongue and I loved it,

He was hungry and I seemed to be his dinner. He was making my body his. Then I felt him push a finger inside of me.

FUCK I shouted out, 'Oh Jacob I'm not…'

'You're not what?' he said with his breath moving across my sex

'I'm not the kind of girl that does these things,' I said, 'This is new to me, I've NEVER done this before.'

He stopped his movements and looked directly at me. I felt my face flush red with embarrassment at that moment and he asked me.

'Riley, have you never been with a man before?'
'No Jacob I have not'

'Oh Riley, this going to be a night to remember' and he continued his movement on my sex. His fingers moved in and out of my vagina while his tongue worked hard probing and licking me good. It didn't take long before I was close to coming and he knew it. He knew my body responded to him in such a way.

He got faster with his fingers and then hit me with the tongue – I couldn't hold back any longer.,

'I'm coming Jacob' I mewled 'Yes, baby come for me' he said

It was like an explosion on my insides and I came hard and fast. My vagina clenched around his fingers so hard he struggled to release them. For me it was even better than the night club moment. If this is what heaven is all about, I never want to leave.

'Fuck Riley I want to fuck you so bad right now.' 'OK' I said in a moment of pure delight.

Jacob removed his jeans and shoes and then his t-shirt. His body was like a fucking god. His cock was strained against his boxers and when he removed them, wow! What a sight.

I had seen a few cocks in my time but this was clearly the biggest I had seen so far. He crawled up over me and placed himself between my legs.

'This will hurt a bit Riley, but I'll be as gentle as I can. Are you ready?' He said with a gentle tone

'Yes Jacob I'm ready'.

He placed his crown against my vagina which was so wet from my orgasm, he then pushed his way into me slowly. I gasped at the feeling as he entered me, stretching me as he went.

'Are you ok?' He looked down at me.

'Yes,' I was breathy and hot. I could feel his length stretching me. He pushed his way all in and then pulled back,

'Oh my god, fuck that feels good' I announced as he filled me again and then pulled back.

As he pushed into me again his mouth found mine and he kissed me so deep it was like a drug and I was tripping.

I placed my hands on his back and felt his hard muscles so close to me, his arms were pumped and he was smelling oh so mighty fine.

'I'm not gonna last much longer Riley, I've wanted this from the first time I saw you.'

'Do it to me then,' I whispered And he did!

My orgasm came again but this time in a wave of heated breathlessness I had not experienced before. My heart was pounding like a steam hammer in my chest and my body went numb. As he climaxed inside of me I felt his hardness expand, stretching me beyond anything I'd experienced before.

As he came his breath rasped harshly against my neck and he slid his hands round to grip the cheeks of my backside. As he continued to pump me, his hands tightened on my behind and it was as if he wanted to crush the life out of me as he drove deeper into my body.

We both shared the moment of no return and I felt him fill me with his seman. It was amazing, I never knew it would be this good because if I did, I would have done this many years before.

He laid on me for a while spent but still inside me and slowly his breathing returned to near normal. I felt great. He kissed my nose and my lips and placed a finger trailing down my face.

'You are so beautiful' he said, gently kissing me again on my lips.

He withdrew his cock which seemed to still be half erect and laid down beside me. As he left my body I felt an emptiness that I could never describe properly, just that I needed him to stay inside me forever.

While we lay there, he trailed his hands under my top again to search for my breasts. My nipples felt a little tender but soon began to rise while he played with them between forefinger and thumb.

'I told you I would taste you Riley and I have,' he smiled

'Oh shit,' were the only words that I could gasp out as my breathing would not let me engage in conversation yet.

He laughed at me and I jabbed him in his side. 'Don't laugh at me Mr. Sylvester.'

'Oh Miss Shure, I'm going to do so much more to you than laugh,' he replied. And the night just got a lot better.

Chapter 8

Jacob

I woke with the sunshine on my body and opened my eyes to the beautiful face of Riley. She was sleeping soundly and had the most amazing glow to her skin.

Last night was beyond any words for me. The connection we had, the mind-blowing sex and the way her body just melted under my touch, immediately started to affect my cock. I must admit taking her four times during the previous night was a high for me as I'd only ever managed it three times with a woman before. But at the start of the evening tasting her pussy was enough to send me over the edge. I felt like a savage wanting more of her, so much more and yes, I took her to the edge many, many times.

Her face as she came time after time her body limp in my hands when she finally gave into her feelings and her body's emotions had been unravelling even for me. Her scent, her taste, her body was amazing and I couldn't help but smile genuinely for the first time after sex. I felt, I was really happy.

She stirred a little and my cock twitched with want.

'Fuck!' I breathed out heavily and hoped she'd heard me so I could devour her again there and then. She didn't so I just needed to wake her.

I moved in closer to her and put my arm around her waist to pull her near to me, she moved to her back still asleep. This was my chance for a perfect opportunity to wake her the best way I knew.

I positioned myself lower beside her and then gently parted her legs. She was accommodating without realising I'm sure, and I went down on her, my tongue teasing her sex ever so gently.

She squirmed under my touch, coming into reality and then I felt her hands move to my head and grasped my hair to guide my tongue deeper into her. She was clearly enjoying this morning's wake up.

A moan left her mouth as I continued to probe deeper. She was still swollen from the night we had just spent together so I was gentle as I placed a finger inside her, again she moaned but this time a lot louder. I couldn't hold back anymore.

The faster I went teasing and enticing her encouraged the wetness down there only more. I kissed her body and when I sank my teeth into her, she moaned and I loved to hear it. My cock was now ready waiting to plunge deep inside her for the fifth time in less than twelve hours.

She moaned low and sultry, 'I want you inside me'

That was all I needed. She was insatiable and I slowly pushed deep into her making her shudder as my length. God she was still tight in spite of the night before and I loved it. I couldn't help myself but to fuck her hard and fast I needed this as it had been a roller coaster of a ride with her since the first time I saw her. She came in no time screaming my name and I followed shortly after exploding deep inside her.

'Good morning,' I whispered to her and kissed her on the cheek. 'Mmmm, morning' she whispered with a smile.

'God you are insatiable, Riley.'

'Thank you Mr. Sylvester, so are you,' she trailed her fingers along my jawline. I kissed her wrist as she lowered her hand.

'You will be the death of me,' I told her.

'I'm guessing that's what virgins do to their prey then,' she laughed.

I laid on her for a while just staring at her. She was gorgeous and I had her, all of her.

I couldn't believe it when she asked me to stay last night. I was so glad because I don't know if I could have left her after seeing her in those shorts and barely there thin top. It fucked with me badly.

Chapter 9

Riley

I was woken up by the skillful hands of Jacob. God he got to know my body like a road map last night, I was amazed at how I felt being the puppet in his game, I orgasmed harder than I had ever done before.

He was an incredible lover. I wondered how many lovers he had before me, but that wasn't really a concern as he was with me and that's all that mattered in the here and now.

The morning ended up as a sexual feast, mainly by him. Jacob knew what my body craved and he gave it to me like no one had done before.

I couldn't believe that morning sex was perfect. He was perfect, this was perfect and laying here in his arms as the sun swept across my room was just pure bliss. I really didn't want the morning to end but as like in all films there is always that element of doubt. Will he just ignore me now we have had sex?

I pushed those thoughts out of my head and just wanted to enjoy this time even if it was the only time.

After what seemed to be like the longest moments in the world I needed to get up and pee. I tried to untwine Jacobs arms but he was strong. He pulled me back so tightly and moaned 'no leave me.'

My eyes rolled but I loved it.

After about five minutes though I just had to get up. I pushed his arms away and disappeared to the bathroom. I was reliving last night's events and this mornings, oh god what a feeling inside, my body felt so different.

So, this is what real sex feels like I thought.

I returned to my room to find Jacob awake and sitting up in my bed. He smiled at me with that gorgeous mouth and I couldn't help but melt. He nodded for me to join him in bed next to him.

'Oh god again?' I whispered as only hopefully I could hear.

I crawled onto the bed and didn't get too far when Jacob grabbed me and pulled me into his embrace kissing me ferociously like he had never kissed me before. I moaned into his mouth as the rush I was getting was exhilarating. The kissing got heated and he laid me down pressing his body to mine, this was what I really wanted.

He placed butterfly kisses along my neck and began to go lower towards my breast when we were interrupted by his mobile.

'Fuck' he said as he reached for it checking who it was before answering. 'I've got to take this, don't move.'

Jacob left my room and spoke on the phone for a long time. I was tempted to get up and get dressed as the mood was now gone. I didn't though as I wanted him to come back and make love to me.

Jacob came back to my room with concern on his face 'All OK? I asked

'I'm sorry I have to go,' he said with anguish in his voice.

'It's work problems. I'm sorry Riley really I am. He had a look on him which I couldn't quite grasp.

'It's OK Jacob, really it is just go. I'll be alright.' He didn't notice my disappointment.

Jacob left me feeling empty. I know he had work but I just wanted this feeling to last but not just for a few short hours. There were so many sad times in my life and he made me feel like I was on cloud nine.

I met with the girls later that day and began retelling the situation with Jacob; they were hyper excited and throwing questions at me like it was a quiz show. 'Soooooo, how was it?' they all said together?

'It was um, you know um - fucking amazing' I said with the biggest smile on my face.

Screams from them all got us looks from other people as we sat in the local diner. 'If I'd known sex was going to be this good, I would have given myself away sooner' I said with a laugh.

'They're not all tens my love' Robin said with a raised eyebrow.

'Sometimes we have to be self-satisfied,' she said quite wryly, waving her hand as she spoke.

We all laughed at her as we were all aware of the large range of toys she kept in her bedroom.

It was a great afternoon of girly chat about guys and stuff. This is what I needed right now, some distraction from a niggling feeling inside. I couldn't quite put my finger on my thoughts but there was something I was missing here.

The afternoon turned into the evening and we ended up having an early dinner at the diner still going strong on our thoughts of men and how they pleased us.

'I need pleasure all the time,' Robin said with an unquestionable sound. 'Oh yeah we know,' we all said back to her.

She laughed and poked Emma in her side. 'Oi' she said, jabbing her back.

I checked my phone and no messages from Jacob. I wasn't sure if I really thought he would text me or ever see me again. He said he wanted to taste me and well yes he did several times and fucked my brains out.

Being a virgin for so long and not having intimacy was a big thing for me and now I'd given it to a man who won't ever contact me again. This made me feel low and used, god what was wrong with me? My friends kinda had sex and left, so why couldn't I?

I left the girls at around seven and made my way home. I was exhausted from last night and this morning's escapades with Jacob and emotionally drained too. I checked my phone again and drew a blank.

Shit what am I doing, he won't call or message me this was a one time thing.

I decided that tonight would be a stay in and veg night and I'd watch the film I was planning to do when Jacob appeared at the door.

I thought I would just check my emails and see if I had any comeback from my phone meeting this week.

When I logged in there was an email from Mr. Quinn regarding our Friday meeting.

Skimming the usual blah blah wording I was alerted to the attachment, so I opened it to see what it was.

There was a listing of my father's entire investment portfolio. Since I was born he'd built quite an impressive list of companies. Some he'd bought in at thirty percent and some at twenty percent. However, I did notice that he had obtained a forty per cent share in the company I work for. Then I noticed Sylvester Media Inc. Again, a whopping forty percent shareholding. This was madness. My father never told me anything about this.

Mr. Quinn stated that they were in what's called a holding account, so no one knew who the owner of the shares belonged to. He also added that I could obtain these shares on my twenty-third birthday which was just a short time away. This would mean I would have to take back my family name officially and not hide who I really was anymore.

Mr. Quinn stated that we could meet up next week to discuss things in more detail and how we should handle things in terms of my identity.

This was something new for me and I wasn't sure what to do for the best in terms of my real name becoming known and also my new status. The shares amounted to a few billions, let alone what I was to gain on my twenty-fifth birthday.

Fuck! Fuck! Fuck!

This was going to change things and not necessarily for the better as I knew my grandmother was sniffing around regarding my father's estate. This was going to be tough and I needed the right support to make sure I wasn't going to fuck up.

I emailed Quinn back and said to let me know when he can fit me in as there was a lot to go over and I needed to plan to get the right support in place before the big reveal and the shit hit the fan. This was going to getscary.

The rest of the night passed in a blur as my mind raced trying to make sense of all that I had been told and read about. What I did know was that I was rich, so fucking rich it was unbelievable. I'm also not sure what the shares meant in terms of who ran what and where would I stand on the board – or if I had a place on the board at all.

Sunday morning got me needing some fresh air so, as it was warm, off to the park I went. I hadn't slept too well last night, what with mulling over the time with Jacob and the email from Quinn Far too much to digest in just one night.

Still no message from Jacob so I guess this was just a ruse to get into my knickers and well he succeeded many times. I guess I learnt the art of fucking in one night but there was so much more I needed to learn and experience.

I messaged Robin as I was sitting enjoying the scenery around me, telling her about the email from Quinn and what it might entail with my name reveal. She was concerned as I was because it would open a Pandora's Box of endless questions and the family that were still around would come out of the woodwork to try and influence me. We were in agreement that I needed to get all my options sorted before I made any decisions.

I slipped into a deli nearby and grabbed a sandwich and a coffee and went to head back to the park when I saw Jacob. He couldn't have seen me because if he hadhe would have been mortified as he was with another woman who was holding onto his arm and smiling up at him. My stomach wretched and I felt like my world was about to crumble, I guess I was just another fuck then. Why did I do this to myself, why?.

The tears were welling up and I needed to get a grip and breath. I went through the park and headed home. All of a sudden I wasn't feeling that great. I thought my lungs were closing and the world was collapsing on top of me. Is this the beginning of the end or was I over dramatising everything. My thoughts went back to Jacob. I thought he was different. I really liked him and I liked the way he made me feel.

When I got back to my apartment there was a package by my front door. I was hesitant to take it at first but convinced myself to pick it up. After all who would want to harm me. There was an envelope stuck to the top of the box. I got inside and placed the box on the table, not yet sure what to do with it. Do I open it or do I just call the police and say it might be a bomb, again with the dramatics Riley stop it!

With a kitchen knife I pried the envelope off the top and sat down to open it. My name was handwritten on the envelope in a scroll type font.

I pulled out the letter and began to read it.

Dearest Riley

You will be reading this letter a month prior to your twenty third birthday.

I know that your mother and I never really had the kind of relationship you or any other normal child would want from their parents. In our defense we did try our best to make your upbringing as adventurous as possible with many activities to ensure you grew up to be strong and healthy.

We know there were aspects of our lives that you don't know about and we didn't share with you. This was to make sure you were protected from harm within the family.

You see, my family was very controlling when I was growing up and I wasn't able to pursue the things I enjoyed and loved. I was in fact dictated to in every way and under the total control of others who did not have my interests at heart. In short I and your mother have had a miserable life with the only enjoyment being you. Your mother and I decided that when you were little we would cut ourselves off from my family and devote our time to protecting you as best we could. To do this we were forced to take drastic and unusual steps. My family believed you died at the age of ten and we hid your identity from everyone including yourself. we know you knew what your surname was and I appointed Mr. Quinn as a trustee for your estate and he is the person who would answer all your questions as you got older.

In the event of our deaths we decided to make sure you would be secure financially and to give you the best start in life. we have invested heavily in shares of different media outlets in the city since you were born and where possible increased them as you grew. Mr. Quinn will contact you regarding this and where you go from here in terms of taking control of certain companies.

You are a strong and brave young woman and will grow into the person we know you will become in time with the right guidance.

Mr. Quinn will be happy to answer any questions you will have and until you are twenty five you will be under the guidance of him and his team.

I'm sorry you're reading this letter as your mother and I would have liked to have been there in person to talk this through with you but our lives took a turn and we well we can't be there with you.

I cannot disclose why we are not around but I'm sure in time you will find out. we loved you, our princess so very much and hope that your future will bring you much love and happiness.

Your ever loving parents

XXXXX

The tears fell from my eyes like a waterfall, they did love me. I knew that but I never knew they were trying to just keep me safe.

My life was about to take a massive turn. Was it going to be for the better or worse?

I opened the box. It contained the most beautiful piece of jewelry I had ever seen. There were also several boxes full of diamonds including necklaces, earrings and bracelets. Finally, I found an exquisite diamond ring and on close examination discovered an inscription from my mother. It simply read:

Happy 25 My Precious.

I picked it up and attached was a little string with a tag at the end. Mum's handwriting was distinctive from mine. I knew she had written the tag.

I hope you love this ring as much as I love you. Mum xx

Wow there were no words right now things were getting way out of control it felt like a bloody bond movie and I was somehow a secret agent.

I put the ring on my middle finger and it was just so beautiful. A ring of diamonds with a sapphire as big as a grape in the middle. It was very expensive looking and really not me but I loved it nonetheless.

Shit just got super real I thought.

I brought the box into my room and placed the jewellery into my drawer for safe keeping. This was an emotional roller coaster and I wasn't sure where it would end.

Going to bed that night I was dreading the nightmares I was going to have and not sure if I could cope.

Chapter 10

Jacob

Just as things were getting good with Riley I had to take that fucking phone call, work / family life always gets in the way of my good times and with her I was having the best time of my life, I've never felt like that before.

My father was taken ill and my mother was concerned for his health and well the shit hit the fan. It was a long day at the hospital with my mum crying over my father, so gravely ill and my sister Bethany not knowing what to say and how to help my mother.

I wanted to call Riley and tell her what was going on, but my mum didn't want me to leave her side and the hospital had no cell phone reception. She must be thinking I'm a right dick leaving her like that and not letting her know that I was ok and we were ok.

My father had to stay in the hospital for observation, they didn't really tell us more than that, so I'm guessing my father told them not to, I wasn't going to press too many buttons as my mother was too fragile for that. I sat beside my father and held his hand. He was awake but quiet.

'Son,' he said.' It's time for you to take over from me. I'm sorry it's earlier than expected but it's time.'

'Dad, you're gonna be ok but if you think I'm ready then I will of course.' He smiled and patted my hand.

'It's all in hand, the board will see you tomorrow and you will be signed in as the new CEO of *Sylvester Media*.'

I wasn't sure what to think of it all, I wanted to tell Riley straight away, but I couldn't leave my father, not right now.

Shit! Why does shit happen to me when I least expect it?

I didn't leave the hospital until roughly eleven thirty, my mum and sister had already gone as per my fathers instructions. It was a little chilly but refreshing after being stuck in the hospital with the claustrophobia-inducing smell of disinfectant.

I thought about messaging Riley, but it was late when I got home and well she must think I'm a dick anyway now. I'll message her tomorrow, I thought and all will be well. Sunday went by as quickly as Saturday did, I took my sister out for some fresh air and a change of scenery, as both her and my mother were again at the hospital, and again I never messaged Riley, I knew shit was gonna hit the fan for sure.

I got into the Sylvester building at eight am on Monday and went straight to my father's office which in theory would now be mine. I sat in the chair and surveyed what was now my domain. It felt good and I was ready more than ready, Dad had taught me well and I guess I did listen to all those lessons he tried to teach me.

The board convened at ten and it didn't take long for them to acknowledge my take over from my father. They congratulated me and showed concern for my father all at once which showed their level of respect and acceptance of the new chain of command.

The rest of the day was a glow of gratitude from employees and members of the board. Lunch was a long drawl of talk about the company and Jeffrey Williams assured us, shares would increase ten fold now new blood was in charge and we were going to go places.

He mentioned shareholders and the forthcoming Gala, which the shareholders were of course, invited. It was a high flyers club if you like, you kinda had to have money to make money and this gave all of them a platform to show off their importance. A necessary and expensive smooze event!

I was exhausted by the end of the day, Margarette Davies, my fathers assistant came in around six o'clock and asked if I was ok after the long day.

'It gets easier Mr Sylvester,' she said warmly with a smile on her face. 'Thankyou I'm sure it will, eventually,' Jacob replied, rubbing his forehead. 'I never knew my father worked so hard,' he said, looking at her in awe.

'He did, Sir you're right. Do you need anything else before I go for the day?' 'No I'm good thankyou, see you tomorrow'

'Good night Sir,' she said.

Alone again, I was left to my thoughts and this train ride I had just embarked on. Fuck! I said aloud, I forgot to message Riley!

I quickly got out my phone to message her. What do I say it's been almost two days since I saw her. How do I break the ice with her?

Ok here goes.

Hi Riley, Jacob here

Sorry I haven't been in touch

I've been dealing with some family stuff and am really busy with the company. Can we meet up? I've really missed you.

X

I was hoping that she would message straight back, however there was no reply. I shoved the phone into my pocket and decided to leave the office. I've done enough adulting today.

I called the hospital and spoke with my father. He was feeling a little better, but still had to stay in 'observations' was all he would say. I knew he was holding back from me, but I couldn't push him while he was still vulnerable.

The drive back to my apartment was hellish, the traffic was far too busy for my liking but I just needed to get home and chill. I glanced at my phone but there weren't any texts from Riley, why? What was going on, why was she avoiding me, had I done anything wrong? Well apart from not contacting her for two days...

86

I had left her apartment and went to get my sister and then went to the hospital. That was all apart from getting some food with Bethany and trying to get her to laugh a little to ease the pressure of our fathers ill health. There was nothing I could bring to the forefront of my mind as to why she wouldn't text me back.

The remainder of the week was meetings with clients and reassuring them the change of CEO would not adversely affect them or us and our priorities had not changed. The marketing team were amazing and I knew my father had faith in their abilities to maintain the focus of where we were going and now with me on board, they were even more eager to please which was a boost for me, exhausting, but a boost nonetheless.

There had been no reply from Riley and I wasn't sure that there would be. I had blown it for sure.

For the first time since taking over from my father I had a moment to just breathe and I felt myself reliving my time with Riley in her apartment. She was spectacular and I could not for the life of me believe she was a virgin as her body reacted to my touch like no other woman had done before. We made love again and again, I know it was rampant fucking, but when I think of it now, I made love to her, I had made her a woman and that was amazing. I got hard just thinking of her and I knew I had to get back in her good books.

I texted her again.

Riley, I'm sorry if I've offended you in any way please talk to me ◡ x

I wasn't sure she would reply.

The ticks never went though, fuck! She's blocked me for sure,

What the fuck have I done, Jesus Christ.

I was tempted to just go round there and demand that she see me. I wasn't an ogre for christ's sake! I wanted to see her and I wanted to be in her arms again, why has she pushed me away?

I went to the bar after work and met with Harry and Aaron. We hadn't met up for a while due to my new status in the company, we had exchanged complimentary words to each other and then got smashed. It was a Friday after all and that's what we did, wasn't it? I would drown out my sorrows over Riley.

Chapter 11

Riley

After no message from Jacob all Sunday and most of the week, I got a message from him and I didn't know what to make of it, so I never replied. I had things on my mind and I wasn't going to lose focus.

I called Mr Quinn first thing Monday when I got into work and told him about the box being left and the letter. He scheduled me in on Friday so I had to mull over it for the whole week, which I wasn't happy about as it would affect my work.

I kept a low profile for the whole week focusing on what I could before my mind strayed elsewhere; to my parents, their letter, Jacob and what was to come for me.

Jacob messaged again. I left it as I had decided it wasn't in my interest to get involved with someone who just wanted a one time fuck.

I blocked him. Yes, it may have been a little childish, but I didn't care. I couldn't be an idiot who gave her virginity to a good time man, who left her for another woman the very next day he had fucked her in the most amazing way.

Nope, no, no thankyou.

Friday came round all too quickly and I was making my way to see Mr Quinn. I managed to get the afternoon off so I didn't have to rush and I had plenty to ask Mr Quinn about my parents' disclosure.

The receptionist was again very pleasant and this time called me by the name, which I preferred and made me smile, glad she remembered as I didn't want to embarrass her again. I sat and waited for Quinn to come get me, as that's how he rolled *the personal touch.*

When he exited from his office I again heard the drawl from Audrey Whitmore, God! this woman never gave up did she. I again hid under a magazine and waited for her to leave before I revealed my existence.

'Riley.'

'Quinn.'

Smiling that great big smile of his was always a warming effect on me which I liked. 'So Riley we have lots to talk about don't we?'

'Yes we do.'

'Ok, so you received the box and the envelope. No doubt you have many questions?' He asked in a business manner.

'Yes. What's it all about? I don't understand it'.

So your parents gave specific instructions for the last three years until you turned twenty five,' he began. 'There are certain things you have to complete in order for the next phase of their plans for you. I'm sorry. It's very complicated, but it's my job to assist my clients in their wishes. Do you understand?'

'I'm not quite sure but I think I may be catching on', I answered slowly.

'So, phase one is the letter and jewellery, some of which is Whitmore heritage, did you get the ring?'He asked.

'Yes I did. What's special about the ring ?'

'Well it was your Great Grandmother's ring. She had it specially made for her and then gave it to your mother for you for when you got older', he said,

'So did she know about me?' I asked, interested right now.

'Yes, she loved you so very much. Your Grandmother didn't like the relationship she had with you, and began to make demands of your father, which he refused and the family rowed about it. Later that year, your great grandmother passed away. Your father distanced himself from her, you were five at the time.

The jewellery that you now possess was hers - all of it. Your mother had the diamonds installed as a reminder of her and your Great Grandmother as she said you were her 'sapphire, shining bright'.

Wow, just wow! I couldn't quite understand all this information coming at me right now. 'So what is going to happen now?' I asked.

Quinn was very business-like for the next two hours going over the shares my father had invested in.

'So this means I am super rich and in some cases very powerful, if I wanted to be, right?'

'Yes Riley you have a very large stake in at least three companies which would make you a majority and a potential major player within them. As well as being financially independent for the rest of your life'

'But why did my father do all of this?'

Quinn replied with his hand on his forehead rubbing it for some kind of comfort I'm sure. 'Your father wanted the very best for you from the first time he laid eyes on you. You were his brightest of stars, the breath he inhaled day to day.

Your mother would fight him over the love he had for you.' he smiled inwardly. 'His family never understood why they only had you and no other children. His mother badgered both Marcus and Felicity over the fact more Grandchildren were needed for this family to survive.'

'I don't understand what's wrong with the family?'.

'I don't know that part, I'm afraid. Only what your father told me, which I have conveyed to you. He was a very secretive man, but with a direct approach to your safety, happiness and care. That's why they faked your death'. Quinn looked sad at this statement.

'I was going to ask about that too, why did they do that?'

'Again, I'm not sure, maybe they didn't want your Grandmother taking control of your life and now you are a woman, she cannot influence you at all'.

'I guess so.' God, there's so much to take in. 'You mentioned the shareholders would be informed in two weeks, so I'm guessing that's the end of next week? And

I turn twenty three in three weeks Quinn, what is coming next? Do you know?'

'Riley I'm not at liberty to tell you until the time of delivery. I'm sorry I am bound by these rules'.

'Oh, ok I guess I will have to wait'. 'Quinn…', I asked.

'Yes Riley'.

'Does this mean I have to declare who I am?'

'I'm afraid it might be necessary, Riley. So be ready in case you do, it's all down to your father and his bequests'.

I was overwhelmed by all the information and left Quinns in a cloud of jumbled thoughts that began to overwhelm me.

I needed a distraction right now and my girlfriends were the right ones to do this for me. On the group chat I messaged:

Girls

Drinks out

Tonight

My Treat.

Clubbing.

Xx

No sooner had I sent the message, the phone went buzzing mad, all three said yes of course and the night would begin.

Dressed up to the nines and feeling fuzzy all over, as I had downed a fair few glasses of fizz, we headed out to the infamous club where my flirting began.

'So ladies tonight we get fucked and well... maybe literally' I shrieked with raised eyebrows and a laugh.

The girls laughed at my outburst and hugged me all the same. I never told them of my appointment with Quinn as I wasn't sure where it was all going, so tonight would be a girls gone mad night.

The club was buzzing and I was ready to let my hair down. Fuck Jacob and his sexy fucking dick, making me come and taking my virginity. Well I didnt mind to be honest it was fucking amazing and lets hope there is at least one bloke here that can do that for me again.

Robin and Hannah got the drinks in, Hannah never came out THAT night as she was delivering a speech to some kind of charity for which she was involved in so we let her off, but tonight she was ours!

Emma and I were checking the dance floor and all the gorgeous people, we were on the prowl for sure. The others came back with drinks and we necked the shots and sipped the cocktails.

Yummy', Hannah said with a big smile on her face.

`Yummy,' I repeated. 'That's just the start of the cocktails girl' I said to her. 'Not the drink silly, the guy over there making 'fuck me' eyes to you', Hannah replied' sipping her cocktail again.

All eyes went across the room to where there were a few guys standing, drinking, I felt his eyes before I locked with him, Fuck!

'Fuck!' I hissed,

'That's Jacob,' I said to Hannah, whose eyes widened dramatically.

'Holy shit Ry, you never said he was that good looking, I would do him for sure'. 'Yes Hannah, and Riley did several times', Robin replied.

We all laughed but I could feel his stare on my flesh burning a hole into me.

I finally gave in and met his eyes, they were so fucking mesmerising I just wanted to float over to him wrap my arms around him and kiss his beautiful mouth hungrily.

I smiled at him, I couldn't help it, I was weak and I knew it.

I don't think he saw me though as my hand was in front of my face holding my straw in place.

I looked away and finished my drink in one whole gulp.

'Right girls, let's dance,' I said firmly. 'I need to get rid of this tension in my body'.

The girls necked their drinks and we moved to the dance floor.

The music was fantastic tonight. My body was out of control and I actually loved it. For the first time I had no inhibitions. My body was my tool and I now knew how to use it properly.

The advances from guys moving in closer to us was inevitable and the girls were all over it like wildfire.

Emma was the first to use her body to attract a partner for the night followed by Robin then Hannah. I was lost, lost in my mind and lost in the music.

I suddenly felt hands coming round my waist and wasn't sure what my next move would be. I knew it wasn't him as I knew his smell. This guy had a different scent and didn't make me feel the same way that Jacob had done. Had he ruined me for other men?

What was I going to do about it?

I held his hands and moved out of his touch, faced him and danced. He was happy at that and there was a distance to us and it was ok, I didn't have to sort him out with a defence move. The girls were around us and we danced in a group which was better for me as I knew things weren't going to end well.

A few more drinks were consumed and I was on cloud nine, the music was awakening something inside me, something free and raw. My hands were working their way over my body in tune to the music and god I loved it so very much. The girls were aware of my change and were enthralled with my moves following suit in some cases.

'Jesus Ry, your fucking on fire tonight girl!' Hannah shouted over the music. 'Go fucking me!' I replied. Alcohol made me bolshy.

Robin threw her head back and laughed, it was so funny.

I was lost in my world when I was brought back to the here and now by his scent. I didn't let on.

I knew he was near but I was super aware, the eyeballing my friends gave me just before he touched me was very obvious.

Warm hands touched my shoulders and then caressed my sides, I licked my lips at his touch but kept on dancing waiting for him to make the move.

I couldn't bring myself to turn him away, my body needed his touch for sure and so what if it was just sex, I needed him right now.

I felt his body close to me as his hands wrapped themselves around me, his face close to me, his breath on my ear.

'I missed you, why did you block me baby?'

'You aired me Jacob, what do you expect?' I was calm, but at the same time wanted to beat the shit out of him and fuck him all in one moment.

He pulled me closer pressing his length into me, he was erect and I fucking wanted him so bad, my pussy tensed at his closeness. God, she was weak too!

'I'm sorry I didn't mean to, I had stuff I needed to attend to'. He sounded remorseful, but I knew he was with another woman.

'Bullshit Jacob, I saw you with another woman on Sunday, was I just the fish you caught in your net and fucked senseless, did I give myself to a man whore?'

'Riley, what the fuck are you on about? I didn't go off with another woman after we made love'.

'Yeah right'. I was pissed off and drunk at the same time. Jacob pulled me harder to his body, my back against his chest.

'Not gonna work this time buddy' I said, turning my body to face him, being bold and brazen for sure. I looked up to him and into his eyes, but before I could say anything else he kissed me hard, forcing my lips apart to access my mouth. His tongue gliding inside, taking me, I kissed him back with all my might and my hands thrust into his hair, his fucking glorious hair.

Everything around me was in a haze; faint music and twirling feelings due to the drink.

I pulled away from him looking at his mouth then his eyes back to his mouth, I couldn't help myself. I pulled him to me and kissed him this time and he reciprocated all too lovingly.

'Jacob, stop, we can't do this, it's not right. Please'.

'Ooh baby I have missed your mouth and your sexy, fucking body, I need you Riley. I've been so lonely without you'.

'WHAT THE FUCK?'

I pushed him away. 'Lonely, you!' I scoffed. 'I just don't get you Jacob, you pursue me and then when I give in and you have given me the best first time ever again and again, you then air me, then after almost a week you decide to message me. I'm not a good time girl for when you feel lonely. Like I said before, I'm not that kind of girl'.

'Jesus Riley calm the fuck down, I was really busy, believe me. I've got shit going on that I can't, I just can't get …'

'We all have shit going on, don't you know that, I've got so much fucking shit going on you could fertilise a whole fucking garden with it'.

'I messaged you and saw you Sunday with a woman, how do you think I felt, hey?'

Before Jacob could say anything I was off the dancefloor and down the hall to the ladies. I needed water on my face before it burnt itself off.

I stared at the woman in front of me not knowing what the fuck she was going to do in this situation, 'Riley girl look at yourself,' I said out loud. Thankfully there wasn't anyone in there.

The door to the ladies flew open and Jacob was there in the doorway, I glanced across to him and his eyes were heavy and seducing me. Fuck why does he do this to me.

'Riley, please'.

He entered the room and the door closed behind him,

I was trapped nowhere to go, yes the toilet I'll hide in there he won't come after me for sure.

I moved towards the stall and went to walk in, I wasn't quick enough as Jacob was behind me in an instant, closing the door and locking it,

'Riley, please I want you, I'm sorry, what else can I say?' 'I cant Jacob, I ca - '

He was on me like the prey I was, his mouth on mine, his hands burning skillfully over my body. His hand was on my back and the other behind my head pulling me in super close.

I moaned at his mouth and his kisses, I was captivated by him and his presence. He moved his hand to my dress and pulled it up around my waist and pulled my knickers down,

'Jacob', I groaned. 'We can't.'

'Oh Riley I fucking need you.' His hands were swift and quickly on my sex, which of course was so fucking wet for him. 'Fuck! Riley, you're so wet for me always'.

He circled my clit with his magic hands and slipped a finger inside of me, I groaned out loud with the pleasure,

'Riley fuck,yes!'

Before I could register much he sprung his dick from his pants and was at the entrance of my slit.

'Yes', I whispered.'Take me Jacob. I want you'.

'Fuck', I moaned as he entered me slowly, filling me up. 'Fuck Riley, Fuck', he groaned.

He lifted me up and I wrapped my legs around his waist. He fucked me good and proper in the ladies toilet and I loved every minute of it, I needed it as my body longed for his touch. It was raw and lustful.

Chapter 12

Jacob

The drinks were going down well and then I saw her with her friends, she looked fucking phenomenal, so powerful, confident, yet so far away.

Her friends noticed me before she did, I couldn't make out what the redhead said because of the music but they all turned my way and she took her time before she caught my eye.

I thought I saw her smile at me but I wasnt sure, I missed her and I wanted her, I wanted to fuck her right now and needed to know why she blocked me. I took my time before making my way over to her and her friends.

The reunion didn't go down as well as I wanted. She was yelling at me about another woman after I left her. That was ridiculous, as I wasn't with another woman that day, well only my sister but how did she know, did she see me? how did I miss her, she was clearly mistaken but she wouldn't listen to reason, her stubborn streak for sure.

I kissed her like my life depended on it, she kissed me back so I thought we were good, how wrong I was.

'I've got shit going on' I said, well it was the wrong thing today she flew at me with her words and then stormed off towards the ladies.

I couldn't let this lie. I needed her to understand I wanted her mind, as well as body and soul.

I followed her making sure no one went in after her.

I made my move and there was no turning back, she flinched when I opened the door, like a cat caught in the lights of a car.

She moved to the stall and I was on her so quickly she didn't have time to lock the door, I took her and she let me. We fucked, yes we fucked and I loved it, we were one again, my body whole; with her touch, I was alive.

She screamed my name and I came hard into her, she shuddered with her orgasm and I felt exhilarated by her.

'Jacob what have we done?' she said to me, eyes heavy with desire.

'We fucked Riley and you loved it, let me take you home and make love to you all night.

'Jacob, we can't, I can't do this, I'm sorry, I want you so badly, but I just can't.' Her words were like a knife to my gut. She pulled away from me and sorted herself out, she was sweaty and beautiful and smelled of sex. Why didn't she want me to take her home? I couldn't understand her, one minute she was hot and then the next cold.

'Riley please listen we need to talk about this,'

She never said a word just looked at the floor as she left me there, again fucking leaving me raw and yearning for more of her.

'RILEY.'

She was gone, again.

Chapter 13

Riley

What the fuck have I done, this is just not right, why do I do this to myself, I need to go right now.

'Girls I need to go, I've done something bad, real bad. Robin was the first to react.

'Oh, Riley what's happened?

'I've just had sex with Jacob again, I need to go. 'Shit, Ry, come on let's go.

'GIRLS!' Robin shouted. 'We need to go right now.'

The ride home was silent. I couldn't face my friends properly. I was disgusted in myself and what I had stooped to do in public of all places, SLUT I thought. Yes I know it happened before but I never had sex with him in the club, anyone could have walked in, just knowing he gave me the best orgasm I've ever had was a benefit.

The girls dropped me off on their way and I went to bed with regret and desire warring in my mind.

I woke to messages from my friends and also Jacob, I hadn't realised that I had unblocked him.

Robin: Ry r u ok?

Emma: Riley hey girl you ok? X Hannah: Riley message me r u ok? Jacob: Riley I need to see you.

Jacob: Riley please answer me, I know you have unblocked me as the message has gone through.

Jacob: Jesus Riley just, message me.

I threw the phone onto the bed and laid back down. I was disappointed in myself, why did I do that, who was I becoming. The fear and disgust run through my mind like a tornado. I can't keep doing this to myself, I'm not a booty call.

I never messaged my friends until the evening. Jacob I didn't message at all. We all exchanged chats with the group and I felt a little better, but not completely.

I got the box that was sent to me and looked again at the jewellery, they were exquisite pieces, the amount of money they must have been was unreal to think about, where would I wear such things I'm not high society I'm just me, little old me the girl who drops her panties for the hot guy. I'm a slut for sure.

My mind went to the conversation with Quinn regarding the deliveries that were due and the impending truth of who I was. Only one more week until the businesses my father invested in knew of me and my place in their companies... Boards I corrected! Shit, what was I going to do? Is there even a choice here?

I emailed Quinn to see what was happening, fishing for info really about Audrey Whitmore, my Grandmother. Eww! I didn't like her the night I met her with Jacob and I didn't even know her.

Once the email was sent I started to research the companies on the list my father had stated:

Krane Media, They were a young company back when I was little, and my father obviously saw potential in them, they are now in the top ten percent in the country which has made them very profitable.

Rogers Marketing Media: These were in the top five percent again, big ballers. God this was extraordinary to say the least.

Clarkes Galleries: These had twenty five Galleries around the world and again were in the top ten percent for gallery profits.

This was becoming more incredible, my shares alone were worth so much just from these companies alone.

Then there was:

Rowthorne Media Marketing, My place of work, wow just wow. I know we were a good company but I was unaware of how much we made yearly and the profits. I was one of the highest share holders for the company so my identity would be known very shortly. Lastly there was the:

Sylvester Media Inc Group. Again forty percent, the company that Jacob's Father was the CEO of. That isn't gonna go down well I'm sure.

Decisions had to be made and made very soon.

I isolated myself from my friends for the remainder of the weekend and just needed to get myself together and ready for what the week will bring. I was nervous for

Friday as that's when the next delivery was due and not knowing was hard.

I messaged the girls first thing Monday in our chat and sent my apologies for my lack of communication as it was not really my style. All was forgiven bythe time I reached my office. There weren't many people in as early as me, so itwas nice to just chill in peace. I was in the break room making a coffee as I forgot to get one on the way due to my begging my friends and getting them back on side. Minding my own business Greta came in with a smile on her face.

'Hi, Riley, how was your weekend?'

'Hi Greta, it was ummmm ok I guess, how about you?' Knowing if I turned it round she would have done something great for sure.

'Oh I went to this great Gallery show on Saturday' she was animated while speaking, 'It was a local artist displaying their work, Clarkes Gallery it's very upmarket.'

I couldn't help but put the biggest smile on my face. Little did she know I was getting rich off her visit, lol.

'Greta, that sounds fantastic, glad you had fun.'

We left the break room together and sat at our desks and I guess started our day. The morning seemed to drag, but I was very productive, finishing briefs for clients and making sure I wasn't behind with my deadlines.

Lunchtime came and I was gonna head to the nearest cafe and just chill. I was starving as I had missed breakfast, so I was ready to eat a whole cow. My phone pinged, as I left the elevator and I looked at it as I left the building. It was Jacob, I rolled my eyes and just didn't need any shit today especially not from him.

Riley, please just speak to me, don't shut me out.

I was tempted not to answer, but it just had to get this done with and move on.

Jacob, I'm not sure what you want from me, our encounters cannot happen the way they have been, I need honesty in my life. I have so much going on that I am making rash decisions, like the one with you at the club.

This has to stop and stop now. I'm sorry.

I hesitated to send it, but this had to be done and said.

I sat in the cafe with my lunch, no answer from Jacob, so I was kind of relieved at that.

I returned to my office with lots of thoughts running through my mind, there were a few people hanging around my desk, I wasn't sure what was going on. As I got closer they looked my way.

'Hi guys what's up?'

The people moved and there on the desk was the most beautiful bouquet. 'Wow, Riley, who have you been impressing?' Emily said.

'I'm not quite sure I get you Em.' I replied.

'Riley, these roses are decorated with diamonds, look!'

I got closer and wow she was right, each rose had a diamond stone set into them, they were exquisite.

'Gosh these are just too beautiful, I wonder who sent them,' I said in awhisper. There was a card set into the side of the bouquet with my name handwritten on the envelope.

I opened the card to see they were from Jacob.

Please Riley, I need to see you. Xx

I smiled and looked again at the flowers. 'Ok guys show's over,they're from a very good friend of mine.'

I placed the flowers on my desk and sat down to work again.

Again it was just me and Greta. She wandered from her area over to mine. I set myself to work with a smile on my face. I looked at Greta and she smiled at me, not asking the question we both knew she wanted to ask. She left me shortly after.

My email went and there it was the email from Jacob.

Riley,

I hope you got my flowers, I wasn't sure your favourites so I got you roses in all the colours I could get.

I think we have gotten off to a bad start for reasons that we can't control.

I cannot stop thinking about you and I really need to see you and explain so many things in my life right now.

Please let's meet up and talk. Jacob

I took in Jacobs email and had to think about how I went about replying. Now wasn't the right time, I had to think. I left the email for the next few days as I wasn't sure what I wanted to do about it.

Wednesday afternoon we all got an intranet message confirming the association with the *Sylvester Group*. I couldn't help, but laugh out loud, Emma looked at me puzzled. I waved to her and smiled.

This week was getting crazier by the minute.

I emailed Jacob about the new found association with his fathers company and congratulated him and his father.

I never mentioned anything about the email he sent me as I wasn't sure what to say and how I felt.

I left a little earlier than usual as I wanted to make plans about what I was going to do with the shares and my identity reveal. Mr Quinn had assured me he would guide me in whatever decision I decided upon. My phone pinged while I was on my way home, it was Jacob.

Riley, I haven't heard from you since my email. Listen, I need to know what's going on.

I put the phone into my pocket and didn't reply. Not now Jacob, not now.

Chapter 14

Jacob

Since the night with Riley she has been silent, I've tried to contact her so many times I'm not sure what to do about her and my addiction to her. We are fucking brilliant together such connection I can't stop thinking about her, its affecting my sleep my concentration, I just want to get things on an even path not the rollercoaster it has been.

My father was released from the hospital under strict orders to rest. They didn't find anything untoward, but that didn't mean there wasn't something brewing. The board was happy he was recovering well and informed him of my success so far, even though it's only been a week. They were in contact with him almost everyday, as there were items still to be discussed with him, as well as me.

We had the Gala coming up and I want to invite Riley as my plus one, however I didn't think she would accept right now, as we aren't exactly on talkingterms, Icy as fuck terms yes, but not talking, not communicating.

I sent her a rather extravagant bouquet of roses, hoping it would break the ice; they were probably the most expensive roses ever, but that didn't work. God what was I thinking she's a chick for christ's sake and I like fucking her, that's all it should be shouldn't it? I cant get her out of my fucking head.

The board sent out confirmation of our association with *Rowthorne Media*, the company that Riley works for, at least this way I can see her without having an excuse, company business and all that. Riley sent me an email and congratulated my father and me on the new association. She didn't know that my father was poorly or that I had taken over. Why would she? We weren't exactly communicating like normal people.. I didn't reply to what I was going to say, tell her everything about my father and that the company is now mine to run, no, I had to wait until it was the right time.

But when was it going to be the right time?

Friday came all too quickly and that afternoon we had our shareholders board meeting, which I remembered I always hated, my father insisted I take part as, 'One day this would be all yours Jacob' he would say.

The standard agenda was worked through, minutes of the last meeting, outstanding actions, finance and then Ronald, he always took care of shareholder interest in all new and old business, dropped a bombshell.

'Mr Sylvester we have been informed a majority shareholder of the company has now come into their own and will need to be filled in with the company's Business Plan. I'm sure your father would have told of the single majority shareholder that had invested in our company. A statement rather than a question.

'Ronald, I'm afraid I wasn't aware, is this something I should be worried about?' 'No sir, the shares are held by just one person who has not shown interest in the company, but we have to inform you they may want to attend future Board meetings or possibly be included in the decision making.

'Ok, well who is it then?

'Well sir the thing is, their identity is still pending; we are not quite sure of their name as yet.'

'WHAT?'

'Yes we are aware of the shareholder, their identity will apparently be shared at the Gala in two weeks' time.'

'Fuck, why so long? whats going on here Ronald?' I was furious. What is this shit I'm hearing?

All eyes turned to the Board member from Legal - he looked around at all the members and said. 'According to the terms of the contract, no details of the individual would be made available until after they 'come of age', that being on the day the Gala is to be held.'

Jacob stood up. 'Gentlemen, ladies, I have business to attend to.' The low mutters as I left the boardroom were very much apparent.

What the fuck was going on right now, a large shareholder silent for what twenty two years suddenly wants in on our business, no fucking way was I going to let that happen. What if they try to push us out! I needed to speak with my father

over this. I had to be calm, he didn't need stress and I well, I didn't need this crap either.

Tonight was going to be a drinking night. I needed to forget shit that's gone down today. Who was this shareholder anyway, why wait until the Ball to reveal their identity, this was all bullshit.

Chapter 15

Riley

The week went faster than I thought it would to be honest. Friday came round and I was nervous as I wasn't sure what was going to happen. I knew I was going to get something today and I had some decisions to be made, but today was going to be a long arse drawl, for sure.

My emails were steady for the day, new clients and old business. There was an email from Quinn suggesting I go to the ground floor as there was going to be a delivery for me at 11:15.

God he is so cryptic. I said quietly so as not to get Emma's stare again. I had been saying shit out loud all week and Emma was getting a little pissed at me because of it.

'Emma I have to go downstairs. There is a delivery for me. Can you watch my phone please, I'm not expecting anything but you know…'

'Yes Riley, sure thing'. She waved me off as I headed downstairs.

And true to his word, as I approached the ground floor reception, there was a delivery man standing there all official. He wasn't a normal delivery guy, black suit, black shirt, black tie, almost like the Men in Black suits. I was quite amused at his attire.

'Miss Shure? Riley Shure?' He said with a strong voice almost commanding, he was a tall man 'built like a brick shit house.' Robin would say, when she saw a big strong guy. He wore sunglasses, why??

He was also wearing an earpiece so he was part of something.

'Yes that's me, I'm Riley Shure.'

"Please sign here', gesturing to me with a piece of paper.

I signed the sheet and he gave me an envelope. Then pulled out from his jacket another envelope, like the one fixed to the box I had received two weeks earlier.

'Thankyou.' I said in a low soft voice, almost a whisper.

I knew the one from his jacket must have been from my father, but what was this other one he gave me and I had to sign for? Confused, I smiled up at him and he turned and left without a word.

Standing there watching him leave he got into a black SUV and then drove off; definitely an MIB wannabe.

I returned to my desk and sat and looked at the two envelopes. Do I open them now or wait? The suspense was killing me, only half an hour to wait for lunch then I would read them.

That half hour was the longest of my fucking life so far, leaving quickly when the clock just turned twelve fifteen. In the elevator I pulled out both envelopes and studied them.

The one I signed for was a thick card and guilt with gold edging, very posh I thought, wondering what's inside.

The other one was just a normal envelope with again my name, hand written on the front.

I stayed close to the building and slipped into a booth at a nearby cafe. I opened the posh one first, as I was excited to see what was in it.

Inside was an invitation to the Annual Shareholders Ball. Funnily enough it was on my birthday, my Twenty Third Birthday. I had to laugh, as this was becoming a fucking joke. I looked round to see where the cameras were 'cause this wasn't real this shit, truly wasn't real.

It was beautifully gilded with gold edging and an embossed floral design. My name was not present on the invite, but attached to the back was a slip inviting me to attend with my name and confirmation.

I'm sure Mr Quinn sorted this to give me the option of going and revealing who I am, or not going and maintaining my secret status.

I couldn't help but think if I chose not to be named, would I still be entitled to the shares etc? That was yet another question for Quinn to answer.

The other envelope seemed to burn into me and I was hesitant to open it. The last one I received opened up Pandora's box for me and a world I was not really prepared for. Jacob's world.

I sipped on my coffee and decided to open it, what more would I have to endure to be me? What more things had my father put in place for me?

I pulled out the letter and opened it up. I instantly knew it was from my father as it was the same handwriting as before.

Dearest Riley

I hope my letter finds you well and not too overwhelmed with what is happening around you and maybe the prospect of you taking on your family name. Your mother and I have always had your best interests at heart and our love for you never faltered in any way.

Riley, your life will change if you <u>choose</u> it to. You will always have support throughout your life, as that's what we have put in place for you.

Mr Quinn has a box for you which he has been holding since before we were gone, it contains documents to an estate that you will inherit if you wish to reveal your identity. I know this sounds as though we are pushing you to make the decision to be a Whitmore again, however, we hope that you choose it for yourself and for no other reason.

My love is always yours

Dad x

There were no words again, things were being revealed to me and I wasn't sure which way to turn.

Right now I wish I wasn't at work cause I needed a drink badly.

The walk back to my office was brief thankfully, as I had seemed to be day dreaming and not concentrating on the walk ahead, god knows where I would have ended up if it was a longer walk.

I was drawn from my daydream by someone calling me. 'Riley! Riley, wait up!'

I turned to find Jacob walking briskly towards me.

'Jacob, I can't stop. I have to get back to work.' I said. 'I'm going to be late.' 'Riley, I need to speak with you, I'll walk with you, as I have a meeting with Mr Rogers.'

'Oh? I thought your dad handled the meetings.'

'Um yeah he would have done, but due to ill-health, he's no longer the CEO, I've taken over'.

'Oh god, is he ok?' I asked gently.

'Yes, we had a scare and he was in hospital for a while, the day I left you actually, and well, he decided that it was time for me to step up and so that's what I have done.'

'Oh,that's fantastic news!' I said.'Congratulations' Focusing on his appointment as CEO, rather than his father's ill health.

I smiled at him. '...and I'm sorry to hear about your father.' I hoped that he could tell I was sincere.

No time for anything further as the lift pinged and we walked into the reception area. Nora, who was sitting at her desk, looked up at the two of us, smirked at me and smiled at Jacob.

'Mr Sylvester, welcome back. Mr Rogers is waiting for you on the Twenty Fifth floor, please go on up.'

'I'll take him Nora.' I said and we walked to the elevators.

As the doors closed Jacob turned to me and lifted my chin, so that our eyes met, he was deliciously beautiful in every way. He seemed to study me then closed the distance between us and kissed me. He was gentle and passionate like a lover, waking in the morning after a night of love-making.

The kiss was long and my hands reached up around his neck and the kiss deepened for a moment. God, my body felt alive with his touch. He placed his hands around my waist and pulled me even closer to him, the kissing was intense and all consuming. I wanted him to take me, it had been too long and I craved his touch. I needed him to take me right then and there. I was drawn to this man, like a magnet; a moth to a flame.

The bell went to announce the floor and we pulled apart reluctantly, both panting, more than a little unfocussed. The doors opened and I walked him to Mr Rogers' secretary's desk and said goodbye before returning to my floor.

I felt his kiss on my lips for the remainder of the day and it was like heaven.

I couldn't help but think about what Jacob had said regarding his father and that he was now the CEO of the *Sylvester Group*. The same company I could potentially hold a majority share in.

I had to smile at myself for even thinking about it, god could you imagine me rocking up to a board meeting and the looks on peoples faces, a nervous little laugh escaped me, before I even realised it. Emma looked over at me confused.

'Sorry Em, thinking out loud again'. I explained. She shook her head and went back to her work.

Around four o'clock I received an email from Quinn regarding my letter from my father, he stated he had something in his office for me and could I come by after work. I quickly emailed him back to confirm I would be there and asked what the contents were.

I didn't expect a reply, as I knew he was a busy man. My email pinged and it was from Jacob.

Riley, I loved seeing you today and I'm sorry I was dominating the conversation. I wanted to contact you about my meeting and then there you were, in the right place at the right time.

I wanted to ask you if you were free next Saturday? I have a Gala to attend and I wanted you to be my date.

I hope you can come as these things are just boring and your company and smile would make it better, a whole lot better.

I smiled at the email, it was sweet and I would have loved to have been his plus one, but as I was invited too and I wasn't sure what I was going to do about it I hesitated answering him initially. By attending, I would be putting myself out there for all to pull at, and my fathers family would be all over me like a rash. And then there was Jacob. How would he feel about my new status and how would I even go about telling him what is going on with my life.

I replied that I needed to think about the invite as I had plans for that day, well I did, didn't I? It was my birthday after all. God what a birthday that could be, ha ha ha.

I said I was happy to see him too and that it would be good to see him again soon.

For some reason I put a kiss on the end.

The trip to Quinns didn't take long today, maybe because I was eager to see him and find out what was going on with this estate thingy, it was getting all a little bit 'out there' if I'm honest. Why couldn't they just put everything on the table instead of all of this bloody cloak and dagger shit going on.

An hour or so later, the outcome of my visit with Quinn was I noun owned a massive Estate on the outskirts of the city. It was roughly 200 acres, mostly landscaped with a lake and some other stuff I wasn't really focused on. The house itself was magnificent from the pictures I was given and had been taken care of since my parents passing, again under a pseudonym, to avoid any link to the name Whitmore. I think there were horses there as well and the stables were managed by a small farm that was near the estate.

'Riley dear, have you thought anymore of what your parents are asking of you?' He said in a gentle tone, concerned in case this was one question too many for me to cope with.

I thought for a moment. 'Well, do you think it's a good idea to do this and be known to my grandmother?'

'Riley, whatever you decide, know that you will be supported at all times. I can assure you, as per your parents wishes, I am here for you until, well, until you no longer need my guidance and, when you turn 25, all the decision making for your trust fund is yours, unless of course, you retain our services.'

'Quinn, thank you, it means alot to me that you are here as I can't, well I don't have anyone really to share all this with and my friends would not understand all this going on, with the secrets and all that.' He nodded.

I could feel the vein in my forehead wanting to protrude out into the air. I rubbed my head and just needed to take a minute and think about what I was going to do.

'Quinn…', I asked. 'Yes Riley'.

'Can I get an invite for my friends for the Gala, is that possible? I ask as it's my birthday and they normally organise something for me.'

'Yes, I don't see why not. Forward me their names and I will make the arrangements.'

'Quinn, one last thing.'

'Yes', his eyebrows raised and he looked curious.

'I think I'm ready for my next chapter. I accept what has been bestowed upon me. Where do I sign?'

'Riley, are you sure? This is great!'. He was excited now rushing round his desk to get the paperwork out for me to sign.

'Yes I'm sure, I don't know the reasons behind my parents death but I can assure you I will not be bullied and I will stand up to whomever comes at me'.

After another hour in Quinns office, signing documents and going over other stuff related to what I had recently inherited, I left with a weight lifted off my shoulders. It was thrilling and scary but when I left I had a little spring in my step.

I messaged the girls that I needed to see them as I had a surprise for them.

We met up at mine for dinner and I sat them down. 'I want to tell you what has been going on with me over the last month or so because I don't want things to affect our friendship.' The girls looked at each other with mild concern. 'It's nothing bad, well not really, but it will entail some major changes in mine - and your - lives...but before I say anything - my birthday this year.' I paused for effect.

'Riley, what is it?' Robin asked.'Stop with the suspense!'

'I want to invite you all to a Ball, next Saturday on my birthday. I know we normally arrange something with just us but I really want you all to come, please say you'll come'.

Hannah spoke first, as Robin was flabbergasted.

'Riley how the fuck did you score an invite the biggest ball ever?' 'Well that my lovely Hannah is what I'm getting at'.

'My parents invested heavily in several companies before I was born, those shares have now been passed to me, and they are not unsubstantial.' I pause again, I have all their attention now because I was using grown-up words. 'But there is a catch. I have to revert back to my family name in order to keep them. It's a big step as for reasons I'm not sure of yet, my parents kept me hidden from the family.'

'Um what?,' Robin interjected.' You've spent the better part of half your life on your own and you have *family*? Like blood relations? Your parents must have had a bloody good reason for keeping you away from them if they thought you would do better with no-on, rather than have them in your life!' Arms crossed over her chest, it heaved, as she tried to understand their decision.

'What is your actual name Riley?' Hannah quietly asked.

'Oh right yeah, it's Whitmore, as in *THE* Whitmore's. Old money and lots of it.' Riley sounded a little apologetic, but just a little.

Emma raised her head to the ceiling and screeched like she had heard the funniest of jokes, 'Riley is going to be a gazillionaire girls! Come on this is hilarious, Riley you're shitting us aren't you?'

As Riley shook her head, she said.'It's very complicated and long winded, but I'm assured I am going to be wealthy beyond my wildest dreams!' The last of this was delivered with her jumping up and down and screaming. The girls all jumped up hugging Riley and each other. This had to be the best news ever!

'But I wanted to do something great for us all so I've got you all invited to the Ball as my guests,' she looked across at each of their faces to make sure they were all on board with this; the smiles on their faces Riley took as a resounding yes to the invite. 'Right...so that means we have to go shopping!'

Again, another shriek that should have broken the window panes but Robin was super excited right now, shopping was her thing and she was bloody brilliant at it.

'Ok, we need to book the salon and then the best place in town for a dress, we need jewellery and shit'.

'Its ok guys. I'm gonna sort it all, they will come to us on Saturday and dress us all. My treat.

We all hugged, a girly mess of laughing, crying and snotty noses; these girls had always been there for me; helped me more than they realised and I wanted to give something back.

Chapter 16

Jacob

Drinking with the lads did not suppress my anger at all; it just consumed me that my weekend was full of anger yet also smothered with desire. I needed to see Riley. I needed to speak to her about everything that has been happening, she would understand better and we could go back to being intimate again. I missed her body, her smell the way she touched me. My mission for the coming week was to see her again and kiss her and make love to her.

I decided to walk to the meeting I had with Rogers, it was a nice day and I needed to clear my head. Maybe I would drop by Rileys desk to see her while I was there, that would be ok wouldn't it.

Before I could think anymore of it I saw her walking across from me and I shouted out her name. She was daydreaming again, I remembered our first encounter and she was probably daydreaming then too, I called out again and she turned to face me this time.

She was breathtakingly beautiful. I wanted to kiss her then but we were close to her building.

She said she couldn't stop as she had to get back to work. I explained I had a meeting with her boss, she looked a little confused and asked why my father wasn't here instead.

'Oh, what is that? I thought your dad handled the meetings she questioned me.

'Um yeah he would have done but he's no longer the CEO, I've taken over. I told her rubbing the back of my neck.

'Oh god, is he ok?' She asked with concern in her voice.

'Yes, we had a scare and he was in hospital for a while, the Sunday I left you actually', I said to her, raising my eyebrows at her, 'and well he decided that it was time for me to step up and so that's what I have done'.

'Oh, that's fantastic news' she said to me.Congratulations'.

She smiled at me. '...and I'm sorry to hear about your father.' Her smile was different to other occasions, it was...intimate, like she knew I could do this.

As we walked into the reception area the woman behind the desk looked firstly at Riley with a kind of smirk on her lips and a glint in her eyes, she then looked at me and smiled.

'Mr Sylvester, welcome back, Mr Rogers is waiting for you on the 25th floor. Please go on up'.

She was polite and flirtatious for sure, but my eyes were only for Riley.

'I'll take him Nora', Riley said and we walked to the elevators side by side. I so desperately wanted to hold her hand.

As the doors to the elevator closed I turned to Riley and lifted her chin so that our eyes met, she was beautiful in every way. I couldn't help myself but to linger on her face before I closed the distance between us and kissed her.

It was a gentle yet passionate kiss. I wanted to woo her with my mouth before I could get to devour her in bed. The kiss was long, Riley drew her hands to my neck and deepened our moment, fuck she felt so good, my cock was hardenening just from our kissing. I placed my hands at her waist to draw her closer to me. I was aching for her, the kissing was intense. I knew she wanted me, as much as I wanted her.

The bloody elevator bell went announcing the floor and we pulled apart reluctantly. The doors opened and I followed Riley to Rogers' secretary's desk.

She said goodbye and left me there.

My meeting with Rogers wasn't too long and he was happy for my involvement after I told him about my father.

'Please Mr Sylvester send my regards to your father,' Rogers said when I was about to leave.

'Yes sure thing, are you coming to the Shareholders Gala, Rogers?' 'Yes I believe so, it's my wife's best night out', he laughed.

'Ok then I'll see you there'.

I needed to email Riley and get her on board, as my date for the ball. I hoped that she would agree and I could again pursue her and her sexy body.

The reply she gave me wasn't exactly what I was hoping for but it gave me a little light to work with. I would just have to be patient.

My initial week was crap, all business and no play. My mind would wander to Riley's face, the encounters we had and our kissing, the way I took her that night and the following morning before it was so cruelly ripped from me, I needed to see her. It was Wednesday now and I'm sure she wanted to see me so I message her on her phone:

Hi, its Jacob

Wanted to see if you were free tonight For dinner,maybe?

I hesitated before sending as I didn't want to be pushy but I wanted her so badly. Send! It was now out of my hands whether she would meet me or not. Now I had to wait.

Almost immediately she replied I couldn't believe my luck when I saw her name on my phone. I opened the message hesitantly as I was expecting her to turn me down, she didn't.

Hi dinner sounds great,

why don't you come to mine and I can cook forus, it would be great to spend some time with you.

I could not believe my luck this was it I was back in the game and I wasnt going to fuck it up this time.

I rushed home to shower and change, dressed in dark denim jeans, boots, a white shirt and blazer, splashed on some cologne before I headed to her place. She messaged me while I was on my way home to say come at seven. Perfect.

I got a driver to take me to her apartment as I wasn't going to drive, collected a bottle of fizz from the local shop near her place and headed up to her. I knocked and waited too eagerly to see her.

She didn't keep me waiting long, she opened the door and she took my breath away. She was wearing a long floral dress with white flowers on it spaghetti straps and low enough I could see her breasts moving up and down, her hair was back curled and looked amazing. She smelt amazing too.

'Hi, come in.' she said smiling.

I entered her apartment and the memories of our time together came flooding back. I closed my eyes briefly to recall the memory and when my eyes opened she was standing close to me looking at me smiling. I couldn't resist, I leant down and kissed her beautiful lips. She moaned ever so slightly which just pushed me over the edge.

I grabbed her round the waist with one hand and the other to the back of her head and deepened our kiss. Her hands went to my neck and her moans continued. Fuck she was making me horny! I wanted to fuck her.

I pulled back from her as my desire threatened to overwhelm me, she too looked as though she could rip off my clothes. I placed the bottle down and took her hand and led her to her bedroom. She didn't resist me, not once. We entered her room and I turned to face her, she blushed a little as I'm guessing she remembered what happened the last time we were here.

I reached out to her to pull her near so I could remove her clothes before I devoured her. She placed her hands on my chest to stop me and told me to take off my jacket, she was warm and confident and she meant business and fuck that was hot. She never came across as the domineering type, well I was her first and I was hoping that she hadn't had sex with anyone else, that would have killed me.

She came closer to me and started to undo my shirt ever so gently, I played with her breasts over her dress and her breathing quickened at my touch.

She pushed my shirt down over my shoulders and traced her hand over my chest, my heart began to quicken and my cock ached for her touch.

I removed my belt and undone my jeans, as I did this she removed her dress in one move and it gently floated to the ground revealing her lace bra and lace knickers.

I swiftly removed my jeans and boxers and my dick sprung out which made Rileys' eyes widen, she licked her bottom lip as she gazed at me, before I could reach for her she pushed me onto her bed and crawled up over me.

'I've wanted to do this to you since our night together, she said.

She lowered her head to my chest and trailed small kisses along it and worked her way down. She nestled in between my legs as she navigated her mouth to just above my cock.

'Yes', I said reaching out to her hair, she placed one hand at the base of my cock and lowered her mouth to my tip. Licking the end sent a shudder through me.

'Fuck! Riley, yes'. I said hoarsely.

I looked at her and saw her take my cock into her mouth, slowly at first, licking the tip and then it went in. I threw my head back to enjoy her mouth on me and felt her head bobbing up and down while she pumped the base of my cock with her hand. God she was good at this, licking me again I needed to taste her so bad. I placed my hands on her shoulders and drew her off my cock and swiftly turned her so she was now under me.

'You are all fucking woman Riley Shure, do you know that?, I told her as my mouth went to her sex.

As my tongue went to her slick clit she moaned out loud. God she was wet! so wet, I began lapping up her juices as she moaned each time my tongue devoured her pussy. I pushed two fingers straight into her and she arched her back and moaned so loudly I wanted to fuck her so bad and so hard.

It didn't take long to reach a climax. Riley came so loudly, she arched her back as the orgasm took her. I reached up over her as she was coming down and pushed my cock into her hard and deep, she screamed my name and I went wild

with desire for her. Fucking her harder and harder, her body working with mine and she came again and I continued almost there myself, it felt almost animilistic our sex tonight and I was raw and passionate.

'Fuck Riley!' I shouted as she tightened her pussy round my cock, bringing me to the edge. As she came down and the tension released from around my cock I turned her over so she was on all fours, her face resting on the bed and her fine ass in the air. I grabbed hold of her hips and pushed deeper into her again, this time more aggressively. Harder and harder until we both came.

'Jacob' her words from her mouth were my undoing there and then. I came so deep inside her it felt like we were one. I rested on her back and massaged her breasts as they hung from her body. God, I loved this woman's body and what it did to me.

I was in a daze when I heard Riley speak ever so gently. 'We need to eat, I'm starving.'

I pulled out of her and she flopped to the bed spent from our sex. 'Come let's shower and eat.' I said, dragging her up from the bed. 'You are fucking amazing Riley, do you know that?'

'You are too', she said back with a smile.

Dinner was a delicious lasagne, which was one of my favourite meals. I especially like it homemade - much better than eating out. We drank the wine I brought and sat and ate in silence just glancing across the table at each other smiling, this was my bliss right here, right now.

'Jacob', she asked, looking at me intently. 'Yes Riley',

'Can you stay with me tonight?' She had the sweetest smile on her face, but I thought I saw a glimmer of wickedness in the corner of her eye, I couldn't resist her, obviously I said. 'Yes, Riley, I'm so glad you asked'.

My heart soared and I felt at home.

Chapter 17

Riley

I'm not too sure why I invited Jacob over but in my heart it was the right thing to do. When he turned up at my apartment, looking so fucking hot and sexy, I felt all my walls crumble immediately.

He wasn't even in my apartment for like five minutes before we were kissing and then fucking, oh yes fucking.

I went down on him, as I had not done it before, before it was always him pleasing me, which was fucking great, don't get me wrong, but I wanted to do this for him.

Taking his cock into my mouth was amazing. He tasted a little salty as his precome seeped from the end when my tongue touched him. I knew I was doing a good job when he moaned, that sexy, half pleasure half pain noise you make at the back of your throat. I sucked him harder and pumped his dick with my hand, he was enjoying it as much as I was. His dick was rock hard and so big, I don't remember it being this big, but when we had sex I felt his size right at my core.

Jacob pushed me away laying his hands on my shoulders and then turned me over onto my back, so I was now under him and god his words were my undoing in my heart.

'You are all fucking woman Riley Shure. Do you know that ?' he said to me as his mouth found his way to my sex. As soon as his tongue touched me I was all out vocally moaning. He was so good at this and my body was his play thing. His fingers entered m,: at least two, I wasn't quite sure, but the feeling was immense. I wanted him to take me so badly, I came hard with his tongue and fingers. As I started to come down Jacob pushed his cock inside me I screamed his name and he went wild with desire, fucking me harder and harder, my body

working with his, in time, I came again shortly after and he just kept going, this was amazing; nothing like we had done before.

'Fuck Riley', he shouted as I screamed out his name, my vagina tightened round his cock, bringing him to the egde as well as me.

As I began to come down from yet another orgasm and Jacob was still going he turned me over so I was now on all fours, pushing my face to the bed and bringing my ass up in the air, so I was now fully exposed to him.

He grabbed hold of my hips tight and pushed into me from behind this time more aggressively, this was the first time we did it this way and he was deep, so deep. He pushed harder and harder until we both came. FUCK! OH MY GOD JACOB!

He came hard. I could feel him fill me with this seed, he stilled his body, his breath still racing along with mine, he laid his body over mine, resting on my back and massaged my breasts. I loved the way he touched me.

I asked him to stay. I was thinking of telling him about my new found inheritance, but I was unsure of how he would take it. Maybe not now in my post coital bliss, was the right time.

The night with Jacob was bliss, we kissed, we touched, we made love, yes it was different than what we had done when he first came to my apartment.

Dinner was great, the company was even better. Strange as it may have seemed this felt like a relationship blooming, I felt so content when he was round.

I drifted off to sleep safe in his arms; his warmth encompassed me as my body relaxed into his. This was heaven, I was hoping it wouldn't turn into hell.

The morning sun shone through my window like it always does which for me is a sign that I must get up. I then realised that I was not alone reaching for the arms snuggled round me, had we slept like this all night? god I slept so well so maybe I did. His scent was all too alluring and I really could have stayed in my bed all day but I had work and literally I had to get up to get ready.

'Jacob, wake up, I have to get ready for work.'

'Mmm, what time is it? He grumbled raising his head from the pillow. 'It's 7:am. I really need to shower and get going.' I tried to sound sincere. 'Shit, I need to go too then,' he laughed.

I smiled at him and threw his jeans at him.

I went off into the shower and returned to see a fully dressed, slightly tousled drop dead gorgeous CEO.

He came to me and unwrapped my towel and kissed my neck and down to my breasts,

'You don't have time for this now.' I gestured to him towards the door. 'Ok, ok, I'm going. Can we talk about my invite for Saturday,' he said. 'Jacob, it's my birthday on Saturday and I have plans already, I'm sorry.' I felt kinda guilty, as I knew I was going to the ball but he didn't.

The week seemed to drag on, I had made arrangements for Saturday for dresses, hair stylists and make-up folk, we were going to have the lot. I wanted it to be a special time for us all.

There were emails from Quinn on what I should expect on Saturday, he said he would be there with his wife to support me and that he was proud of me and that my parents would have been proud too. He really was turning into a sweetie!

Jacob and I exchanged flirtatious messages right up until Friday night when he said he wanted to see me, he had a gift for me. The only gift I wanted from him was him, all of him, forever, I think I was falling for him. My heart sang when we were together and it wasn't just the sex whihc if course was awesome, but the connection we had, whether sitting eating across from him at dinner or falling asleep in his arms, everytime our bodies touched we seemed to know what each wanted, two halves of the same coin - I had heard that phrase before but now understood juast what it meant.

Friday came and Jacob invited me to his apartment. I was a little uneasy, as I felt safe in my own place. I'm sure his was much bigger than mine.

He sent a car for me at seven, a tall guy with jet black hair opened the door for me, as I stepped in. It was the Bentley again. I recognised it from before.

The drive wasn't too long but I wasn't paying too much attention; I was nervous, why, I didn't know but I was.

We had arrived at the most beautiful building I had ever seen, it was Thyme Towers, rich list properties, of course it was, he was from money.

The concierge escorted me to the lift and then punched in a code

'Mr Sylvester is waiting for you miss,'he said smiling.

My mind went crazy how many other women have been here before me, the thought crept in and jealousy shot through me. Stop it Riley, you are overreacting.

The lift ride wasn't too long. I was daydreaming about a previous encounter in a lift when the doors opened and Jacob was standing there waiting for me. 'Daydreaming again Riley are we ?' he mused, as I blushed a little.

'Caught me.' I said laughing at him.

'Come let me show you round my pad,' he reached for my waist and pulled me into him and kissed my head.

'You smell great,' he whispered, as we entered the main room.

There were floor to ceiling glass windows on two sides showing the city in its full glory, it was breathtaking. His apartment was pretty much open plan, which made the apartment look huge; there was so much space. The kitchen was beautiful, glossy cupboards in grey and dark slate worktops, nothing hanging about on the sides. In fact it looked like it had never been used!

There were three bedrooms, two of which he said he never used of course he lived alone. The bathroom was massive and there was a study, decorated in an old style like rich woods and leather, you could smell its heavenly scent from the doorway. It was very relaxing. He took my hand and led me down a short corridor through some double doors, it was his bedroom for sure.

There was an ensuite to the left that could have fitted my own apartment in and a walk-in wardrobe opposite it, the corridor continued for a short walk and opened up to a beautiful bedroom, a king size bed dominated the room, with views to die for from the windows.

'Oh this is spectacular,' I said, mouth open wide and in awe.

'The windows are one way in case you were thinking…' He smiled at me with a wicked grin.

'I wasn't thinking anything so rude Mr Sylvester,' she scolded him, with an equally naughty smile curving her lips.

We went back to the main room and had a glass of fizz, the expensive kind. 'So I wanted to wish you a Happy Birthday, early,' he said, and presented me with a gift box.

'Jacob you really didn't have to, honestly.'

'Please I wanted to, if I can't spend the night with you on your actual birthday then tonight is your birthday with me.'

I smiled at his kindness and opened the box.

There right there was the most beautiful diamond bracelet.

'Jacob, this is too much.' I stammered, running my fingers over the exquisite piece of jewelry.

He held his hand up and whispered. 'It's never too much for you baby.' He kissed my cheek so gently and helped me put on the bracelet.

I kissed him back, reaching my arms up to his neck and twirling his hair. 'This is the most loveliest present Jacob, you're so lovely, I Lo -'

I stopped myself, as I was going to say the L word. Not yet Ry, what if he doesn't like you like that, you know the heart stuff.

Thankfully Jacob did not notice my potential slip up, as he kissed me again. 'You're quite lovely too, Riley,' he mimicked, close to my lips.

This time instead of ripping each other's clothes off we ate the most delicious meal. He made me steak, with a side salad; it had a zesty lime and ginger flavour dressing - it was amazing. It was a perfect night, just perfect. I wanted it to be like this forever.

'Riley, will you stay tonight, so at least I can wish you a Happy Birthday in the morning?'

'Ok, I'd love to.' I was happy, he was happy this night was going so bloody well, I was thinking what could go wrong.

Jacob slowly led me to his room and slowly took my clothes off and laid me down on his bed.

He removed his clothes while I watched him, he had the most incredible body, muscles rippled. I wondered where he found the time to train unless he was actually a god. He crawled up over me and placed his arms either side of me, I couldn't help myself, I ran my hands over his torso and the electricity between us ignited a flame at my core.I was biting my lower lip as I traced my hands down to his cock,, I ran two fingers gently down either side and as my fingers came up his shaft and added a little more pressure, I was learning what he liked. He let out a little moan. 'Tonight baby, is your night and I'm going to pleasure you until the sun comes up.'

Instead of ravishing me which I was more than up for, he took me by surprise...

⚬⚬❖⚬⚬

Chapter 18

Jacob

Last night was just so perfect, Riley came to my apartment. I'm not sure what she was expecting but I'm glad the cleaner had been in! Not a dirty sock in sight.

We ate steak, as I know she loves it, it was just perfect. I could have ravished her from the moment she walked in, but this was a special time for her and I wanted to make an effort, little did she know I'd never cooked for a woman before...well apart from my mother and scrambled egg and toast didn't really constitute cooking, did it?

After dinner I undressed her and laid her down on my bed crawling on top of her, not making love to her right then and there was the hardest thing I have ever done especially when she ran her fingers up and down my cock. I kissed her, then drew her up from the bed towards the ensuite where I had secretly filled my oversized bath just for us. Her face was glowing at the sight laid before her, candles around the bathroom which softened the masculinity of the room. I helped her in and got in behind her. The water was hot, not too hot, but it felt good on my skin. She had goosebumps, as she sat down. Her skin was so soft and I couldn't help but stroke it. I lathered up a natural sponge pouring a generous amount of soap on it, stoking up and down her arms and slowlyI moved it forward to caress her front. She tilted her head back towards me; my hands replaced the sponge and went down under the water gently pushing her legs apart to gain access to her.

She let out a little moan or it could have been a purr, letting me know she was enjoying herself.

Reaching down and stroking her made me hard and my cock pushed against her resting in the crease of her perfectly formed arse. Kissing her neck and shoulders, one hand massaged her breast tweeking and pulling at her nipple, whilst the other explored her slit. Circular movements around her nub made her breath come in short gasps. She was so close to climax, her pussy became slick and I could see the blood surge up from her chest to her face. I wanted it to be perfect, perfect for her

I wanted her to come for me. She was irresistible and I knew I was falling for her.

After the longest bath pleasuring Riley, I wrapped her in a huge, fluffy towel and lifted her from the bath, walking her into the lounge in my arms, I dropped onto the sofa keeping her firmly on my lap, we held each other close watching the night sky through the windows, occasionally murmuring about the amazing view, pointing out a shooting star or potential UFO; this was bliss, pure bliss.

Cuddling, we turned to kiss, which turned to making out on the sofa, she took hold of me and wanted to pleasure me, I moved her hand. 'Tonight is about you Riley, not me.' I said as I went down on her.

Saturday 24th July, Riley's Birthday

Waking up next to Riley was... perfect; it felt like home. I felt content.

I didn't want to wake her up because it meant she would be closer to leaving but my body was craving her touch; I wanted her so badly.

I went and prepared some pancakes for her breakfast and juice, I hoped she liked them. Everyone does, don't they?

When I returned to the bedroom, breakfast in hand Riley was laying on her front, her back exposed and a peak of her breast showing, I could feel my length growing instantly.

Placing the tray on the bedside table I layed down next to her and began kissing her back and neck bringing her into consciousness as gently as I could, without taking her sexually.

Not long after my kissing Riley awoke with a smile 'Morning J, she said.

'Morning beautiful,' I replied with a smile, so big Colgate would have paid a fortune for it!

She turned and sat up drawing the sheets around her. 'I've made breakfast for you, I hope you like pancakes ''I love pancakes, thankyou.'

'Oh, Happy Birthday by the way.' I smiled again, as her bright eyes touched mine.

'Thankyou Jacob, this is just wonderful,' she looked alive and so beautiful, wrapped in my sheet in my bed; my heart was racing. With a small peck on her lips I left to eat her breakfast while it was still warm.

We spent the morning just chilling in bed and holding each other close. She said she had to leave at lunchtime, as she had made plans with friends.

I really didn't want her to go, but it was out of my hands. I had really wanted to take her to the ball tonight, to be my date and to lea#ve with me at the end of the evening….Alas it was not meant to be, so I am taking my baby sister instead, she never comes to these things, but she agreed to for me tonight.

When Riley left at lunch I headed to meet my parents for a wellness check on my father, he was doing great, in fact he was more than great.

We had lunch and I suggested, if my father was up to it, that he and my mother should attend tonight as the board would be pleased to see him. He agreed of course but it only for a short time; didn't want to overdo it on the first outing! My mother was beside herself, she hadn't missed a Gala Ball yet and was looking forward to attending this one in particular.

My suit was delivered at 4:00pm and got myself ready - men don't seem to take as long as women do, my sister was still getting ready when I turned up at my parents house to collect them in a limousine.

Bethany looked like a true lady in her plum gown and flowing locks, she liked the dressing up part even though she would always say she didn't.

Royal Compton House was on the outskirts of town and was an impressive piece of architecture, with immaculate lawns to the front and rear. The drive leading up to the house was lined with the most beautiful pink blossom trees. The ground around each looked like it had been sprinkled with confetti.

The entrance hall was gilded in gold with ornate murals on the ceilings, a true masterpiece if you were into those things. The main ballroom was down a flowing flight of stairs; when standing at the head of the stairs, you could see the whole ballroom before you.

We were greeted by members of the board who shook my fathers hand first and were smiling, clearly pleased with his presence at the ball.

'Good to see you sir,' said one colleague. 'Thankyou Jeffrey,' my father replied.

It went on like that for about five minutes, before my mother suggested we move on to find our table and meet other guests. Dad smiled and left with her.

Bethany was skimming the room looking for someone. I think she was looking for Bradley Moore who worked for a rival company to ours, as she had been seeing him for a little while. She thought no one knew, but I had ears everywhere.

The room was filled with the cream of society. I was engrossed in a group conversation with a couple of media heads, when I became aware of raised whispers around us. Bethany walked up to me with my parents in toe indicating for me to turn toward the staircase.

'Who are they? She whispered near to me.

My eyes took in the vision before me; four beautiful women, dressed to kill and totally hypnotising.

' I'm not sure they must be guests of someone, I haven't seen them here before, ' I answered her. I turned away to carry on my conversation when I heard Old Mister Charles comment, 'look at that beautiful woman, wow if I was thirty years younger.' He chortled and sipped his brandy.

I turned to see which of the four beauties he was referring to. I didn't immediately see who he was talking about but when I did I felt the breath leave me.

'Wow!' My sister said in barely a whisper. 'Who is she?' My mother asked quizzically.

I had to look twice before I saw the woman who had my heart. Riley.

'Ah, yes that's Miss Whitmore if I'm not mistaken.' Mr Charles said, gawking at her.

I was dumbstruck! What did he say?

'Mr Charles, that's Riley Shure,' I corrected him gently. 'She's the woman I am seeing,' I said to myself.

My mothers turned questioning eyes to me.

'I'm afraid you are wrong this time, Jacob my boy. Her name is Riley Whitmore, from 'THE WHITMORES.' Raising his eyebrows now.

What was going on I was confused and aroused all at the same time

She was stunning in a long red halterneck dress showing a hint of cleavage and her beautiful neck; the bottom of the gown flowed perfectly around her shapely body. Tasteful jewelry adorned her ears, throat and wrist. She was a vision!

My only thought now was why is she here and why did they say she was a Whitmore?

Chapter 19

Riley

Waking to the soft kisses from Jacob this morning was... god there were no words, it felt just perfect. He made me breakfast, it was such a sweet gesture from him. I must have looked like a mess, but he didn't say a word.

We spent the morning in bed cuddling and stuff. It was a great start to my birthday, I felt a pang of guilt though, as I hadn't told him what was going to happen tonight and he would be shocked. I'm sure of it.

These thoughts were quickly erased, as I wanted our time this morning to be fantastic, my feelings for him were so much more than I had wanted right now. Not love, but not lust either.

Meeting the girls' at lunchtime was exciting. We were all giggling about the night ahead and the preparations I had set up for us all. We stepped into Rialdo's - a small pizzeria, where the food was delicious - the best of the best, in my view.

A few glasses of fizz and we were off, back to my apartment to await hair, make-up and....the dresses! I was so excited!

Preparations began with our dresses. Rolled in on a rail, they were just the most beautiful and elegant gowns I had ever seen.

'Riley, these are incredible.' Robin said.

'Oh they are! Riley, are you sure? Emma joined in. Hannah was awestruck, fingers skimming over the gowns. 'These are breathtaking Ri.' Hannah whispered.

'Ladies, this is to say thankyou for your support and our futures ahead.' I said with barely contained glee.

Emma was first to find her dress, a baby pink gown with lace straps full in length and plunge front that had a semi flare from the waist, perfect for Emma. Hannah was drawn to the navy fitted dress with a bardot top perfect to accentuate her auburn hair.

Robin went for a traditional black dress, however this one was off the shoulder and oh so perfect for her.

There was a bag that Ricardo had sent over with a note on the front addressed to me; **This my treasure is your perfect dress, enjoy your night**

Ricardo xx

I unzipped the bag and drew out the most exquisite dress I had ever seen.

Full length red dress, a halterneck top and flared from the waist. It had a secret slit in it which showed the leg when you walked.

'Wow, girls look at this". I said, feeling like all my christmases had come at once.

'OMG', the girls said together. "I know, right". I replied.

The makeup and hair stylists turned up a short while later and we were then pampered to the max. God it took forever, but the results were stunning, truly stunning. I hardly recognised myself.

After what felt like an eternity, mixed with giggles and oohing and ahhing, we were dressed, I honestly felt like a princess. I took out a few pieces of jewellery that my parents had given me. A single strand diamond halo band that went onto my hair, oh my god my hair was just perfect, curled but pinned back loosely followed by the bracelet Jacob had given me and then there was the ring; it slipped on perfectly and shone brightly reflecting on the walls as the light caught it. I wanted to wear the choker, as that too had been my mothers, or had it been a Whitmore piece? I wasn't too sure.

'Yes! Riley, wear it", Robin assured me it was perfect.

Shoes on, glasses emptied, we made our way to the waiting limo. "OMG, Riley, a limo!" squealed Hannah.

'Yes ladies, we go in style. We will rock this night, a night to remember for sure".

I was just hoping it wouldn't go tits up, especially when I come face to face with Jacob and my Grandmother.

Inside the limo, the champagne popped again. The girls were all so excited, I on the other hand, felt nervous the more we left the familiar surroundings of the city and headed towards the venue.

'Riley, we have a gift for your birthday", Emma said as the others smiled.

"Girls you shouldn't have, I told you it was on me tonight". "Well we have; here and open it".

Robin handed me a cute little box, red velvet with a little ribbon surrounding it.

I gently pulled the ribbon and opened the box, there shining up at me was the most beautiful locket, gold with a diamond on the front.

"Oh girls, this is too much", I whispered.'Open it Ry go on" Robin pushed on.

I opened the lock to find not only a picture of my parents, but my three best girls, tears formed in my eyes at the beautiful gift.

'Girls," I whispered, trying not to cry.

'NO,NO,NO, No crying allowed, not tonight," Hannah wiped the tear that fell from my eye to my cheek,

"Tonight is gonna rock! So, let's rock it".

We clinked glasses and made a vow to enjoy tonight, as we were princesses all of us.

We arrived at the Royal Compton House, it was just beautiful. Warm brick gave the house a welcoming feeling despite its size; cherry blossom trees lined the

drive and what I could see of the landscaped grounds, they were immaculate. I made a mental note to come back here and photograph it for some personal work.

There were limos all around us and people being ushered into the house. My hands were twitching as we pulled up; photographers vying for the best position to photograph from. I began to get nervous.

'Riley it's gonna be ok", Robin said as she gently took my hand in hers.

The door opened and the girls began to get out. Flashes all around as each girl stood up from the car, it was my turn and I was crapping myself. I can do this, I whispered to myself, as I exited the car.

Flash, upon flash in my face. God it was awful! Just smile Riley, I thought, just smile. And I did. So did the girls who were a force to be reckoned with.

Just then one of the reporters shouted out, "Who are you representing Miss?"

As I turned to the voice coming from behind, flash again; the perfect shot. I poised myself, and took a deep breath before replying;

"I am Riley Whitmore, daughter of the late Marcus and Felicity Whitmore, in the flesh and back from the dead!"

The girls' mouths were aghast at my outburst, if I was gonna do it I had to go big, I thought. No backing out now!

Then they all started shouting out questions, which I never answered, merely walked up to the entrance of the house, before disappearing inside.

'Shit, Ry what was that?" Robin asked, eyes wide.

'I couldn't help myself." The shit is gonna hit the fan now for sure. I smiled, not really feeling quite so blase now.

The walkway was again beautifully decorated in an old style like the renaissance paintings I had admired so much.

I took a moment to myself as the girls walked on into the great hall and the stairs. I had to be calm and together tonight. It was going to be a difficult one. I know that now. Was I really ready for this or was this just me playing pretend? I walked up behind the girls as they stood waiting for me, as I approached they moved so I could come into the middle. The room was just out of this world. I couldn't help, but stare at all the glamour and glitz before us. What I didn't seem to notice was the number of eyes looking at us from the floor below.

My feet seemed glued to the floor and fear rose up inside me. For a brief moment I couldn't move a muscle. Then I was brought out of my trance.

'Riley", I heard a man say from behind me.

As I turned I saw Mr Quinn and his wife walking towards us.

'Quinn," I said, catching him in an embrace. "These are my friends, Robin, Emma and Hannah.' They all responded with hellos and how are you.

We followed Quinn and his wife down the opulent staircase and into the fold of people again staring and whispering to one another.

'Yes, a Whitmore, can you believe it! Where has she been all this time? 'I'm sure she isn't their daughter, didn't she, you know, die?', 'A W Whitmore really, oh.'

The whispers carried on as we sashayed our way through the crowds.

I felt him, his presence, before I could see him. The girls followed Quinn, as I turned to face the onlookers behind me, there he was in all his god damn beauty. Jacob looked intense, truly fuckable.

Before I could reach Jacob I was set upon by some of the guys from work, Mr Rogers being one of them.

God, I wish I could just get to Jacob to talk. At every opportunity I glanced his way watching him from afar. He moved gracefully between groups, in and out of a conversation but always just out of reach. I mustered a little smile towards him. I wanted him to come get me, hold me, take me, love me.

Chapter 20

Jacob

Watching her turn to face me from a distance was like a scene from a movie when the leading man gets his woman - could that be me?

She looked like she was going to come my way at one point, when she was stopped by Rogers, her Boss - I never took my eyes off her as he spoke to her.

"Jacob, how long have you been dating a Whitmore?" My sister spoke low for my ears only.

"Not long Beth, not long at all." Not looking at her when I spoke. "Thought you said she was Riley Shure Ja -'

I cut her off mid sentence, as I needed to speak with Riley urgently. I didn't get far when a few shareholders walked in front of me, looking quite concerned.

"Ahh, Mr Sylvester, we have some news sir." Ted masters spoke low, but earnestly.

I just wanted rid of them, my eagerness to be close to Riley was building at a rapid rate.

'What is it Ted? I said, rushing my words.

'It appears the hidden shareholder is none other than Miss - "

'Ted I know, I've figured it out for myself, Miss Whitmore! Am I Right?"

'Um yes sir it is.

Rage. Unbridled coursed through me. Then fear; what was she doing? was she playing me? We got close, so close, what was her deal? Thoughts competed for attention, twisting around in my head. I closed my eyes trying to calm myself from imploding.

There were a few dings around me coming from phones. I wished that they had banned them from this night, as I didnt want crap bringing me down, then my own phone buzzed in my jacket;

NEWSFLASH:

MISS RILEY WHITMORE BACK FROM THE DEAD

God damn instant news app I cussed under my breath.

Riley seemed to have disappeared, glancing up from my phone, where she had gone? I was scanning the room. I just caught sight of her perfect back as she began to leave for the dining entrance with her friends. Just as I began to make my way toward her the announcer spoke to let us know dinner was served.

It was like a mass rush of people moving like a snail, I couldn't get to Riley - I would have to wait now - damn it.

I was seated not too far from Riley and her friends. There were a few others there at the table too, men single and sharing jokes I'm sure, as there was laughing coming from the table.

Staring at her wasn't gonna get the desired effect. I had to speak with her. Bethany and my folks sat down sharing looks between each other before my mother spoke in soft tones:

'Jacob dear are you ok? You seemed somewhat preoccupied.'

'Um, what mum?' I turned to face her, now breaking contact with Riley's table. 'I said are you ok dear? You seem...' She fumbled for a word. '...elsewhere.' Her words brought me back to reality.

'Mum I must speak with Riley, there are things that need to be discussed.' I said distractedly. In reality I wanted to fuck her so hard and hear her scream out my

name - where? I didn't give a shit, as long as I didn't have to wait too long. Anger and frustration were competing for attention, both decided that fucking Riley would go some way to easing things.

'So, J -,' my sister began in a nosy tone. 'Spill the beans, who is she? Where did you meet?'

'She works for the company we took under our wing Rowthornes Media.' I deliberately left out how we met and obviously stayed away from all the details of our sexual encounters and how I fucked her over and over again and how she made me feel; and her screams... Yes, her screams were wild like she was. She didn't need to know all that.

'It's not at all interesting Beth, really.' I try to close down the conversation.

On our table there were a few shareholders from some of the larger companies in the city. Krane Media, two from Clarkes Galleries and the two from Henshaw Digital Media. As if a fuse had blown their phones started to ping too. Why the fuck aren't those things on silent? Do they have them on loud?

Looks turned to frowns and they began to scan the room. My guess was they were all now privy to the secret shareholder, otherwise known as Riley Shure... Whitmore, I corrected myself. I had to chuckle a little to the discomfort of those nearest me.

The shit had well and truly hit the fan, these were companies that I'm sure Riley's father had invested in. I was now curious as to what percentage of shares she now had, maybe it was the businessman in me or was I just pissed at her, either way I needed to find out.

'Gentleman. everything ok?' I asked nonchalantly.

'Um, yes news info in; about shareholder stuff you know what it's like Sylvester.'

'Yes. Shareholder crap,'another said.

'So how much of a percentage has she got guys? Come on, we're all now in the same boat it would seem.'

'Ah, um, well let's just say she is now a major player in Kranes.' Craig admitted. 'A single shareholder too.'

'Without going into detail Sylvester, our position mirrors Kranes,' said the Clarkes CEO.

Eyebrows raised, the men looked at each other. These captains of industry now found themselves in equivalent positions; all pondering the potential threat to their Companies, given the shares Riley now owned.

Dinner became a bore, so when dessert arrived, I made my excuses and got up to leave.

It was as if by magic, Riley had done the same and made her way to the restroom I'm sure. Without hesitation, I followed her through the tables and down to the east wing where the powder rooms were located.

Just as she was going to enter the room I grabbed her arm, turning her towards me and kissing her hard.

She responded after a moment's hesitation. Satisfied I had her attention, I pulled away from her.

'Riley what the fuck is going on? Why are you here?'

I didn't give her a chance to answer, as my lips swooped down on hers again. This time Riley gave me access to all of her mouth immediately, her tongue stroking mine, as our mouths were hard pressed together.

'Jacob, I need to explain,' she stammered, sounding breathy and seductive; her voice sent electricity right through me and my cock hardened instantly.

'Riley, I don't care at this moment, I want you, you look so hot, too fucking hot,' I ground out.

She was speechless. I was in no mood for pleasantries or foreplay; I was hungry for her.

Looking round there was a small room adjacent to the powder rooms, unlocked thank god. I whipped her into the room and locked the door.

I turned to face her with heavy eyes god she was so beautiful, but right now I wanted to fuck her raw. Reaching out to her I grabbed her by the back of the neck, we kissed hard and aggressively, each of us trying to dominate the kiss. There was no thought of pleasure, just the overwhelming need to fill her, to brand her with my cock. My hand moved to her dress and lifted it up around her waist, her lace thong was precious little defence for her soaking pussy and I ripped it off. I moved her to the back of an armchair pushing her down so that cute arse of hers mooned up at me. We were in some kind of reading roomsmall but traditionally decorated with hard leather furniture and rows of shelves with books.

'Jacob…'

She gasped as I plunged my hardness into her in one thrust. My breath caught as she tightened around my cock.'I'm home' I thought, before I thrust into her again. She was wet and warm and moaning in that sexy throaty way only Riley could do. She cried out gripping the sofa tighter as her climax gained momentum.

'Yes Riley,' I said hungrily, pounding again each time harder than the last. 'Jacob, I'm coming!' she cried out, as her climax exploded from her core to every nerve ending in her body. Her legs started to tremble from the intensity of her orgasm, I grabbed her hips more firmly, I wasn't finished yet! I tilted her pelvis up slightly and again thrust deeply into her, establishing a rhythm that had her panting for more.

'Faster Jacob,' she pleaded.'Oh my god I'm nearly there!' I could barely hold on but all at once I felt her muscles clap around my cock as another orgasm shattered through her body, I pushed harder up into her as my cock burst.

'Yes, fuck yes!' I came into her, filling her with my hot seed.

She gingerly sorted herself out, looking unsuccessfully for her thong as I straightened out my own clothes.

'Jesus fucking christ Riley,' I said, we both stood looking at each other. 'What the fuck is going on?'

She stared at me for what seemed like an eternity before she spoke.'I'm sorry Jacob, I couldn't say anything about all this until today. We do need to talk, but not here, not tonight, do you understand?'

Her words were sincere and I wanted to shout that no, I didn't understand, Didn't she trust me, or was she just fucking with me?

'Ok. Tomorrow we talk.'

She nodded and we made our way out of the room, checking the coast was clear, Riley continued her journey to the ladies room and me...I hit the bar!

Chapter 21

Riley

We were shown to our table by Quinn and his wife, she was a beautiful woman stunning in fact, I would say Quinn was really punching above his weight with her, he adored her you could see that by the way he looked at her and well she was the same, it was lovely to see.

'So Riley Quinn's wife stated, 'you are going to be getting a lot of attention, are you ready?

'I'm not quite sure if I'm honest, I thought I was but all of this, I waved my hand around is quite overwhelming.

'It is my dear but you will soon realise it's all bullshit.

My eyes widened at her cursive manner, wow she was a real time person no snob at all, I kinda loved her after that quote.

I could feel Jacob's gaze upon me for most of the dinner, it was making me wet just knowing he was close and deep down wondering if my formal arrival was enough to put him off, god I needed him right now I was horney and nervous all in one.

Dinner was great, there were ten of us at a table which was kinda intimate in a space this grand, there must have been over 150 people here at least, it was huge.

Apart from Quinn, his wife and my friends and I there were four guys from I'm not sure what company as we weren't introduced properly, just a hello and a wave.

It was funny watching them all go to their jacket pockets as their phones went off either buzzing or pinging at im guessing notifications. My phone was on

silent so even if I got a message I couldn't care less right now, it was my birthday and my coming out evening all in one.

The thing I was dreading was coming face to face with my Grandmother if she was here. Which I'm sure she is somewhere lurking. Faces in their phones and looking up told me that the information was regarding me and the attachment to their company.

'You must be Miss Whitmore, ' one said opposite me. "I'm Hugo Reynolds of Krane Media. Welcome to the circus," he smiled as did the others.

I couldn't help but laugh and we all then laughed. The meal was more pleasant after the ice was broken.

'So Miss Whitmore another gentleman began to curiously ask, why have you been silent?.

That question held me for a moment but before I could speak Mr Quinn replied for me.

'Well gentleman it goes back a long time and Miss Whitmore, Riley has been in the custody of a great team for almost two years. It was her Fathers and Mothers wish she carried on the family name and registry, we are looking forward to Rileys successes in the future.

Not tonight though as it's her birthday.'

Said with utmost respect and a don't fuck with me attitude the questions stopped and glasses were raised for my birthday.

My friends were chatting and flirting with the guys. They were slightly older than us, not much though, cocky little bastards if I'm honest but the girls were lapping it up, little did they know my friends would eat them alive if they went down that! Road.

As dessert was presented I made my excuses and left to powder my nose, actually I was so fucking wet I needed to sort myself out, I needed Jacob and his cock to just keep me going.

After following some instructions I made my way down to the east wing where the powder rooms were located, god this place was magnificent as I walked along the corridor which was laden with portraits and landscape a plenty.

Finding the rooms I was about to open the door when someone grabbed my arm turned me around and before I could even say a word his lips were on mine hard, god his mouth was like magic.

'Fuck! He said when we came apart.

'Riley what the fuck, why are you here, you look fucking amazing'. He said dominantly. He didn't give me a chance to answer when his kissing began again, giving him access to my mouth with ease as I wanted him as much as he needed me.

167

'Jacob I need to explain, breathy from our kiss I tried to speak coherently. 'Riley I dont care for just a minute I need to fuck you, you look too fucking good not to. There were no words at that statement, it was like he was reading my fucking mind.

Jacob began looking round us searching for something. He spotted the small room near the powder rooms unlocked to his amusement and he pulled me into the room and locked the door.

When Jacob faced me his eyes were dark and seductive like a lion before they devoured their prey, me being the prey for sure I was willing to be devoured. He grabbed me behind the neck and pulled me into his embrace this time hard and somewhat aggressively, I liked this, it was primal. He drew his hand up under the skirt of my dress and rubbed his fingers across my lace panties igniting my sex.

We were in some kind of reading room and it smelt of leather, sexy as fuck, hell my arousal was on fire now. I vaguley heard Jacob say to me to hold onto the chair as he was gonna fuck me hard, shit the bed I could have come just by his words. He pushed into me with one hard push forcing me to cry out and gripping the chair hard. He was like a fucking hard ass machine pushing into me harder each time making me reach that point I knew all tofamilarly.

'Yes Riley, he said hungrily as he pushed into me harder, gripping my hips with each push.

'Faster I said whispering in delight, Faster Jacob I'm coming.

He took that as the go to fuck me harder than he has done beofre making me scream out his name before I came hard around him squeezing his dick

'Yes, fuck yes. Jacob said as he came, filling me with his hot seed.

'Jesus fucking christ Riley, he said as we were putting ourselves backtogether. I was blushed from the sex and my face was hot. I was staring at Jacob and his amazing face before I could speak.

'I'm sorry Jacob, I couldn't say anything until today we do need to talk but not here not tonight, do you understand?I said these words with honesty now as I couldn't afford a fight nor too much attention as the night was young and I needed to be strong.

'Ok, but tomorrow we need to talk. He said with a look meaning just that.

I nodded in acceptance and we made our way out of the room, checking the coast was clear.

Jacob went before me and I made my way to the bathroom to clean up, realisng yet again we had unprotected sex, thinking about it we had only used protection once, fuck!, registering my thoughths and the amount of sex we have had since we met this could be dangerous. Thankfully I was on the injection contraceptive even though I was a virgin until the wonderful Jacob came into my life. Reality check 101 I thought.

After what seemed too long I made my way back to the others with a smile on my face and a sated feeling inside.

Horny girl no longer, check! Fucking in a posh place with hot guy, check!, fucking check!

'And where have you been?' Robin asked, raising her brows and nodding to the other side where Jacob was sitting, I blushed at her question and she didn't need my answer. It was written all over my goddamn face.

Giggling turned to more drinking, more glasses being raised, this night was going to plan so far.

Dinner was pleasant and the company was too but it was time to move again back to the ball room for a civilised array of music, yeah snob shit for sure I thought.

Quinn and his wife had left us to speak with other patrons from other trustee facilities and we decided we would go check out the posh music, it was truly an experience watching people's reactions as we passed them. It was like we were royalty, the stares, the whispering, especially from the women. It was hilarious and the girls made it known they thought it was funny, taking on catwalk style walking. God I love my friends, they are so normal it makes me giggle just watching them.

We enter the ballroom and refresh our glasses with more champagne, it's free so we don't care.

As the patrons fall in, the music is already playing a melodious tune, I'm guessing it's to allow the food to go down gently, I laugh again at the poshness of it all. This is truly not me.

A hand slides it way around my waist and a kiss is bestowed upon my neck as my friends watch with open mouths.

'Ladies, he says with teasing eyes as he draws himself away from my neck.

'Jacob these are my girlfriends, Robin, Emma and Hannah, I say encouraging them to stop gawking.

'Pleasure to meet you, ' he said, taking each hand and kissing the back of it. Well thats just gonna get them all tangled up and horny, fuck why does he have to be so good at this shit. Thoughts are maybe a little off the mark.

'Nice to meet you; was Robin's lame response, probably feeling flustered because I know what that touch does to me.

The others just said hi and then excused themselves off mingling, yeah on the prowl more like.

Once gone Jacob pulled me into his arms and kissed me ever so gently.

'Riley I want you to come and meet my parents,' he said excitedly, reaching down for my hand before I could respond.

We walked to a table where there was seated Mr Syvelster Senior whom I recognised from the day he came to the office with Jacob, I'm assuming his wife and a younger woman, all smiling as we approached the table.

'Mum, Dad, Beth this is Riley, he said confidently yet somewhat different in tone to his normal level of speech.

His father stood up from the chair and so did the other men in attendance, 'Lovely to meet you Miss

Whitmore he said, 'oh no just Riley please' I said in response.

Beth was next to greet me, 'I'm Jay's sister Beth, pleasure Riley.

She was beautiful and I had a flashback to the Sunday when I saw Jacob with a woman, it was his sister as I recognised her.

I felt stupid at the memory of my first seeing her and thinking the worst. Jacob's mother pulled me into an embrace, it was strange but I welcomed it willingly, 'Ahh Riley you are a beautiful woman and you look like yourmother she said with no hesitation.

'You knew my mother?' I asked

'Yes dear very much so. Her words were kind and loving. "We were friends you know for a long time. I was sad to hear of their passing, I am truly sorry for your loss."

I wanted to quiz her but she was somewhat guarded after her small disclosure. Did she know something about my parents, did she know about me?

After pleasantries Jacob and I began to circulate the room, he was pointing out the companies to which I was now linked to through my shares. He never once asked me though about his company and what percentage I held, I guessed that he already knew otherwise he could have been super pissed at me.

The music changed and Jacob asked me to dance. It was a strange request really but looking at the floor it seems not to be.

I hesitated at first as Jacob looked at me. 'Do you dance Riley? He questioned.

'Well yes I do actually, very well in fact. Never had to though so I might be a little rusty.' winking at him.

'Right come on.'

Dragging me to the floor and spinning me round to face him we glided around the floor, my dress swishing as we went.

'So miss secretive what style of dance do you know? Jacobs eyes were boring into my soul and making me all hot again.

'Umm, most really my parents made me study all dance. I smiled my sweetest of smiles. When I now think of it, they were preparing me at a very young age to be just this person I am tonight, how wise, clever parents really.

Jacob broke off our dance and went to the band who were playing, spoke to the guy and returned to my side.

'Ok let's see what you're made of then Whitmore, shall we'. He had the cheekiest of grins on his face that could only mean he was gonna do something rash.

Oh and he did.

The music changed to a tango style, oh god I rolled my eyes, this was a steamy dance he was gonna get me riled up in the best way for sure.

His eyebrows raised and his eyes were wide at my response to the dance, oh I matched him perfectly, it all came back to me instantly. When our bodies collided I made sure I teased him where I knew it would. Accentuating my moves to the music drew a crowd including my friends. They hadn't seen me dance properly only at a club and that wasn't this type of dance, not really.

By the time we concluded the dance we were surrounded by an audience, Jacob dipped me and kissed my neck.

The crowds applauded and I blushed. 'Take a bow Whitmore he smirked.

And I did, my friends instantly came to us and was like congratulating me on

my moves

'Wow Riley I didn't know you could dance like that, Hannah said 'Umm thanks, lots of dance classes.'

'Yeah Riley you kept that little secret yourself' Robin teased.

We all laughed a little before returning to the side for a rest, well I needed it. Jacob went off to I don't know where and we just mingled in the crowd.

An uneasiness krept up on me, not sure where it came from but I didn't like how it made me feel.

Chapter 22

Jacob

I never really knew my body craved Riley, as much it did. Taking her so aggressively was a first even for me - but from the moment I saw her this evening it was at the forefront of my mind; like I was in perpetual readiness to fuck her - she felt so good and smelt even better. Sex has always be unique with her and this evening just proved the point.

Walking back to my table where my folks were sitting, I had a smile on my face and a lighter step as I walked; I hadn't finished with her yet. That was merely the starters for what I had in my mind and I wasn't going to let her slip away tonight without being inside her again.

'You ok son?' my fathers words directed at me as I approached the table. 'Yes Dad - all good,' smiling again.

My mother never missed a beat on that one. 'Where have you been?' she asked suspiciously.

'Um, just stepped out for some fresh air that's all.' I smiled innocently at her, as I sat down.

Trying not to engage in the talk, I watched as Riley surreptitiously, she stood from her table with her friends; wow she was breathtaking. All eyes were on her and her friends, as they moved through the tables, back through to the dance area of the hall. The faces on people were hilarious really, like she was some kind of princess floating among her people. Yes, she fitted the role perfectly, too perfectly.

My mother stood first and the gentleman on the table rose; manners and respect. We followed her too and all left for the other room to enjoy the evening and the rest of the festivities.

I couldn't help but to slide up to Riley and place my arm around her slender waist possessively. She was too delicious to not touch and I placed a kiss on her neck to the surprise of her friends.

'Ladies.' I said pleasantly, drawing my face from Rileys neck and smiling. 'Ah Jacob, these are my girlfriends, Robin, Emma and Hannah,' she said, looking weirdly at them.

'Pleasure to meet you.' I responded, taking the hand of each one and kissing the back of it.

'Nice to meet you.' One of her friends said giggling..

The others just said hi and then excused themselves to somewhere other than with us.

Once her friends had left us I pulled Riley into my arms and kissed her gently, not caring who saw us.

'Riley, I want you to come and meet my parents.' I asked. I reached down for her hand before she could respond.

We walked a small way to where my parents and sister were standing making small talk and nodding to friends and acquaintances who they knew.

'Mum, Dad, Beth, this is Riley.' I said as we approached the group. My father bowed slightly and took her hand.

'Lovely to meet you Miss Whitmore,' he said. 'Oh no, it's just Riley please,' she said quietly.

Beth was next to greet her. 'I'm Jay's sister Beth, it's a pleasure Riley.'

My mother surprised me by pulling Riley into an embrace, it was strange to see my mother acting in such a tactile way. 'Ahh Riley, I am so pleased to meet you. You are indeed a beauty; you look like your mother.' She said with no hesitation.

I never knew Mother knew Riley's parents, but then that was never a conversation I would have started.

'You knew my mother?' she responded.

'Yes dear, very much so.' Her words were kind and loving. 'We were friends for a long time. I was sad to hear of her passing and your father of course. I am truly sorry for your loss.' She was sincere in her condolences.

This made me quickly turn to Riley, she looked somewhat puzzled, but she recovered quickly.

After introductions I felt the need to take Riley away and circulate the room. I pointed out the companies I was aware of that she had links with. I didn't pry to ascertain if they were the extent of her holdings.

I never spoke about her percentage in my company, as I didn't want to cause a scene tonight. But it angered me and yes, I was pissed off, but tonight was her birthday, and I had decided to leave that particular battle for another day. I could wait… until after I had taken her a few more times tonight!

The music changed in the background and I asked her to dance. She seemed to hesitate at first while studying my face. I couldn't help asking, 'Do you dance Riley? I raised my brow challenging her.

'Well yes I do actually - very well in fact.' Winking at me. 'Right, come on then, let's go.'

Pulling her onto the dance floor and spinning her round to face me, we glided around the floor, like we had partnered for years. Her dress flowed gently round my legs, wrapping us up in a shimmering red cocoon. She was elegant and more with all the grace and rhythm of a professional dancer.

'So Miss Secretive what style of dance do you know?' I questioned her, wondering whether we could raise some eyebrows by taking this up a notch or two.

'Enough to make *you* sweat.' She called my bluff, and now we needed to test it! 'Wait there.' I trotted over to the band, then back to Riley.

'Ok. Let's see what you're made of then Whitmore, shall we.' I said with a cheeky grin on my face.

The music changed, the orchestra playing the intro to Roxanne by Police. 'Tango?' I said to her, she rolled her eyes at me, knowing full well what I was prepared to do to her.

'Let's make it an *Argentine* tango, shall we!'

I was taken aback, wondering if I had actually bitten off more than I could chew.

She matched me perfectly, not a step out of place and the way her body moved was incredible. When I pulled her into my chest, she made contact with my chest, stomach and cock, causing it to twitch. She flicked out her leg and I turned her, she slid down my body and beads of sweat broke out on my upper lip. I slowly drew her up and as |I did so, she dropped her head back and her chin came into contact with my hard on, her lips twitched. The little minx knew exactly what she was doing to me!

She continued to tease me where it would make the most impact, my groin and I found myself wishing for the song to end before I embarrassed myself!

We had drawn a small crowd on the edge of the dance floor, including her friends and when we concluded the dance, I dipped Riley and kissed her neck. The crowds applauded and she blushed.

'Take a bow Whitmore.' I smirked at her.

And she did, her friends came to us and were smirking. 'Wow Riley you are a darkhorse.' Hannah said.

'Umm thanks, lots of dance classes.' She responded.

'Yeah Riley, you kept that little secret to yourself.' Robin teased.

I whispered in Riley's ear that I would see her shortly as I needed to go and cool down. She beamed up at me and raised her brows. 'Something to remember Jacob,' she whispered back. 'I always rise to a challenge!'

I left her then, shaking my head and chuckling to myself. I was hot for her even more now, she had set me on fire and I needed to either cool down or throw her on the floor and fuck her senseless!

I moved out onto the terrace area where it was cool. It had been lit up with fairy lights wrapped around the pergola and climbing roses; it looked magical, but was wasted on me at this moment when I was trying to get my cock under control. I pulled out my phone and started checking my emails I had received since Riley's announcement. I wasn't aware of someone walking up to me.

'Hello Jacob. I thought it was you on the dancefloor doing your thing, she said before coming into the light looking up from my phone towards the voice and to the face of my previous girlfriend Amelia Castle. Tall slender blonde and sexy as fuck, well that was until I met Riley who outshone her so many times over. 'Amelia what are you doing here, suddenly feeling uncomfortable in my surroundings.

'Well daddy wanted company and mother was sick so I stepped in, I'm glad we bumped into each other as I've been missing you terribly.'

She moved in closer before I knew it she had pressed her lips to mine. Memories of our time flashed passed me in a second and my response was to kiss her back, tongues and all.

I pulled away it was only seconds I thought but I was doing wrong it felt wrong but right, fuck what was my mind doing to me all of a sudden.

'Jacob, what's wrong?' she asked, holding her own and staring at me blankly. 'I um, I'm seeing someone Amelia, this can't happen, not now not ever right'. 'But Jacob' she started to feel me up, 'You know how I make you feel, we both know you want to fuck me like we used to do, dont you?

God her touch was magic and my senses were playing with me. There were no sparks, no ignition, just a primal feeling nothing like I had with Riley, nothing like that at all.

She continued her touch to my groin and grabbed me there. 'You know you want me J. Come with me.'

She grabbed my hand and led me through the many trees outlining the garden area where it was dark.

Once out of view she turned to face me and dropped to her knees and unzipped my pants. I don't know if it was the combination of the drinks, dancing and my lust for Riley but I didn't stop her. Her hands reached for my length and she proceeded to take me in her mouth. The sensation was sending me over the edge. I wasn't thinking straight, she sucked harder and harder pumping with the other hand before I could feel myself building up. Before I knew it I filled her mouth with my seed groaning as I came.

My head was spinning with many emotions right now but when I looked down it wasn't Rileys face I saw it was Amelias, what the fuck have I done I thought, regret almost flooding me senseless.

'Shit Amelia what the fuck, pulling my dick back in my pants. She stood up wiping the side of her mouth and smiling.

'Knew you still wanted me babe' she said before turning around and walking back to the house.

Fear swelled up inside me. I didn't know what to do, she was not a woman to be reckoned with, remembering the times we were together she used me for her needs and wants. I was a puppet in her playful games and it seems she got the better of me tonight aswell, fuck!, what was I gonna do if Riley knew what just happened.

Think Jacob, think the words stumble from my mouth before I know it.

Just as I was walking back to the house I saw one of Riley's friend's lookingmy way, fuck! Did they see Amelia, shit I was now worried as I approached her, the look she gave me was not the look I was hopingfor.

'Good time there Mr Sylvester?' The blonde one said she was called Robin. I was speechless for the first time in my life, caught fucking red handed Jacob you dick.

Chapter 23

Riley

The girls and I chatted for a while before they went off to scout the single guys. I trailed along behind them looking for Jacob, as I carefully moved through the glitterati.

'Riley *Whitmore,* I presume.' A voice behind me drawled, the hairs on my arms stood up. I knew who this was and by the tone in the voice, my fight had just begun.

I turned to face my Grandmother, shoulders straight and chin held high.

'Hello Grandmother,' I said confidently, looking her straight in the eyes. I gave her a dazzling smile.

'So, you are my Son and Daughter-in-law's child I am given to understand.' Her words hit me hard, but not as much as her scornful look.

'Yes, I am. My father was Marcus, your son and my mother, Felicity, your daughter-in-law.' Holding control of my feelings, I spelt it out for her, keeping my tone light, so as not to *fully* disrespect her with my tone of voice.

'Well, I'm not sure I believe you. You see, my granddaughter died when she was ten years old, and you are clearly a lot older.' Her words were as rigid as her posture and her face looked hard. I don't think she had ever been spoken to in this way before.

'Well, believe it. For reasons I do not yet know *Grandmother*, my parents kept my existence, not just from you, but from everyone…until today that is. So, cheers.' I held my champagne flute up. 'Here's to my resurrection AND my 23rd birthday.' I took a sip from my glass, turned and left her standing there looking at my departing back.

My body was shaking, as I walked away. Holy. Fucking. Shit! How the hell did I do what I just did? I was never confrontational; it was not what I was about. I was a mouse really, but all of a sudden, I had grown some balls!

I quickly scanned the room to find my friends; Hannah and Emma were chatting in a small group over towards the french windows.

'Hi,' I said, approaching them.

'Riley, come and meet these wonderful gentlemen,' Hannah said giddily, holding up her glass in one hand and tugging my hand with the other. Looking at her eyes, she had definitely put away a few more glasses, than when I had last seen her.

They had eyes like saucers, as I met their gazes.

'Holy shit!' one said. 'You're Riley Whitmore, aren't you?' 'Yes, that's little old me,' I confirmed, giving them a huge smile.

'Well, you are the talk of the evening let me tell you.' Another chimed in. 'Back from the dead I heard someone say.'

We all smiled, mine was a little strained though. I definitely didn't have the energy to hang around here feeding their curious little minds, but I think the look on my face prevented any further questions. Where was Jacob? My eyes swept the room again. I really could do with a bit of support right now.

We talked for a while. Hannah was flirting with one of the guys and he was lapping up all her attention. Emma too was right on it with the other guy; he looked as though all his Christmases had come at once.

Robin was nowhere to be seen, probably pulled, I thought. She was beautiful and could pull all the right guys for sure and here it was easy pickings as there were a fair few single men.

Taking stock of the evening so far, I had met with Jacob, met his family, and came face to face with my Grandmother *AND* held my own with her! I seemed to be winning tonight, which was good, as it was making my birthday one to remember.

Still, I couldn't shake that feeling though - as something is about to go horribly wrong. If something was too good to be true….

Again, scanning the room to see if I could find Jacob, I made eye contact with Quin, he gestured to me to go over which I did as the girls were getting close to the guys, while me, I was just a bystander.

Quinn and his wife were in conversation when I approached, the conversation stopped, and all eyes were on me.

'Riley, this is Harold and Gregory, Thomas and Michael, we are members of the Board of Trustees at the firm your parents hired.'

'Oh, hello' I muttered quietly. I smiled at each of them.

'Pleasure to meet your acquaintance Riley.' Michael, clearly the youngest of the four, he oozed sophistication and confidence. He took my hand and kissed the back of it. I looked into a pair of piercing blue eyes, blonde hair and a tan. He was VERY attractive and when he smiled, WOW! I caught my breath for just a second; he was dazzling.

The others just said hello as Michael had taken the lead in introductions.

'So Riley,' Michael began, 'What is it you do, work wise?' He was direct and his voice deep and melodic.

'I um, work at Rowthornes Media.' I stammered, feeling like a school kid. This was not me! What the fuck was happening? He made me feel like losing control, I could feel perspiration at my hairline and my cheeks were flushed around him.

Where the fuck was Jacob? I needed rescuing myself right now.

They chatted amongst themselves for a while, asking whether I had started thinking about my inheritance and what I might do in the future. Michael and I skirted the very edge of flirting the more I relaxed.

'So, I saw you dancing with Sylvester before. Are you guys an item?' He asked, smiling broadly and butterflies started in my stomach, at the mention of my earlier dance with Jacob.

'Um, well, I think so, we have been seeing each other recently.' I said not very convincingly.

'Oh, right. I assumed he was still with Amelia Castle as I saw them outside earlier in the gardens.'

My throat was immediately dry, like I had swallowed hot coals. I began to cough, trying to catch my breath.

'Are you alright my dear?' Mrs Quinn said as she patted my back. 'Yes, thank you. I'm ok,' I said after a few deep breaths.

Rage, fear and many other emotions began to wash over me. What was he doing with another woman, who was she? Was that why I couldn't find him?

My mind was numb, my thoughts lost, my face vacant.

'Riley, do you want to dance?' Michael said drawing me away from my dark thoughts.

Necking the rest of my champagne I had been holding for like an eternity, I took the hand he held out for me.

He twirled me onto the floor and pulled me up into his chest. My head fitted just beneath his chin; our bodies touched all the way to his knees. My breathing shifted and I peered at his face through my eyelashes, catching a glimpse of a smile on his face. He placed my hand on his chest with his own hand over the top of it. His other hand slowly moved to the small of my back, holding me firmly, but with enough room to move.

It was so intimate, maybe too intimate.

I was blushing, it felt like we were wrapped in our own private cocoon. His head dipped and he whispered in my ear. 'OK?'

It must have been the heady aroma of his cologne, his breath on my ear and his hand on my back; his thumb gently stroking circles, which was unsettling my pulse, but I leaned into him.

'Yes', My response, breathy.

His hand was warm and soft, and my pulse settled down. There were no fireworks, no sparks, just warmth, I felt very protected. I can do this, I thought.

As we returned to Quinn and Michael's colleagues, I saw Robin coming in from the garden terrace. I waved her over to us as Michael was still standing by me. 'Robin, this is Michael Rhodes, he is one of the Trustees looking after my portfolio.' Michael gave a slight incline of his head toward her, but Robin gave him a cursory acknowledgement and a very quick 'Hi', she then proceeded.

'I need to speak with you, it's important.'

I smiled toward Michael apologetically and away from the group so as not to be overheard.

'What's up Robin, what's happened?' Something had obviously upset her, maybe one of those men who had been chasing her earlier.

'Riley, I don't know where to start really,' She was wringing her hands and quite clearly upset. I knew bad news was coming, that feeling I had had all night was right!

'I-It's Jacob,' That was the last thing I expected. 'What about Jacob?' I frowned at her.

'Well, I saw him *with* another woman tonight. I'm sorry, I wouldn't usually say anything, but it's not good I'm afraid.'

I knew Robin and she would never say anything unless she had seen or heard something with her own eyes, gossip was not her thing.

Those words hit me like a brick to the head, Michael had mentioned a woman before and I just internally laughed it off, but now with what Robin has said, this was different, she never lied to me and I honoured our friendship for that fact alone.

'What did you see? I need to know.'

'Ry, I'm not sure you want to know,' she said quietly. 'Tell me Robin, Tell me NOW, please.'

Robin put her hand up to her chest nervously. She took a breath. 'He was getting sucked off by a blonde in the trees by the garden,' I blanched; she delivered a hammer blow in one quick breath, hoping no doubt, it would make less of an impact, it hadn't worked. 'I'm so sorry Riley, I really am.' Her head bowed defeatedly.

Anger rose like bile in my throat, I clenched my fists. This was that feeling fucking ruining my night! What a fucktard Jacob! Why? That was the only word I could muster in my brain, why would he do this?

Robin held my hand, as I tried to control my breathing, thankfully I had moved away from Quinn and the others before this disclosure was outted, however Michael was still near enough to see my distress.

'Are you ok, Riley?' he asked, touching my arm.

'Well,' I hesitated, then made my decision. 'That depends, Michael. My 'sort of boyfriend' has just been seen getting his cock sucked by some woman in the garden.' Michael had the grace to look shocked. I looked him straight in the eye. 'What would you do in my situation?'

I threw the question out flippantly, as I was going to blow a gasket any minute now, especially if Jacob was to appear.

'Well as I see it, you have two choices,' he said. 'One dump the mother fucker or two, get even,' a smirk crossed his face, and I knew where he was going with the second one.

'Mmm. Hold that thought for a while,' I said to Michael, as I turned towards a waiter walking by with a tray of champagne, I reached out with both hands and took two.

'Thank You.' I said, as I necked one and returned the empty glass to the tray, then sipped at the other flute. Robin and Michael looked at me as I contemplated my options.

Hurt, disappointment, rage; all bubbled just beneath the surface. I turned to see the man who had wronged me walking towards me.

'Riley-,' he called towards me, his arm outstretched.

'Nope, not interested Mr Sylvester,' I stated, standing my ground and keeping him at arm's length.

Trying not to create too much of a scene I lowered my voice, seething.

'If you think you can stick your fucking dick inside me when someone else had just been sucking you off, you can think again! I am and will only be a memory to you now *Mr* Sylvester. I will never give you another opportunity to degrade me, *never! You DISGUST* me!' I had never been so venomous towards another human being in my life, but I meant every single word!

Jacob blanched, Robin disappeared into the throng of people and looked for Emma and Hannah.

I put my hand on Michael's arm and drew him to the dance floor. 'Dance with me please Michael, before I lose my shit.'

Jacob stood at the edge of the dance floor open-mouthed and stunned. He was rooted to the spot, staring at me.

Not ever in my life have I ever been treated like this, I was devastated. I could not even fathom why he would bother introducing me to his family, if I meant so little to him, that he would have sex with some else – well not sex but a god damn fucking blow job! Maybe Michael was right and I should get even.

Michael held me in his arms not saying a word while the music surrounded us, I was so furious I was shaking. Michael gave me a few moments to gather my thoughts and calm down.

'Riley, do you want to leave, I will take you home if you want to.'

I smiled up at him, appreciating his consideration. 'I, I'm ok, just give me a minute or two please.'

'Ok, if you are sure.'

'I'm sorry you had to be around to hear and see this happen, I don't even know you.'

'Well let's sort that out now and get to know each other,' he said, smiling sheepishly at me. I knew what he was trying to do, so I went with the flow.

'My name is Micheal Rhodes, I'm twenty nine years old, *single,*' he emphasised. 'and I'm a senior handler for Margetson Trustees Corp. I like to take walks in all weathers, I love photography and all that is beautiful,' he said the last word looking at me into my eyes. 'I like to ride horses when I'm out in the country and I love to dance with beautiful women.' He looked at me directly in the eyes and smiled.

'Ok,' a genuine smile played on my lips as I joined in the game. 'Thank you for the resume. I guess it's my turn now. I'm 23, I heard him give a 'happy birthday' as I continued. 'I love the outdoors too and I also ride, not that I've done it in a while. Photography is my passion and until tonight I hadn't danced in a long time, which I now realise I should do more often as I love it. Oh and one last thing, I'm well trained in self-defence.' Smiling at Michael as his eyes widen at my defence quote.

'So, I guess we are now acquainted, Miss Whitmore.'
'I guess we are,' feeling a little more at ease.

Jacob had gone from where I had left him, which was good, as fuck, I could have killed him.

Robin had found Hannah and Emma and were seated with some guys chatting, Robin however, never took her eyes from me and Michael on the dance floor.

My night was only saved by Michael and his skill at dancing. Having to concentrate on dance steps was taking my mind off things, even if it was only for a short while.

We joined my friends and Michael and I chatted some more. I was drained if I was honest with myself and couldn't wait to leave. But I didn't want to cutthe girls' evening short. Just then Robin turned to me.

'Riley shall we go?' Robin was looking glummer than I had ever seen her.

'I guess we could go, I'm knackered and need to sleep. The limo is outside ready when we are.' We all seemed to be on the same wavelength.

Michael lent into my side, drawing his face to my ear, so only I could hear. 'If you want to play this out a little more Riley, take my hand and walk out with me.'

His breath on my skin sent shivers through me, not sure if it was the drink, the adrenaline, or the fact I was super pissed, but I liked the idea.

'Ok,' I said in barely a whisper.

We all stood including Michael, the girls looked at me quizzically, especially with what I did next. Reaching out to hold Michael's hand, we weaved through the crowd and walked out together.

My eyes were drawn to the bar and there was Jacob drinking on his own. He turned to face me as we walked past him. The sadness in his eyes pulled on my heart strings, but no he fucked up, not me! I didn't do anything wrong and what I was doing now wasn't wrong either.

Michael added salt to the wound in a big way by acknowledging Jacob, 'See ya Sylvester. She's a keeper isn't she?' He smiled at him and god you could actually see the anger rise up in him. It was just the right amount of salt. 'Riley can we speak?' Jacob pushed himself off the bar towards us.

'I'm afraid not Mr Sylvester, I guess I will see you at the emergency shareholders meeting. I am going to be pushing for a meeting this week.' We continued to walk to the exit.

Fresh air hit me like a tornado, affecting my stance and senses. I swayed a little and almost lost my footing before Michael caught me.

'Jeez Riley are you ok? seriously.'

'I'm good, just too much fresh air and booze,' I said.

Michael was a true gentleman and kissed my cheek as he guided me to the limo where my girls were waiting for me.

'Thank you for tonight and again, I'm sorry for involving you.'

'Riley, it's ok. Believe me it was no great hardship holding you in my arms.' Michael came closer to me this time and kissed me gently on my lips, soft and tender and romantic.

I could have reciprocated but I didn't. I stood my ground and accepted his kiss as it was given.

'Until we meet again' he said and left for his own ride.

'Fuck my life!' I said exhaling at the same time opening the door and getting in with the girls.

Chapter 24

Jacob

I had fucked up badly, so badly in fact, Riley wouldn't even talk to me.

Her friend clearly told her, fuck!

Damage control couldn't be done tonight, not now. she was too pissed at me. Watching her with that guy Michael from the Trustee's Company was tearing into me. It should be me dancing with her, kissing her, shit! What if she has kissed him? Rubbing my face with my hand trying to come to terms with my actions and trying to think how the fuck I was going to win Riley back was killing me and what was that crap about a shareholders meeting? What was she planning?

Feeling more than a little sorry for myself I downed the bourbon still in my glass and asked for another. I contemplated calling her. Looking at my phone and was about to dial her number when Amelia walked up and sat beside me.

'Penny for your thoughts Jay?' she asked while tapping her nails on the top of the bar.

'Are you fucking kidding me right now, Amelia?' I stared at her with a mixture of disgust and disbelief. I shot daggers at her.

'Babe…' she started to say before cutting her off –

'No fucking 'babe' Amelia! I don't want to see your face ever again. Do you understand what you have done? Any comprehension at all? You have destroyed my life right now!'

'*Excuse me* Jacob. I didn't see you stopping me if you're referring to our little rendezvous earlier. Is that what this is all about?' She lifted the drink the bartender had poured her and took a sip. 'You wanted me and we both know it,' she purred.

Amelia stood and smoothed out the non-existent creases from her dress, lifted her chin and walked away like she was gliding down a catwalk. I watched her retreating, oozing confidence and sex appeal; the woman had no shame.

I messaged Riley before I left Compton House and made my way home.

Riley, I don't know how to start this message I fucked up in a big way.

I know your friend told you what happened between me and Amelia.

I was high from our encounter and the dancing and drink and she took me by surprise, in the moment I thought it was you.

I'm sorry please forgive me I love you

J X

Send. There was no going back from this, I just had to wait.

Waking up to my phone buzzing on a Sunday morning was not a good thing. I had the hangover from hell and felt like shit.

Looking at the screen I saw it was my father, 'Not now dad, sorry.' I mumbled while declining his call. Falling back into bed I started reliving my actions from last night, then drifted back not a restless sleep.

I woke around eleven with several missed calls from my father, my sister, but nothing from Riley.

A shower and food was called for and although the hangover improved I still felt a right fucking bastard.

Dragging my arse to my home office I decided I needed to face whatever my father had to say. Hopefully nothing about Riley, I wasn't prepared to go there with anyone but her.

Dad answered after the second ring, I was tense. 'Jacob,' shit, something was definitely up. 'Dad', sorry I missed your call, what's up?'

'I've had some members of the board call me regarding an emergency shareholders meeting asked for by Miss Whitmore, Jacob. What's going on? Why has it been brought forward?' My father's voice was stern.

'Dad I'm not really sure. I'm just going through my emails now' - I tried to keep my voice neutral, not giving anything away.

'You do realise if she gets even one person on her side, shit could hit the fan. In terms of your position Jacob, what the fuck have you done to piss her off?'

'Dad, nothing honestly.' I didn't want to admit what had actually happened; he would have torn me a new arsehole. My dad and cursing never went together, so I knew he was angry.

'So when is it then? I asked.

'Friday! Jacob, sort your shit out before then or else.' He hung up on me. Fuck my life I thought.

News flashed up on my phone this time it was a report on Riley with a stunning photo of her. It was questioning who she was and where she had been all this time.

God, looking at how beautiful she was, chewed me up inside. Why didn't she message me back? Fury rose in me, by not answering me she was putting off my apology. FUCK! My mind wandered over the conversations I had lastnight, snippets here and there. I remembered my mother saying she knew Rileys' parents, well, her mother at least.

Fed up waiting for Riley to contact me I decided to go round there. No doubt I would get my balls busted, but at least I wasn't a coward. But no amount of banging on her door and yelling through the letterbox got her to open the door. Sunday was written off for me, damage control wasn't working at all.

Took myself to the gym and met the lads, training seemed to help with the thoughts racing through my head. Punch bags were the best, I could literally beat myself up! After three hours and sweat pouring out of me, I hit the showers.

We went out for a bite to eat after, and I shared what had happened at the Gala. They knew I was into Riley, so weren't impressed. They both knew Amelia and what she was like. I felt even more of a shit than I had done before.

The coming week was going to be intense, that is for sure.

Chapter 25

Riley

The tears started to stream down my face as we rode the forty five minute journey home. Robin held my hand and so did Emma. No one spoke. My eyes were closed and I felt lost, lost in many ways right now. This was supposed to be my night, a celebration and a new chapter in my life and I was hoping it included Jacob. Well that shit isn't gonna happen now is it!

I dropped the girls off first, even though they said they would stay with me.

'Riley don't be on your own tonight love,' Robin said.

'I'm fine honestly,' I reassured her. 'Look no tears!' I tried a little humour.

My phone buzzed in my clutch, I looked down to see there was a message from Jacob, I couldn't open it to read it. I was too raw right now.

My phone rang and it was a private number, I wasn't sure about answering it at first. 'Hello,' I said nervously.

'Miss Whitmore, my name is Richard Hague, your Grandmother has requested your presence at the Manor tomorrow lunchtime. A car will collect you at twelve noon.'

'I'm afraid that will not be possible Mr Hague, was it? It's late. My Grandmother can call me herself tomorrow when it's more convenient, Thank you goodbye.'

I wasn't going to deal with more shit not tonight.

I was tempted to call Michael for a revenge fuck, but I didn't take his number. Fuck Riley, you are shit at this.

Sunday morning found me hungover, but not as much as I thought I would have been. Messages from my girls came flooding in by ten.

'Riley, are you ok?' 'Riley you ok babes?'

'Riley I'm sorry for the info. I hope you're not mad at me,' The last one was from Robin. There was no way I could be cross with my friend. She told me the truth and better now than down the road when more feelings had been invested in that bastard!

After eating and making myself feel almost human, I set off for a walk to clear my head; walking is always good therapy for me.

Grabbing another coffee from a street cart and a danish, I set off for the park. A long walk, fresh air, freedom, no interruptions.

The sun was shining today and the warm rays on my face were very much needed. I found a bench and sat enjoying my surroundings facing the sun, eyes closed. It was peaceful, apart from the odd jogger passing by.

The birds singing was a treat, eyes still closed, I was in a nice little bubble appreciating the sounds, when a shadow fell on my face. Opening my eyes they were met with a wide smile and a pair of piercing blue eyes. Michael, god he looked good, fresh handsome, his hair loose doing its own thing.

'Michael' I said surprisingly.

'Well hello there Riley, fancy seeing you here.'

'Well it is a public space Michael.' I said sarcastically. 'Are you stalking me?' He smiled and sat beside me.'I didn't know you lived around here.'

'Yeah, not far, I like coming here. It's quiet most times,' raising my eyebrows to acknowledge he was invading my space.

'I'm glad we bumped into each other. I wanted to say I had a good time last night, even though it was to piss off Sylvester.' There was a hint of regret in his voice, which pulled at me inside.

I smiled. 'You helped me no end Michael, I'm very grateful.' Michael smiled at me; it was the sweetest smile.

'How are you feeling after last night?' he asked.

'Well considering I had a bit of a hangover and all the shit that went down, I'm doing ok thanks.'

'I hope I didn't offend you by kissing you last night,' Michael said in an honest tone.

'To be honest with you Michael, if I had your number I would have called you last night, but we both know that it wouldn't have solved any of my problems.' I gave him a self-deprecating smile.

Michael looked at me and was astonished at my honesty. Michael held my hand and looked me directly in the eye.

'If you want to we can, no strings attached.'

I looked at him then, I mean really looked at him. I've never known anyone like Michael, so forward and confident in himself. But I just couldn't go there. It wasn't right.

I shook my head. 'Two wrongs don't make a right. I need to deal with my shit with Jacob first.'

Even though Michael seemed like a perfect fit for me; he liked what I liked, we had similar passions and he was drop dead gorgeous, maybe he was too perfect.

Michael closed the gap between us on the bench and kissed me hard on the lips, moving his hand behind my head to deepen the kiss. He was forceful, but gentle and I caved. He was teasing me with his tongue and it felt really good. My hands went to his chest to stop the kiss, but not before I enjoyed a fair time with it.

'Michael I'm sorry I can't do this, as much as Jacob has hurt me, I still have feelings for him. I'm sorry.'

'I'm sorry too. I shouldn't have, but you are too darn irresistible and I couldn't help myself.'

I held his hand and smiled.

'Fancy a walk,' I said trying to diffuse this situation. 'I would love to.' he said.

We walked the park until the warmth started to fade, it was great. We chatted about random stuff and I laughed a lot. He laughed too. It was good to hear, he was easy company, very knowledgable and there was no sexual tension surrounding us.

'God I have to go,' I said looking at the time on my phone.

'Thankyou for this afternoon. I had a good time.' He sounded a little surprised. 'I can't remember the last time I just relaxed. 'It was great seeing you, we should do this again…as friends.' he bowed ever so slightly.

'I would like that Michael, I really would.' This time I initiated a kiss and it was on his lips, he pulled me closer just for a moment and I let him.

'I have to go,'I said.

He smiled and we both walked away in different directions.

I felt a little bad for kissing Michael, but I had to remind myself, Jacob did a lot more than that and I was done with him.

I sent an email to the shareholders confirming my request for a meeting on Friday, considering my share holdings, this should not be a problem. I could do this and demand some changes. I just need a little backing. He, Jacob, had fucked with the wrong woman.

As I walked back to my apartment building I opened the message from Jacob, my mouth dropped open at the last part. He loved me! Well fuck me! If he truly loved me then he wouldn't have lost his dick in some woman's mouth! I didn't know how to reply to his message, so I didn't.

Chapter 26

Jacob

By the time I got back to my apartment I was more than a little drunk. Checking my phone I had seen that Riley had read my message, no reply though, fuck! I needed to call her, make amends, do something.

I dialled her number, it rang and rang and then went to answer phone. I didn't leave a message. I needed to speak to her face to face. Do I go over to her? It was late, but I knew she would be awake.

I contemplated it for more time than I should have, even walked down to the front of my building, only stopping as I realised in my state she wouldn't have entertained me at all.

The night went from bad to worse. I couldn't sleep, tossing and turning, thinking of her and what I had done to ruin it. I needed her more than she could have ever imagined.

Monday came way too soon and I was nursing a biggest fucking hangover, forgot the water before bed and the mind was racing, everything felt like shit. Coffee and paracetamol was taken and as I entered the building of Sylvester Media, the receptionist, as always smiled and I dutifully smiled back. It wasn't her fault I was a grouchy bastard.

The ride up the elevator seemed to take forever and my patience was wearing thin. Once in my office I closed the door indicating I didn't want to be disturbed.

The usual emails were waiting to be responded to. There was one from the Board of Shareholders regarding the emergency meeting with our new shareholder, Miss Fucking Whitmore.

They had scheduled it for Friday. This was going to be a long fucking week.

The day seemed to drag on forever and I had sent Riley several text messages;

Riley I need to see you.

Riley please get in touch.

Riley come on you can't block me like this, we need to talk.

Riley if you don't answer me then I'm coming to your work

I mean it.

Do I really mean I would go to her place of work? Yes, I believe I would. I needed to sort this out before Friday, otherwise I don't know what will happen. What if she makes decisions the board likes, it could have serious implications with my position as CEO.

My phone rang and I thought it would be her, but it wasn't, just another news story about Riley, she was all over the internet now, lots of questions being asked about her.

My father had emailed me demanding I sort stuff out with Riley. My reply obviously wasn't going to placate him one bit, I was trying but she was blocking me.

Monday turned into Tuesday and still nothing from her. I was becoming more frustrated as time went on. Another message should push her along to talk to me, I thought.

'Riley listen I know you hate me but I really need to talk with you before Friday.

Nothing, no reply then my phone went pinged just after lunch.

'Mr Sylvester,

I believe we can discuss anything you have on your mind on Friday where all our laundry can be aired, you hurt me and I will not forget. Be prepared.

What the fuck does that mean 'be prepared', I messaged back.

She never responded, which infuriated me even more. What the actual fuck is she playing at.

I got up from my chair and paced my office running my hand through my hair, this won't do at all I thought. I was done with this shit. I needed to see her and I was going to have it out with her whether she liked it or not,

I called my secretary. 'Get me a car please, I need to go to Rowthorne Media.' 'Yes Mr Sylvester right away.'

Today this was going to be sorted one way or the other.

The drive was quicker than I thought, which gave me no time for strategy to get her alone, however I just had to see her make an excuse to Rogers that she was needed for sensitive talks and we needed some privacy. Yes, I will call him now to arrange it.

'Good morning Rowthorne Media, how may I help?' The women seemed super chirpy.

'Good morning this is Jacob Sylvester from Sylvester Media. I would like to speak with Mr Rogers'

'Yes sir of course please hold the line.' The hold music wasn't as bad as some, but I was nearing their building and shit needed to be done quickly.

'Mr Sylvester how are you?'

'Very well Rogers, I need to make an urgent appearance to speak with Riley Shure, I mean Miss Witmore, can you arrange a private room?'

'Ah yes our secret shareholder, of course Mr Sylvester, I will arrange that now for you.'

'Excellent thankyou I should be with you in five minutes.'

I hung up. Right, what the fuck am I going to do when I get her alone, I know what I WOULD like to do, fuck her sensless, as she has gotten me really fired up.

Nerves pricked me inside as I approached the front of the building, god I was actually sweating.

I was greeted personally by Mr Rogers who escorted me into a room on the twentieth floor of their building.

'Thankyou Rogers for sorting this. I appreciate your speed and urgency.'

'No trouble actually she is in demand at the moment so getting her some time away will be good for her.'

'Ahh ok, - great.'

'Riley is in room 213 down the hall to the left.' Then he left me.

I hesitated at the door, before I reached for the handle and opened the door. Silence filled the room. As I closed the door and gently locked it, I saw Riley coming from the room behind, must have been somewhere to get refreshments. She was startled at first I could tell.

'What are you doing here?' she said dismissively. 'I'm here to see you like I said I would.'

'I have nothing to say to you Jacob.'

'Then just hear me out will you.' I moved in closer to her. She stepped back; she did this several times, before she was against the wall.

God she smelt good my nostrils full with her scent, making me warm inside and waking my dick up.

I moved into her personal space and placed my arms on the wall either side of her head, almost pinning her to the spot; her arms were down and she didn't fight me.

'God Riley I have missed you so much, I'm a dick, a fucking dick to be exact, things were going so well and I fucked up really bad, I can't tell you how sorry I am that I done that to you.'

I placed my forehead to hers and she closed her eyes, a single tear falling onto her cheek.

She was silent, so silent it scared me.

'Riley please talk to me.' I wanted so desperately to kiss her and tell her I would do anything to take back what I had done.

She just needed her to talk to me. I stayed forehead to forehead for a few minutes before my urge to kiss her overtook me.

I leant down with my hand and lifted her chin so that our eyes could meet, she opened them as my lips pressed against hers, she softly moaned into my mouth and I embraced her, holding her close as our kiss deepened her mouth opening to let me in.

'Fuck Riley!' I moaned, momentarily breaking our kiss.

She looked at me with sadness in her eyes. I released her arms and she took me by surprise by wrapping them around my neck and pulled me into a passionate kiss. I was animalistically aroused by her forwardness, she wanted me as much as I wanted her.

'Riley I want you,' I breathed.

'I want you too,' she said in a whisper.

That's all I needed to hear. I lifted her up and carried her over to the desk placed her juicy ass on the desk and hitched her skirt up revealing stockings, fuck!

'Fuck Riley you are killing me here.'

She smiled but there was something else in her eyes, something dark I hadn't seen before.

She pulled me close again and kissed me as though her life depended on it.

I reached down to her sex and removed her knickers lace fucking lace again my dick was harder than fucking rock. I slipped my fingers over her clit and she was so fucking wet it was glorious.

'Fucking hell Riley you're so wet for me.'

She sniggered as she was kissing me, her tongue teasing mine over and over. I rubbed her clit and she moaned louder into my mouth, slipping into her my fingers playing and teasing her. God, I wanted to fuck her so bad, but it would have been over in just a short time. I needed this to last as long as I could.

Her moans grew as I worked my magic on her, she began rubbing herself up onto me for more. This drove me wild. I couldn't leave it any longer, so I undone my trousers and dropped them to the ground. My boxers were next freeing my hard cock. I teased her with the head over her clit and spread her juices over it; she was so ready for me. With one push I slid into her like a fucking glove, I couldnt stop my own moan escaping from my mouth.

She joined me as I pushed into her again and again. I grabbed her legs and pulled her closer to me, pushing her body to the desk, pulling on her hips as I thrust into her.

'Oh my god,' she moaned.

I pulled out of her and drew her to stand then I turned her over and pushed her front down onto the desk, she held the top of it as I grabbed her hips and thrust into her from behind.

Fuck she felt good, her moans were coming quicker now. 'Fuck you feel so fucking good' I said horsely.

'Yes Jacob yes,' her words encouraged me to fuck her harder.

I reached my hand down to her slit and rubbed her clit as I fucked her. She came hard squeezing her vagina tight over my cock, until I came inside her releasing my built up juices just for her.

'Jesus fucking christ Riley,' I said as I lay on top of her back, panting. Her face was to the side and flushed.

I pulled out gently and eased her up from the desk, turning her to face me.

I put my dick away and tucked my shirt back in, she just sat there watching me.

'Are you ok? I said, worried now.

'I'm very well thank you,' she answered primly. She smiled but it never reached her eyes. 'Riley we need to talk.'

'I don't think I can at the moment, Jacob. I have a lot on my plate right now and I can't deal with us as well.'

Her words hit me hard, we had just fucked! Did that mean nothing to her? 'Riley I thought -'

'What? You thought you could have sex with me and it would all be done? sorted? back on? I'm afraid not, however I am grateful that you came here to fuck me, I really needed that. I could have refused you I know, but why would I? You're a great lover, my first, my only, up to now.'

Every word hit me like a body blow.

'What do you mean for now?' I gulped at the implication. I didn't want her fucking gratitude!

'Just that, I'm a rich woman now Jacob I can have who I want, when I want. Today I wanted you and I had you. Thank you.'

With that she walked towards the door. I was confused and hurt, and used. Yes, very used.

She stopped at the door and turned my way and paused for just a moment,

'I'm looking forward to Friday Jacob, maybe I'll see you before then if I want to. I'm a busy woman now.'

With that she unlocked the door and left me there.

I blindly left the building even more confused than I was in that room. She had fucking used me and now I was just a fucking pussy. What had happened to her? Is this what my actions had turned her into? Where was *MY* Riley!

Chapter 27

Riley

Monday morning found me with so many texts from my friends.

Apparently I was all over the internet. I was super newsworthy, it was quite amusing. I had a message from an unknown source as well. Opening it up, I immediately wished I hadn't. It was from my Grandmother asking if I would meet her this week, not telling me but asking. How thoughtful of her. But she can wait. I have other fish to fry this week, I thought.

It was like a switch had clicked inside me. I was determined, more than ever, to be stronger and not take shit from people, anyone. There were two people on my list: Jacob and my Grandmother. He had to be dealt with first.

The doorman buzzed my intercom and said that there was a car waiting for me to take me to work.

'Ok, thanks David' I said.

I never ordered a car, I wondered who called it? Was I going to be kidnapped or something, foolish, dark thoughts for a Monday.

I exited my building roughly ten minutes later, as I wasn't ready when the call came up. A tall man opened the door for me.

'Thankyou,' I said. 'Who sent you?'

Hearing a shuffle in the car I bent down. Mr Quinn sitting there smiling at me. 'Quinn' I said, smiling back. 'How are you? This is a surprise.'

'Riley, great to see you. How are you this morning? Lots to take in no doubt. Have you seen the news?'

He was smiling again, but there was concern in his voice.

'I'm not sure if I'm honest, Saturday didn't go like I had planned, but I'm ready to take on what I need to. I know there are going to be companies that are a little perturbed right now. As for the news, no I haven't. I've tried not to engage in it. Is it bad?'

Foolishly I had not seen any news reports and didn't want to get caught up in any of it even though it was me being reported on.

'Actually there are some great photos of you, you look like your mother in some of them. As for your story, they are digging now. Looking for any information about you. I think we need to do a press release, so you can be on top of it all.

What do you think?'

'If that's what you suggest then, yes I guess we can sort that out.'

We discussed what happens next and about arranging meetings with the 'Big Three -Sylvesters, Rowthornes and Krane Media. The others could wait for now as my stake was smaller.

'Can I leave it to you to organise please Quinn, I do have to speak with the Sylvester group on Friday, can you be there with me for that one?'

'Yes of course. I will arrange Krane Media for this week as well. Is Thursday good for you?'

'Yes all good.' I thought for a moment. ' I'll actually speak to Mr Rogers when I get in, and sort something with him. Let's meet as soon as possible this week for the press release.'

'Good good. That's settled then.'

'Excellent. Thank you Quinn I really appreciate your support.' 'That's what I'm here for.'

I touched his hand as a thankyou, he was my rock through this and I needed him so I could be strong.

Rowthornes was busy as per usual and I seemed to go unnoticed which was good. I didn't need the extra attention, not yet at least. As I was heading for the elevator, I was joined by a few other staff, thankfully not making eye contact with me. Staying quiet they began chatting in excitement.

'Did you see the news? Back from the Dead the headlines said, well there's going to be dirt I bet. No-one can hide then just appear like that without there being something to hide.'

'Yeah what is that all about, I heard she's worth billions now. I bet she was just biding her time.'

'Apparently she works here, I haven't seen her though, she looked amazing on the front cover though, a real hottie.'

They left the elevator three floors below me. God, I was the talk of the town it seemed. I needed a strong coffee right now.

Mr Rogers met me on the way to the breakroom, smiling as he always had done so thankfully no change there.

'Morning Riley, are you ok?'

'Um well I think so sir.'I smiled at him. 'Please call me Hugh.' Mr Rogers offered.

'Oh no. No, Mr Rogers is fine with me, you are my boss after all.'

'Ok,' he swallowed a little chuckle after my response. 'But if you want to then I'm ok with it, obviously we need to have a chat after the weekend news.'

'Uh yeah I think we should. I said, trying to be low key.'

'I tell you what, have your coffee come see me in an hour. We can have a chat then.' He walked off with a nod in my direction.

I exhaled not realising I was holding my breath.

I sat at my desk sipping the hot delicious coffee letting it burn my throat as it went down. Pain was good. I was dealing with a lot right now, it was a release I thought.

The emails kept coming all morning, my chat with Mr Rogers did not happen, as he was called away. He left a message to say he would come see me when he could. I understood there was a lot going on.

Emma who was sitting across from me was just as normal as before. 'So Riley, you kept that little secret to yourself?' She said amusingly.

'No secret. I just had to make a decision and well I made one. The consequences will be either good or bad. We will just have to wait and see. I'm no different than last week.' I said keeping the conversation light.

She scoffed, unbelievingly. 'Well, I hope you can hold that thought. One thing is certain, you'll have a few more suitors and if you're not careful a fair few gold diggers.' She laughed and I laughed. Things were cool.

I put off the inevitable conversation with my Grandmother for most of the morning then decided now was as good a time as any. Do I call or message her? Hmm, she messaged me first, so maybe I should just do the same. It was easier as I don't have to actually speak with her!

Good morning Grandmother, Riley here.
I believe you would like to meet up this week?
Well I can be free Thursday if you are available
Maybe we could have lunch together.
Please let me know your schedule as I'm
Sure you are a very busy person.
Regards your Granddaughter Riley

Right that's one down I thought, as I pressed send. Hopefully just the right kind of coolness to show I am not a pushover, nor will I ever be.

Now that was done it brought me to another message I had received from Jacob. The thorn in my side and right now my thoughts were a jumbled mess in my brain. So nope, I can't deal with him today. One at a time and he can wait. I will have to face him on Friday anyway.

Monday drew to a close and everyone was leaving. I was finishing up a small project draft for a new client, when Rogers walked along the corridor.

'Ah Riley you're still here?'

'Yes, I had some work to finish off today, new client.' 'I see, do you have time for a quick chat?'

'Of course no problem'. I stood and followed him into his office. He gestured for me to sit. The sofa was near, facing the city heights.

'I'm sorry I haven't been available today,' he said with concern in his words. 'As you can imagine your news has caused quite a stir within the company.'

'It's all good. I've been busy anyways.'

'So,' he began. 'You are now a major shareholder in our company, you have a voice. I knew your father had shares and that they were held in trust. Do you know what you want to do, I mean keep them or sell them or because of your background consider a more active role in our company. I mean more so than you are now?'

'Er wow. In truth, I'm not sure what I am going to do Mr Rogers. I thought I would attend a meeting and listen to what the Board had to say. Obviously, I am getting guidance from my Trustees but they are just that, offering guidance.' It was the only answer I could give him at the moment, as I really wasn't sure where I was heading.

'Ok no need to worry right now, I will have my secretary send over the last quarters' papers and have details of our Board meetings sent through, you can decide if you want to join us or not. You're pretty much in the know of what we do, so that wont be new to you.'

I nodded, thankful for his understanding.

We had a general chat for a while before I excused myself; it was late and my stomach was rumbling too loudly.

'Thanks for the chat' I said as I left his office.

'I'm always here if you need to talk, Riley please remember that.'

He smiled and I left. He was like a surrogate father and I knew he meant well with his words and concern.

I was exhausted Monday night and needed some quiet time to myself. My friends were messaging me non stop, but I didn't have the energy to answer any of them. I fell asleep after a cheese and ham sandwich, I couldn't even be bothered to cook.

Tuesday morning came all too quickly as the alarm drew me from a glorious sleep; lying on a warm beach sea rippling in the distance sun beating down on my body while being devoured by Jacob and his mouth. Gripping his hair, as he licked me tenderly exciting my clit and making my body tremble with desire, an array of tongue and fingers exploring me bringing me to the edge, then the buzzing noise, fuck! The alarm.

'Shit the fucking bed!' Sweat on my brow, my pussy wet, so wet. Annoyed with myself and my dreams I got up and showered.

Tuesday started off better than yesterday, my emails were not so hectic and it seemed the news people were quiet too, thankfully.

I was busy with my work and keeping my head down when I got a message through on my phone from Jacob.

Riley listen I know you hate me but I really need to talk with you before Friday.

Friday was all he was bothered about, his precious job probably. He *was* a man after all, however, I couldn't get the images of my dream out of my head. God I missed his touch, I could get wet with just that thought of him. Maybe I could play this right for my pleasure only. I'll let him stew for a while and text him back after lunch.

Mr Sylvester, I believe we can converse on Friday where all our laundry can be aired, you hurt me and I will not forget. Be prepared.

I kept it deliberately formal. Somewhere deep inside me, I needed him to pay and pay he would. His message came back straight away which I wasn't surprised at.

what the fuck does that mean be prepared?

I didn't reply and carried on into the afternoon just as busy, Mr Rogers came around and said there was an urgent meeting I had to attend in room 213.

'Of course sir I'll go now shall I?' 'Yes please. Thank you Riley.'

'No problem Mr Rogers' I said as I left my area and went to the boardroom.

There wasn't anyone here yet, that's good, then thought I'll get a drink from the back and be prepared, not knowing what the meeting was about or how long it would take.

As I walked from the back room I came face to face with Jacob. He startled me for a moment, not sure what was going on.

'What are you doing here?' I said to him directly. 'I'm here to see you like, I said I would.'

'I have nothing to say to you Jacob.'

'Then just hear me out will you.'

He seemed genuine, but I couldn't let my guard down. He moved in closer towards me. I had to step back from him, he did this again, so I had to move back until I was up against the wall, nowhere to go.

He was so close now I could smell his cologne, god he was as delicious as I remembered him even though it hadn't been that long. The smell and his proximity was like an aphrodisiac.

He got so close to me, almost touching, he placed his arms on the wall behind me, I was pinned to the spot. I didn't react, I was waiting for his next move - before I made mine.

'God Riley I have missed you so much, I'm a dick, a fucking dick to be exact, things were going so well and I fucked up really bad, I can't express how sorry I am that I done that to you.'

He placed his forehead to mine. I closed my eyes trying not to get too emotional but a tear escaped.

I didn't say a word. I had to keep control here. 'Riley please talk to me.'

I couldn't let my guard down even though my walls were crashing around me just by being in his presence.

His forehead pressed to mine for what seemed like an eternity before he made his move.

His hand rested on my chin, then he was lifting it so our eyes would meet.

I opened them as his lips pressed against mine, I couldn't help but moan, he was my destruction right now.

He pulled me close as our kiss deepened. **'Fuck Riley!'** he said momentarily breaking our kiss.

I looked at him and emotions flooded through me. Before I realised what I was doing, my traitorous body had taken over, my arms reached around his neck and I pulled him into a kiss. I was doing the taking now.

'Riley, I want you.'

'I want you too.' I could hardly deny what I was feeling.

With that he had lifted me off the floor. When he hitched my skirt up to my waist he noticed I had worn stockings today.

'Fuck Riley you are killing me here.' He said, looking down at me.

I smiled at him knowing I had gained some control over my fickle body. I wanted him to fuck me hard, because thats what I needed from him now. I pulled him close again and kissed him urgently, giving the idea I needed him more than he needed me.

I was ready for him well before he removed my knickers, I had been ready since my fucking dream last night.

'Fucking hell Riley you're so wet for me.' I could sense his burning desire.

I giggled, as I began kissing him, deliberately teasing him with my tongue over and over. I just needed him to fuck me now, so I could move on.

He rubbed my clit and my desire grew. I moaned louder into his mouth as he slipped his fingers inside me playing and teasing me. As he played my body with his fingers, I couldn't help but rub myself against him wanting more, so much fucking more.

This did the trick. He undone his trousers and removed them then his boxers allowing his fantastic cock to be free, so big and it was all mine now and forever.

He began to tease me with this dick across the front of my pussy. I wanted him to just stick it in and do me hard across the table and then he did. With one push he was inside me, stretching me, filling me like I wanted, like I needed right now, electricity shot through my body from my core.

I couldn't help myself as he pushed into me again and again. I wanted his body to merge with mine, I just wanted to feel not think. Pulling at my hips, he thrust deeper into me. God help me, I wanted, needed this and he knew my body so well. I know I was using him for my own pleasure, but I didn't care.

'Oh my god!' I could barely get the words out, it felt so good.

He withdrew from me and pulled me to stand up, this wasn't in my plan I thought, but then he turned me around to face the desk. This time he pushed me down onto the desk, I splayed my hands across the top as he grabbed my hips and thrust into me from behind. Oh that felt sooo good! I was losing control and this wasn't supposed to happen, I was supposed to be using him, not the other way round. My voice gave me away far too much and he knew it.

'Fuck Riley you feel so fucking good' he said hoarsely

'Yes Jacob yes! I couldnt help it, I was now lost to his fucking.

He pushed into me harder again and again, then reached for my clit and teased me until I came. My mind went numb as I absorbed my climax and felt it vibrate through to every fibre of my being.

Then I felt him come inside me. 'Jesus fucking christ Riley,' he groaned, as he pressed himself across my back.

He pulled out of me gently then turned me around to face him. He sorted himself out while I just watched.

'Are you ok?' he said with a worried look on his face.

'I'm very well thank you,' I smiled, but again it never reached my eyes.

'Riley we *do* need to talk.'He went to reach for me but I moved before he got a firm grip.

'I don't think I can right now Jacob, I have a lot on my plate right now and I can't deal with us as well.'

'Riley I thought -'

'What? You thought you could have sex with me and it would all be done? sorted? back on? I'm afraid not, however I am grateful that you came here to fuck me, I really needed that. I could have refused you I know, but why would I? You're a great lover, my first, my only, up to now.'

I needed him to know I was in charge even though the words coming from my mouth were hurtful.

'What do you mean for now?

'Just that, I'm a rich woman now Jacob I can have who I want when I want, today I wanted you and I had you.'

With that I walked away towards the door, hoping he understood what had just happened.

'I'm looking forward to Friday Jacob, maybe I'll see you before then if I want to. I'm a busy woman now.' I said before leaving him.

Leaving Jacob open mouthed was a slight win for me even though I was shaking like hell, as I tried to keep my shit together.

Tuesday was a win win for me.

My Grandmother messaged back later that afternoon saying she looked forward to lunch and she had booked us a table at The Wallflower - very swanky I thought and full of *her people.* It had an exclusive waiting list and by all accounts the food was to die for.

I emailed Mr Rogers and asked if I could have an extended lunch. As it was shareholder stuff, he immediately agreed, suggesting I take the afternoon so things were not rushed.

Sweet I thought. Preparation had to be perfect, because this was going to be tough.

I hadn't heard from Jacob by the time I left the office, thankfully. I was still feeling the buzz from earlier, but I told myself, it could be a while before I get my next fix so enjoy it while you can.

Chapter 28

Jacob

There were no words as to how I felt on the ride back to the office on Tuesday. She had changed so much. I could understand how pissed she was with me because of THAT incident, but she had already forgiven me - at least in part, otherwise we would be trying to rip each others' clothes off at every opportunity. One minute she was keeping me at a distance, thenext….

She was driving me crazy!

I had to keep my eye on the ball when it came to my company and where and how I was dealing with things. I wasn't going to let her push me out, not now, not ever. If she was playing with me then game on Miss bloody Whitmore, game on.

My relationship with her was going to have to take a back seat to some extent, so I could focus on what we needed to do to protect all that we had worked for. I wasn't going to roll over without a fight for my company…and the woman!

Preparing for the shareholders meeting was my only priority right now. Wednesday was intense with near on back to back meetings. It didn't help with the numerous emails back and forth from my father and the constant nagging about the situation with Riley. Trying to placate my father was more difficult than I ever thought it would be.

'Dad, I assure you all will be well on Friday, you need to calm down.' It was utter crap, but he didn't need to know that. The last thing I wanted was for him to have another health scare.

'Please Jacob, we have worked too hard to build up our reputation and client base for it to turn to shit now.' He was pissed for sure.

I worked my arse off all of Wednesday to prepare for every eventuality we could come up with and things were looking better by the end of the day. I thought about messaging Riley to gain some insight as to how the meeting would go, but decided I would message her in the morning and see how the lay of the land was.

I was hopeful at least.

Mid morning came and I messaged her that I wanted to clear the air, following our liaison on Tuesday which was left on a strange note.

Riley,canwemeettoday.? Letstalk

Message me

I waited for an age for a reply, and I allowed my thoughts to drift back to our time in the office. The way her body accepted me, her passion and her smell. God her smell! The feelings between us, even though she tried to deny it, were stronger than ever. I needed to remind her of that.

Her response came shortly before lunch;

I have a lunch date today, I can meet you at 4pm at the diner on 4th street if you are free.

This wasn't gonna do it. I needed her alone.

Come to my apartment Riley. I need to speak to you alone.

I don't think that's a good idea do you ?

Please Riley.

Ok, ok, I'll meet you there just after four.

Yes, at least I would have her in my apartment, I needed to ensure the hostility she was directing toward me did not get reflected toward the Board.

I was nervous all of Thursday leading up to the afternoon, I couldn't mess this up, not one bit.

All I could do now was wait and hope things went my way.

I paced the apartment as it approached four. I dragged my fingers through my hair, a sure sign I was anxious.

Four pm came and my hands were now sweating, any moment now she would be here. Don't fuck this up Jacob; I couldn't fuck this up, it was too important.

It was four fifteen before the buzzer went from the ground floor. 'Mr Sylvester I have Miss Whitmore to see you down here.' 'Yes thank you, please send her up.'

The elevator drew close as I watched it intently from the foyer to my apartment.

The doors drew open and there stood the most - fuck she looked beautiful. Oozing sophistication and confidence, it was hard to believe we only met 6 weeks ago.

'*Mr Sylvester.*' She drawled, a hint of steel in her tone.

'Please Riley,' Jacob rolled his eyes. 'It's Jacob. I think we can dispense with the formalities given our history, don't you?'

'Hello Jacob.' She smiled and nodded; there was my Riley.

'Come in please,' I gestured her into my apartment and followed her behind. She smelled good.

My mind briefly wondered where she had been, dressed to kill and looking sensational. Jealousy crept into the outer reaches of my mind.

The long dress she wore was open at her chest giving a glimpse of her perfect breasts, her hair was curled just a little and framed her face…she looked elegant.

'You look beautiful Riley,' I said in a low voice appreciating her. 'Thank you.' she paused, then continued. 'I've just had lunch with my

Grandmother.' She wrinkled her nose. I couldn't be sure but I don't think she meant to tell me this little tit-bit. 'How did it go?' I was interested. 'Um, ok thanks.'

'Would you like a drink? I have some champagne on ice if you want one.' I was keeping it cool, not being too eager or needy. Trouble was I wanted her as soon as the elevator doors opened and now I was trying to keep my cock under control!

'Yes please, thank you.'

I poured two glasses and handed her one, as our hands met I could feel the spark between us and my eyes went straight to hers, she felt it too as her breath caught in her throat.

She held the glass to her lips and sipped the champagne closing her eyes as she did so. I watched her. I wanted to reach out and kiss her, touch her. And well, fuck her, the pull between us was so strong. I was aching for her body to be close to mine.

She walked to the windows and looked out at the city all the while sipping her drink. She seemed lost in her own world, as I approached her I stood behind her. I could feel the heat radiating from her body. Just being in her space was doing things to me emotionally and physically.

I took a deep breath before I put my hands on her shoulders.

'We need to talk. Really talk.' I said quietly. I released her and she turned on her own free will.

'Yes we do'. Her words were quiet and I knew I had to try and win her forgiveness.

She finished her drink and walked past me to the table to refill it. 'This is good,' she said, raising her glass to me.

'Yes it's a good year' I replied inanely. I could get whiplash with her changing the subject! She was acting a little strange, here but…not.

'Are you ok Riley?' I asked, looking puzzled by her.
'Yes, I'm good, thank you. Shall we sit?'

She moved over to the couch and sat down. I came and sat near her, almost touching but not, she looked me in the eyes.

'Riley I know you ha-,' I started to say, but she put a finger to my lips. 'Shhh, don't speak, she said quietly.

What happened next blew my fucking mind.

Chapter 29

Riley

Thursday morning I had gotten up extra early and dressed to impress.

I decided on a long, flowing, floral dress with my hair curled enough to emphasise my features, just like my mothers. I put on the ring my parents had given me just to piss her off. I topped it off with some sandals that gave me a little more height and I wore the bracelet Jacob had bought me.

The morning was slow but steady, and the moments were ticking by until I had to meet with the dreaded Grandmother, Viper in disguise.

I had arranged to meet Jacob at his apartment after my lunch date, not sure why I agreed to his apartment. Maybe deep down I wanted to be alone with him. I wasn't sure as my emotions were somewhat off kilter probably due to the meeting with my Grandmother.

The Wallflower was extremely impressive, the decor was white with pure white roses everywhere, and a gold patterned Aubusson carpet swept through from the reception desk to the restaurant. The doorman was a delightful man with a welcoming smile and a glint in his eye. I was taken by a waiter to the far side of the restaurant where a private area was set up in what seemed like, a light room surrounded in glass and a garden on the far side.

There she was, Grandmother, seated on the far side of the room, dressed from head to toe in haute couture and looking like the epitome of old money glam. She was sipping tea with her pinky aloft. God why do old people sip tea? The irrelevant thought jumped into my head.

'Riley dear,' she said in a pleasant manner, putting her teacup onto the saucer without even taking her eyes off me. The creases in her face deepended with her smile.

'Hello Grandmother,' I said respectfully. 'Please sit.'

She was smiling and looked somewhat different from the first time I saw her. 'So I guess you have a great many questions for me?' I broke the silence.

'Yes, I believe I do and no doubt you have more than a few for me, but for now, I would like to have lunch with you and get to know you.'

I was slightly taken aback by her response. From what I gathered from my fathers letter I was expecting a grilling from her.

'Ok, sounds good to me.' I smiled, she smiled and then she sipped her tea.

The waiter hovered inconspicuously. 'Would you like something to drink?, wine, tea?'

'Wine would be nice, thank you.'

'Jeffrey, wine for my Granddaughter please and some iced water too, thank you.'

'So Riley, what do you do here in the city?' she asked.

'I work for Rowthornes Media, I'm in the special projects department.' 'And have you worked there long?'

'I've been there almost two years now. It's rewarding in it's own way, my father helped me get it before he and my mother passed away.' This conversation was beginning to become hard.

She raised her brows at the mention of my father, which was curious.

'I miss him, your father,' she clarified. 'And your mother. You look like her, but you have your father's eyes.' She smiled and sipped her tea. Her eyes were a little glazed. I thought she was going to cry. Cry! That was definitely not an emotion I was expecting.

At that moment the waiter - Jeffrey, came back with a bottle of wine and some fresh chilled water. He poured a little wine into the glass for me to taste,

'It's lovely, thank you', smiling up at him, he smiled back and filled my glass. 'So where are you living Riley?'

'I have an apartment not far from work. It was my twenty-first birthday present from Mum and Dad and I've been there ever since.'

Food arrived before more talk could be done. It was a light salad and fish, it was delicious fragranced with lemon and hints of something smoked. It was delightful.

We chatted about my job in general terms whilst we ate, leaving the bigger questions until after.

'I know you want to know why my parents kept me from the family, unfortunately I can't answer that, as I have no idea.' I swept a strand of hair away from my face with the hand that I was wearing in my GG's ring.

I could see her eyes widen as she looked at it and glared.

'That's a lovely ring you are wearing Riley, where did you get it from? It looks expensive.' Her lips stern as she spoke.

'Oh this ring?' I held it up, 'It was a gift from my parents and Great Grandmother, it used to be hers apparently. My mother had diamonds put around it. It's beautiful isn't it?' I smiled at her, moving the ring so the light could catch it.

'Yes it's a family heirloom, it has been in our family for generations.' She sipped her tea again.

'Wow! I never knew that. My Great Grandmother said that she would leave it to me when I was a 'big girl.' I smiled reminiscently.

'There is a lot you are not aware of about your family my dear. I think it would be a good idea to come to the Estate and see for yourself. But for today, let's just enjoy our lunch and arrange another date. I do want to get to know you Riley, I have missed out on so much.'

I drank my wine and nodded. My second glass of wine was almost finished and was making me feel a little nauseous. My nerves had not helped either.

She kept looking at me and smiling which was making me uncomfortable so I was fidgeting a little to distract myself from looking at her.

I was too curious for some answers myself and decided to bite the bullet. 'Did you love my father?' I asked, looking at her from under my eyelashes.

Without pausing she answered. 'Yes I did, your mother too. Your father became distant after my Mother passed away - your Great Grandmother, and slowly over the next five years or so, he shut himself away from the family entirely.

The next and last time he contacted me was to inform me you had passed away, a mystery illness took you. He never contacted me even though I tried to reconcile with him. For the life of me I cannot understand why he would tell such a dreadful lie'

Tears filled her eyes and for the first time, I felt sorry for her. Why *had* my father lied about my dying? What was going on? I really needed to find out what the fuck was going on with this family *MY* family.

Lunch ended with more questions than answers although I had agreed to visit with her but no date had been set.

Making my way to Jacob's apartment the sickness started up again, and the butterflies did not help. I had to stop the cab twice to throw up. I didn't think I had that much to drink. Hmmm well I did end up finishing the bottle, but I ate too. The cabbie was nice, in fact he gave me a bottle of water to help after I was sick for the second time.

Arriving at 4:15 to the apartment building, I was shitting myself. The doorman was nice and sweet. I informed him of who I was, he smiled and rang up to Jacob's apartment.

'Mr Sylvester I have Miss Whitmore to see you down here.' He nodded, smiled and looked my way.

'Please go on up.'

He called for the elevator, pressed his key and then left me there to continue up to his floor. I was nervous, but despite being sick I knew I looked good. I knew I had to be strong, because I had zero willpower where he was concerned and it would take very little for me to cave.

The doors drew open and he was standing there waiting for me, the look on his face told me I was winning and made the right choice with my outfit and hair.

'Mr Sylvester.' I said trying to keep it cool and under control.

Please Riley, it's Jacob. I think we can dispense with the formalities given our history, don't you?'

'Hello Jacob.' I couldn't help but smile and remember the time when we played with our names.

'Come in please,' he said, gesturing to me to go in, he smelt good as I walked past him.

We entered the open lounge area when Jacob turned towards me.

'You look beautiful Riley,' he said in a low tone, which sent chills down my spine in a good way.

I thanked him then blurted out. 'I've just had lunch with my Grandmother.' 'How did it go?' He seemed interested in my grandmother.

'Um ok thanks'. I didn't want to say it was crap really.

'Would you like a drink? I have some champagne on ice if you want one.'

'Yes please, thank you.' I said in a more normal manner. I kinda had to really. I threw up the last lot I drank, a little dutch courage needed now.

He poured two glasses and handed me one, as our hands met I felt that spark between us, our eyes met, as I caught my breath ever so slightly. I held the glass to my lips and sipped the champagne, closing my eyes to try and keep control.

I walked over to the glass panels and looked out at the city sipping my drink trying to hold it together. I wanted him so much my body was beginning to tremble.

I was lost in my own world when I felt his hands on my shoulders; a jolt of electricity shot through me straight to my clit and I could feel myself getting wet.

'We need to talk. Really talk'. he said quietly.

He let go of me and I turned to face him looking at him and his beautiful face. 'Yes we do.'.

I finished my drink and walked past him to the table to refill it. My courage was failing me, however the champagne was providing me with a great big dollop of dutch courage.

'This is so good,' I said, raising my glass to Jacob.

'Yes it's a good year' he replied. Jesus, why was he talking about good years?. He looked at me with a puzzled look.

'Are you ok Riley?'

'Yes, I'm good, thank you. Shall we sit?'

I took myself to one of the couches and sat down making sure my leg was exposed. Short of jumping on him I couldn't be any more blatant!. My desire

inside was at a point where my walls were down and I needed all of him. Desire was controlling me now, or the drink and my desire, I wasn't sure.

Jacob joined me on the sofa, almost touching me. I could feel the pull between us. It was so strong, I looked at his face, not moving.

'Riley I know you ha-,' He started to say but I placed my finger on his lips. 'Shhh, don't speak,' I said quietly.

I placed the glass in front of us on the table, turned to face Jacob and stroked my hand across his face and trailed my finger across his lips. Slowly I moved my hand down to his chest where his shirt was slightly open, his chest waiting to be touched. I leant in and gently touched his lips with mine, his lips automatically reacting to mine a small sound escaped from his lips. I think I shocked him!

I pushed my tongue into his mouth forcing him to kiss me back, which he did. He went to touch me and I moved his hand away, I wanted to control this.

My next move took me to the point of no return.

I lifted my dress and straddle Jacob's lap, as I did this, his hands followed mine and he grasped my ass as I sat on him.

'Riley fuck,' he looked at me, desire burning in his eyes.

I wrapped my hands around his neck and pulled his mouth to mine, deep, passionate kisses, breaking only to catch our breaths before beginning again.

Jacob released my mouth and began kissing my neck sucking and kissing all at once. I shivered, so turned on I couldn't wait..

I ground myself into his groin, feeling his cock, so hard in his jeans. He massaged my breasts, still kissing me.

I wanted this so much, the feeling was growing inside me, steadily building.

Before I could bring myself back to reality, Jacob had moved to the edge of the sofa and lifted me up, I wrapped my legs around his waist. His hands were on my ass as he walked me to his bedroom.

Jacob slowly released me, gliding me down his body so I could feel the hardness of his cock. I stood facing him, so close, I could feel his breath on me. He leaned down and kissed me gently, then began to unbutton my dress.

I went to undo his shirt, slowly, seductively, never taking my eyes off of his.

After what seemed like hours we were both naked standing in front of each other.

There was a moment where we both hesitated, wondering who was going to make the first move.

I did.

I dropped to my knees and took hold of his cock and drew it to my mouth, lapping the end with my tongue, running my fingers gently down the underside of his cock, to cup his balls. I massaged them before moving my hand back up, where I clasped the base firmly at the same time taking him further into my mouth. Jacob breathed in sharply and placed his hands on my head. Slowly, I began to move my head back and forth, my tongue licking and teasing, whilst my hands started to pump from his base.

He was enjoying this; his groans were testament to that. His body twitched and his hands were in my hair pushing my head down to match my movements. The air of doubt tried to creep into my thoughts after what he had done with *her,* but I brushed them aside.

'Riley stop, I want to taste you,' Jacob's words were breathy and needy. I sucked harder and pumped faster, until he pulled away from me.

'Jesus Riley, fuck!' he said, as he leant down towards me. I smiled and he picked me up and threw me back onto the bed.

His eyes were now darker than I had ever seen them, his hair falling in front of his forehead as he leaned over me staring at me laying there.

'You are a bad woman Riley, teasing me with that mouth of yours.' 'I'm a woman who knows what she wants, Jacob.'

'Oh and I'm going to give it all to you Riley. Trust me!.'

With that he went down on me, homing in on my core with unerring accuracy. He licked and nuzzled me gently with his magical tongue, each lick making me arch on the bed. I was so near an orgasm that my legs started to shake, my eyes rolled back into my sockets.

When I came I exploded. It had been so long. Jacobs' mouth and fingers knew my body so well; he set off a fire inside me that burned just for him, and I craved his touch. My body stiffened and I called out his name, I was lost in a sexual void, my walls I had tried to build around my heart, well and truly down.

Before I had a chance to come down off my sexual high, Jacob was on me and pushed his dick deep inside me making me gasp. He was still rock hard and keen to join me in a climax.

He thrust into me roughly, determinedly. Pushing deeper inside, makingmy body come alive again as that intoxicating feeling started to run through me again. It was electric.

'Oh god Jacob, yes fuck, yes harder'

He stilled, as my eyes met his. Dark desires in them, as in mine. He brought his body on top of me and kissed me resting his elbows on either side of my face. His cock buried deep inside of me, his kissing intense. His tongue matching the thrusts of his cock. He lifted himself up again, and pushed into me. I could feel my own cum making me wetter; he knew I was close to another orgasm. He briefly withdrew from me and flipped me onto my front, quickly lifting my hips; my ass was up and my head down, he entered me quickly and oh so deeply. God it was the best feeling! The deeper he went, the more intense I felt it.

He grabbed my hips with one hand while wrapping the other round to the front and played with my clit. I came almost immediately he touched me, I screamed or groaned, I couldn't tell, But it brought Jacob to his own climax.

We both called out together. It was raw, it was love.

Jacob drew me up to sit on his lap, his cock still inside me and held me there, his arms wrapped around me and his face nuzzling into my neck.

'Mmm, you smell like you have been fucked Miss Whitmore.' 'Mmm, and how can you tell Mr Sylvester?'

'Because of the smell we make together.'

For the first time I blushed and giggled making the muscles inside my vagina tense.

'Riley you keep doing that, I'll fuck you again.' 'Promises, promises,' I giggled.

I had gone past the point of no return now, so I might as well roll with it I thought.

I could feel Jacob's hard length inside of me waking up for round two, I squirmed in his lap before I moved to the bed Jumping under the covers before Jacob devoured me again.

He made love to me. It was slow, seductive, and drove me crazy, coming again in a soul shattering climax. The feeling was utterly intoxicating.

After Jacob came, he laid there looking at me intently again resting on his elbows.

'Riley I hav- have to tell you something,' he said, closing his eyes then opening them, staring at me. His eyes were shining.

'What is it? I played with a strand of his hair.

'I, I love you.'

I couldn't speak, no words would come out, he stared at me for the longest time. Until eventually he asked, 'Riley, are you ok, Did you hear what I said?'

Just as I was about to speak I had this sudden urge to vomit, 'Move quick,' I said, shoving him off me.

I managed to get to the toilet before my guts entered the bowl, heaving several times, until my stomach was completely empty. I felt like shit. Sweaty, shivering. I was a collapsed mess on the bathroom floor.

Jacob went to come and see me but I pushed the door closed and managed to lock it before he could see me. I retched again, but there was nothing left to bring up.

'Riley, are you ok? Let me in' 'Mmhmm,' I was incoherent.

'Let me in honey?' He was growing concerned.

'I'm ok, I'll be out in a bit, can you get me some water please.'

I heard him leave the room, I washed my face a little and made sure I looked ok. Yeah right! Pasty white with my hair clinging to my scalp, where I was sweating. God what is wrong with me, come on pull it together!

I put one of Jacob's robes on, walked into the bedroom and sat on the bed.

I smiled wanly as he walked back in. He had glass in hand and his boxers on, thankfully, I expected him to be naked.

'Here take these too,' he said, handing me some tablets.

'Thanks, sorry I kinda ruined the moment there.' a half hearted smile on my face.

'It's ok, I was getting worried there for a bit,' he chuckled a little, rubbing his hand through his hair.

God, he was so good looking. My anger towards him and what he had done was temporarily squashed.

'I think I should go, I'm not feeling too good,' I said, trying to stand on my wobbly legs.

'You don't have to go right now do you?' He was sounding panicky now. 'Let me look after you.'

'I think I should go, I have a lot to do before tomorrow.' I didn't want to go, but I was feeling rough and did have to sort things out before our meeting tomorrow.

'Ahh yes the meeting, I wasn't going to mention it, but seeing as you are preparing, what am I to expect?'

'Don't be worried Jacob, whatever comes out will be beneficial to us all, I'm sure.'

I dressed quickly and kissed Jacob gently on the cheek. 'Until tomorrow Mr Syl-.'

'Jacob please.' 'What? just Jacob? 'Yeah just Jacob.'

I couldn't help but laugh with him and smile. 'Until tomorrow Miss Whitmore.'

'Riley'

'Just Riley?'

'Yes, just Riley'

He smiled back, as I walked out to the elevator.

I waved as the doors closed. Fuck my life what was that shit going on, I exhaled.

Still feeling nauseous I couldn't place what it could have been. The food was well cooked and I hadn't had that much to drink, well not really considering I had eaten too. As the elevator hit the ground floor I could have died, checking my phone as I left the building I brought my calendar up. Fuck! Shit! Fuck!

Fuck! I hailed a cab.

'No, no, no' I said, shaking my head.

I gave the driver my address, then said. 'Can you take me to the nearest chemist before dropping me home please.'

I sat back in the seat and tried to figure out what was going on, google was my friend right now and after a few taps on some pages it came to light that I could have had a defected jab and I may not be covered and well, over the last 6 weeks I've gone from a virgin to having lots and lots and lots of sex.

I called my clinic and asked to speak to my Doctor, telling the receptionist it was urgent. I was on hold for a while. The music was crap which irritated me.

'Miss Shure I'm going to put you through to Dr Abrahams, please hold.'

'Miss Shure, hello, Dr Abrahams here, What seems to be the matter?' He listened as I asked for details about the jab I had received.'I'm looking at your notes now. We have had a batch of injections that were reported as being potentially defective in their protection. It has only come to light this week, and we are in the process of contacting those who were prescribed it.'

'Oh god no,' I began to cry.

'Miss Shure it's ok you just need to use additional protection for a while.'

'Too late for that now Doc.' I said through the tears that were now streaming down my face. 'I think I'm pregnant.'

There was silence at the end of the phone. 'Ahh, have you taken a test?'

'No, but I'm pretty sure I am, I've got one to do at home.'

'Ok, call the surgery in the morning and we can do one here for you as well.' 'Thanks Dr Abrahams. I'll call back in the morning.'

With that I hung up and we pulled up to my apartment building. I paid the driver and hurried to my floor. Threw my bag on the side and went to the toilet.

Three minutes is like a century when you want the outcome to be in your favour. I hesitated before looking at the result, I was scared, so scared.

Two blue fucking lines! Fuck. This is not possible! I screamed to no-one in particular. But it was. It is, it really is. Lots of sex and no cover equals a baby. I needed to think. How far gone could I be? Anything up to six weeks I answered myself.

I threw up again. Fuck. Why me?

Chapter 30

Jacob

I told Riley that I loved her, played on my mind for the remainder of the night once she had left.

Did I really mean it? I think I did. She was everything I wanted, but never knew it. She was passionate, funny, caring, not to mention annoying and contrary.

There was no doubt she was clever; she had had to deal with a major change in her life, but had managed to keep her feet on the ground, well to date anyway. It had given her a new found confidence in herself and I was the lucky guy who had reaped the benefits yesterday. But despite all that she was forgiving too and although we had not spoken about my tryst with Amanda, I was sure Riley had put it behind her. Behind us.

Just thinking of her got me hard, and shouldn't a man lust after the woman he loves? I started thinking about her eyes, her mouth around my cock; it was enough for me to pull on my dick and wank.

Friday came. I didn't sleep well last night. I could still smell Riley on my bed clothes, which made me want to play with my cock every five minutes, but the expectation of the unknown tomorrow wormed its way through my sexual daze.

I sat bolt upright as my alarm went off and groaned aloud as I held my head in my hands - I definitely should NOT have told Riley I loved her. It was too soon, we hardly knew each other…outside of the bedroom. Maybe I was overthinking things, and whether this was love or not I felt for her, I'd give anything to take the words back. My timing was crap *and* she never reciprocated them. I pushed the thought away to concentrate on the upcoming meeting. Christ! I hope she didn't think I said I loved her because I was worried about today!

Once showered and dressed in dark blue Armani, I grabbed a quick coffee before leaving for the office.

By the time I got to the office I was starving, lots of sexual activity meant I had to eat more. As I approached my secretary I asked her to grab me something to eat from the diner near our building.

'Of course, Mr Sylvester, anything in particular?'

'Something tasty and loaded with carbs,' I smiled sheepishly at her. 'Thankyou.'

I grabbed another coffee from the staff room and retreated to my office and closed the door.

I sat looking out of the window taking in the panorama before me. The city was just beginning to come alive; I could see people the size of ants scurrying to their jobs along the pavements. Glancing at the sky I grimaced. Let's hope for a good day, maybe some sun.

I was tempted to text Riley to see how she was feeling, but decided I would grab her after the meeting instead.

The boardroom began to fill around 9:45. The room was filling up nicely and I took my place at the head of the table, the Chairman opposite me. Two chairs were conspicuously empty, as we waited for our new major shareholder to arrive. We'd heard nothing from reception, so I buzzed my secretary to check whether she had signed in. She hadn't. Why isn't she here yet?

Five to ten and still nothing and now I was worrying, had she taken a turn for the worse after being sick last night? The door opened for what seemed like the hundredth time, a gentleman came in smiling at the many of the people in the room. He wasn't someone I knew or had seen before, so I was curious as to who he was and why he was here.

Curiosity got the better of me and I approached him just as Henry Derwent, our Chairman, announced we should all sit.

I sat back down and everyone not already sitting, found their chairs, all seats were taken with the noticeable exception of Riley's.

'Where's Riley?' I asked Henry as he sat.

'Just one moment Jacob.' Henry coughed, drawing all eyes toward him. 'I have a short announcement, Miss Whitmore, who called the meeting, is unable to attend today due to ill health, but has sent her representative to attend on her behalf. May I introduce you all to Mr Quinn, who is one of the Trustees appointed by Miss Whitmore.'

I was a little taken back by this. Just how sick was she? I know she was sick last night but surely she would have let me know if she couldn't make today's meeting. Frustration brewed inside of me.

'Thankyou, Mr Derwent.' Mr Quinn acknowledged the chairman with a slight incline of his head.

'Henry please.'

Quinn smiled. 'Henry.'

'I am Roger Quinn and as Henry has said, I am here on behalf of Miss Whitmore. Firstly she sends her sincere apologies to you all and said if there had been any way she could have attended, she would have. She acknowledged in lieu of her attendance, for the following considerations to be minuted, in order for them to be discussed, at a later date, when she is well enough to attend herself.

'Those considerations are that Miss Whitmore take an active *advisory* role into the running of the company, within her own area of expertise, with the view to explore emerging new business. Miss Riley is looking at expanding into other developments and stresses these are not currently part of your own business plan, with the backing of the Board she hopes that it can begin very soon.'

'She is excited to be a part of this company. She believes she has a valuable contribution to make towards the future of the company. She also wanted to meet everyone, and will do so, once she is back on her feet.'

Roger Quinn smiled at the table, everyone of them, they seemed to be happy - and a little relieved - that she wasn't going to disrupt the company like they had originally thought.

The meeting was brief and the pleasantries afterwards were even briefer. I had to text Riley so I went to excuse myself from the room, however Mr Quinn caught me before I left.

'Jacob right?' He said.

'Yes it is, how can I help you Mr Quinn?'

'I have a message from Riley, she sends her apologies to you personally and advised she would like to meet with you regarding a private matter.'

'Did she say what it was about?' I was curious now.

'Private being the operative word Jacob,' he smiled and then moved to excuse himself from everyone.

Once everyone had left I went back to my office and tried calling Riley.

No answer, it went straight to voicemail. Shit, what was going on, the next best thing was to text her.

Riley hi, hope you're feeling better and nothing that can't be fixed with medicine.

Quinn said you wanted to speak to me. I can come to yours today if you want.

Let me know, we need to talk.

Jx

I wasn't expecting a reply straight away, as she rarely picked up when I called. I did, however, pace my office for a while, until the phone rang. I answered in a strangled voice.

'Good news then Jacob,' my father said on the other end of the line. 'Well done son, whatever you did worked.'

I could hear the joy in his voice, but I wasn't overjoyed.

'Yes it's a good result Dad, I just need to finalise some of the details with her.' He seemed happy and promptly hung up.

Alone again with my thoughts I wondered what this private matter was she wanted to talk to me about.

I had been lost in thought when my phone pinged.

Hi Jacob

Sorry I didn't attend today

Hope you weren't too disappointed with my rep

I told you I was going to surprise you.

So I need to see you. Can you come over maybe tomorrow.

Rx

I replied shortly after accepting to go over to see her. I wanted to see her so badly, even though I only saw her last night. I needed her close to me.

Saturday morning came quickly as I was all too eager to see Riley. I had arranged to see her in the morning straight after my gym session with the boys.

Having some energy sapped from me would help with my need to ravish her I hoped. Showered and dressed in a casual T and jeans, I was ready to face what was coming.

The drive to her building was a little longer than I wanted due to the traffic. ThankfullyEdward was driving me today, I didn't think I had enough concentration not to end up on someone's bumper…

'Thanks Edward, I'll make my own way home.' He smiled as I left for her building.

The front door was opened so I didn't bother to buzz into Riley's apartment building.

I took the elevator to her floor and briskly walked to her door, hesitating momentarily before knocking.

I stood there for a while but there was no reply, I knocked again and waited, but again no reply.

I called through the door at Riley but there was nothing.

I called her number and it went straight to the answerphone. I left her a message;

'Riley, it's me. I'm here open the door.'

I hung up and waited. There was nothing, I was confused. Where the fuck was she?

Chapter 31

Riley

Friday came and I was feeling, well there was no right way to feel with what was now going on with me. I went to the clinic first thing, and after half an hour of waiting I had my test done which confirmed what I already knew, I was pregnant.

Dr Abrahams was busy, but I had already made an appointment to talk to someone about what happens next.

Leaving the clinic I was in a daze, finding my way to the nearest store and walking through the baby aisle without thinking.

Suddenly my mind was clear. I had to leave here and think about what I was going to do, telling Jacob right now wasn't going to work out in my favour or his.

So I just left. I knew I had the Estate, so I decided I would go there. I stopped at Quinn's office to collect my keys and paperwork and Quinn organised a driver to take me there.

I had messaged Jacob regarding the meeting and that I needed to speak with him knowing that I wouldn't be at the apartment when he arrived.

My arrangements with my grandmother were on hold too. I couldn't face anyone while I was dealing with my news and deciding what to do next.

It was roughly an hour out of the city and finally we came to a vast estate surrounded by tall trees and a drive that lasted a few minutes.

We pulled up to the front of the house which was beautifully lit up. I got out and was greeted by a lovely older woman, she must have been in her fifties, well put together, she smiled when I approached her.

'Miss Whitmore, lovely to finally meet you, I'm Mrs Chester,' she said smiling and holding out her hand for me to shake.

'Hi, please call me Riley,' I said as I shook her hand. 'Please follow me, and welcome to your new home.'

She was so friendly and showed me around the very large house. We went through room by room and then she took me to meet the staff who were employed by the Estate, it was far beyond anything I expected to what I was used to.

Once formalities were completed I retired to the lounge area and sat for a while just taking it all in.

'Can I get you some tea miss?' a kind lady appeared like magic. 'Oh yes please, that would be great, thank you,' I said.

There were lots going on in my mind right now, I was feeling remorseful at the prospect of Jacob turning up to my apartment tomorrow and me not being there. Shit my life was spiralling out of control and I couldn't stop it.

Afternoon turned to evening and a light meal and water as I now couldn't drink because of the little peanut inside of me. Guilt flowed over me too at the thought I had been drinking while pregnant, but I didn't know, so I had to lock that thought away.

Nerves again bubbled up with the prospect of Jacob and having to tackle him with my news. I went to bed early still going over my feelings about all this and where it would leave Jacob and me. I still hadn't really forgiven the incident at the ball, how could I not, but I'd also had him too many times for make-up sex to use it as an excuse to break with him, what was I doing to myself.

My room was to die for, a truly old style decor, with a french renaissance theme. A four poster bed commanded the centre of the room with deep pink and cream upholstered curtains and bedding, the overall effect was very feminine, There was a walk-in closet bigger than my apartment for sure and an ensuite with a tub so big you could swear it fitted at least three people in. This was luxurious through and through.

I woke up later than I expected on Saturday. It was good to get some sleep, the sun was shining, it seemed clearer out here in the countryside, there was so much green.

I pulled on my dressing gown and went downstairs to make a drink. I was welcomed by Mrs Chester who was busying herself in the kitchen.

'Good morning Riley, did you sleep well?'

'I'm just going to make a drink, would you like one?

'Thank you for the offer Riley but I've already eaten. I'll get you something my dear, what would you like?'

'Um tea please if that's ok, oh and maybe some toast.'

'Of course, would you like to take it in the sunroom? It's a lovely morning' 'Oh ok, sorry Mrs Chester where is it please?

'Oh yes, sorry dear, it's back through the kitchen door and down the Hall, to the right.' She pointed to the large wooden doors across from the stairs.

God this place was not me at all.

I found the sun room and she was right. It was wonderful. The sun was beating down onto the roof and it was super warm, a relaxing warm. I sat for a while just looking at the gardens, they were beautiful.

Tea came and some toast and I just relaxed in the sun room, not a care in the world, no really I wasn't thinking of anything, just this bliss right now. I don't

think I left the room until about midday to which returning to my room my phone had gone, it was Jacob seemed he had left me a message;

'Riley, it's me. I'm here open the door.'

I held my hand to my chest at the thought of him standing there and me not answering, guilt, so much guilt.

I messaged my friends to tell them I had gone away for a while and that all this stuff surrounding me was too intense and I needed time to adjust; they were all supportive, but concerned too.

'Are you ok Riley, Robin messaged

'I will be just need time

'We are here for you, you know that right? Emma posted

'Big love babe, Hannah posted too.

'Thanks guys means alot xx

I love my friends, but if I tell them I'm pregnant, they will be mad, especially since I've only slept with Jacob. More importantly, what he did to me at the Gala

- they were less forgiving than me. If only they knew I had taken him back, it would have been much easier to explain my pregnancy.

My heart belonged to Jacob and there was nothing I could do to change that.

I sent out a few emails Saturday afternoon, one asking my boss asking if he would mind me working from home, as I was finding this new found fame a little overwhelming and I needed some quiet time. He was straight back saying, he was happy to agree in the short term and he would check in on me regularly. He was a good man and I had a lot of respect for him, so I felt safe in the knowledge he had my back.

Quinn was next. I told him everything regarding the pregnancy and that I wasn't sure what I wanted to do about it. He messaged me and said he would support me as much as I needed and would only contact me if absolutely necessary.

Covering all my bases was a big relief for me, and I just enjoyed being somewhere everyone else wasn't.

The first week in the new house was interesting. Getting to know its geography and Mrs Chester telling tit-bits about its history; the gardens particularly were my favourite, it was blissful. Swathes of lawn, lush and green, the flower beds an abundance of colour.

I had many messages from Jacob asking where I was and why I hadn't called him. He sounded frantic, but I pushed him mentally away. I couldn't cope with him yet.

Thursday came and I had an appointment with Dr Abrahams for an early scan to see actually how far into the pregnancy I was. I was nervous to go back into the city. in case I bumped into jacob. Thankfully I didn't see him and I was back out on the road within an hour.

'So it looks like you are roughly 6 weeks, possibly 7, and there's the heartbeat there, look!'

I was overwhelmed and tears filled my eyes. It was a tiny person inside of me. Looking at the pictures while returning to the estate was very surreal. Twenty three and knocked up by a CEO after a whirlwind of a fuck fest. What a mess!

I had to be an adult about things now, after seeing that little heartbeat there was no way I was going to terminate. I was going to be a mother with or without Jacob by my side.

When I got back and sat with my tea in the sun room I decided to check my emails. There was one from J;

Riley-tellmewhereyouare? What's goingon?

You're not at work, I've checked and you're not at your apartment. WTF is going on?

You seemed to have vanished off the planet.

Jacob X

Subconsciously touching my stomach as I read the email, feeling a little guilty for just up and leaving, I needed to tell him, but not today.

Mr Rogers checked in with me on Friday and caught up with my workload and my response to the projects I was working on.

He seemed happy that my productivity was more so, while I was away, I'm guessing the quiet agreed with me.

Saturday came and I had to let Jacob know what was going on as it involved him as well. I was nervous to send the email as calling him, I would have chickened out, yes I would.

Jacob, there is no easy way to tell you this news, and I am sorry for telling you over email but I cannot deal with anything remotely emotional at the moment.

I was scared at first but I believe it's your right. I am pregnant, 7 weeks. There was a problem with my birth control injection, a defect apparently according to the doctor and as we didn't use anything else, well….I am under no illusion of a relationship either. I am however prepared to go this alone, but the baby is yours.

Please don't be mad at me, these things happen. I just wanted you to know.

Riley

Send -

The nerves grew inside of me to a tremble, I walked the whole of the house for about half an hour as I didn't want to see the reply if any.

Would he be mad? happy? Indifferent?

When I returned to the sun room there was an email from Jacob, I was so scared to open it.

Riley,

Are you joking with me right now? You don't answer any of my calls and then you lay this on me!

What were you thinking??? getting pregnant! I thought you were protected!!!!

A defective jab, come on, really pull the other one. You saw a rich man and thought there's a meal ticket. Fuck! Riley how could you be so stupid.

I can't believe you right now, You're getting rid of it right?

When I read the email initially I thought he must have used his quota of exclamation marks for the year... for the second time though, I just could not believe it, truly.

I replied with tears in my eyes and anger in my heart.

Do not ever contact me again Jacob, to me you are nothing now but a bad memory.

Saying that you loved me, REALLY - fake, totally fake. A meal ticket come on Jacob be realistic about it I dont need your fucking money as if you hadn't noticed I'm a wealthy woman, in fact I really don't need you for anything.

As if I could ever love someone like you, I see your true colours now. don't wish you well at all, you conceited arsehole.

Send -

Grrrr I sent the email overwhelmed with anger and wept. Tears streamed down my face, I felt like my heart had been ripped from my chest.

What the actual fuck was wrong with him, he was charming, adorable the chemistry was like a lightening bolt through my body, but now, how could he have been so hateful! It was an accident, a truly unforeseen accident that this happened.

I was done with him. This journey I would now undertake on my own.

⊷⊷⊰❮ ❯⊱⊶⊶

Chapter 32

Jacob

Feeling like a twat, I left Rileys building confused - where the fuck had she gone to?

The weekend went by in what I can only describe as a blur. How could she just disappear, I fucking told her I loved her for gods sake and then she just ghosts me!

Well it was bloody obviously how she felt about me wasn't it! Otherwise she would have told me back, wouldn't she?

Going to work Monday I looked and felt like shit. The day got worse with meeting after meeting. The only reprieve was I had plans with my friends and I was to leave work early - before 7 anyway.

I was playing pool and drinking beer, but definitely wasn't on the 'ball' and was losing.

'Jacob, dude what's up? You're not here,' Aaron said. 'I, um yeah sorry.' I didn't know what to say.

The game finished with Aaron beating me, for the first time - he was jubilant in his accomplishment.

'Whatever has you brooding I am eternally grateful,' - he said bowing with a smile on his face.

The first week of Riley being MIA, was killing me. There was no trace of her even, Mr Rogers, her boss, didn't know where she was, only that she was working from home! Home my ass, she wasn't at her apartment.

I tried to carry on with my work, but concentration was difficult especially when she was on my mind 24-7.

By Thursday I was desperate. I emailed her, just wanting some contact. I was missing her and her touch, her smell, everything.

Riley - tell me where you are? What's going on?

You're not at work, I've checked and you're not at your apartment. WTF is going on.

You seemed to have vanished off the planet.

Jacob X

I got nothing back, feeling frustrated and honestly, very pissed off. It put me in a bad mood for the remainder of the day and I found myself growling at everyone.

Not sleeping and feeling irritable wasn't a good combination. Every meeting I had on Friday ended with me blasting off at something. I was irrational I knew, and I made at least three members of staff upset to the point of tears. I felt like a wanker and made a mental note to apologise.

Anger was rising in me now, her deliberate move to not contact me was making me irrational. I was *so* angry at her. I tried taking my frustrations out at the gym instead of going out with the lads. I wanted so desperately to try and get rid of this feeling inside, I wasn't his person. Yeah, I can be aggressive with deals and stuff, but genuinely I am a nice guy or so I thought.

Saturday found me aching from the gym, but still feeling like shit. My phone pinged letting me know I had an email, it was from Riley. At last, I thought. God I had missed her.

I sat at my kitchen table with a coffee and opened the email. What I read sent my blood pressure shoot up, I read it again and the anger that had already brimmed, exploded!

Jacob, there is no easy way to tell you this news, and I am sorry for telling you over email but I cannot deal with anything remotely emotional at the moment.

I was scared at first but I believe it's your right. I am pregnant, 7 weeks. There was a problem with my birth control injection, a defect apparently according to the doctor and as we didn't use anything else, well....I am under no illusion of a relationship either. I am however prepared to go this alone, but the baby is yours.

Please don't be mad at me, these things happen. I just wanted you to know.

Riley

'What the actual fuck' was the first thought that went through my mind. Was she having a laugh? Because it wasn't funny at all. I ran my hand through my hair and before even thinking about it I emailed her back, it was like someone else took control of me and then the email was sent.

Once I sent it I reread what I had written not believing the words that were on the page, but it was too late now it was done;

Riley,

Are you joking with me right now? You don't answer any of my calls and then you lay this on me! What were you thinking??? getting pregnant! I thought you were protected!!!! A defective jab, come on, really pull the other one. You saw a rich man and thought there's a meal ticket. Fuck! Riley how could you be so stupid. I can't believe you right now, You're getting rid of it right?

I couldn't believe it, she emailed me back almost immediately and then I knew I had crossed the line and thinking of how I would make it good was gone.

Do not ever contact me again Jacob, to me you are nothing now but a bad memory.

Saying that you loved me, REALLY - fake, totally fake. A meal ticket come on Jacob be realistic about it I dont need your fucking money as if you hadn't noticed I'm a wealthy woman, in fact I really don't need you for anything.

As if I could ever love someone like you, I see your true colours now. don't wish you well at all, you conceited arsehole.

Fuck! What have I done?

I read again, what she had written, realising how difficult it must have been, the fact she was pregnant and dealing with everything else that was happening to her and what do I say…I was a dick for sure. Those words were not mine, were they, really?

Jacob Sylvester you are a prick, an absolute fucking PRICK! If you can get back from this point it would be a bloody miracle.

But I was going to get her back if it was the last thing I did.

———◄❖►———

Chapter 33

Riley

Second week in my new home, I was becoming more aware of my surroundings. Mrs Chesters was completely invaluable, I would never have settled in so quickly if she had not been around to help.

My current workspace was in the library. It was a luxurious room completewith dark mahogany wood and leather chairs, a sofa positioned in front of a fireplace and a desk set by the window, which looked out onto thegardens.

There were books of all descriptions around the room set in floor to ceiling shelving. The desk I assumed belonged to my father, it had a few photographs set on top, one of these was a picture of the three of us from when I was about fourteen at one of my sports events, one of me as a baby in my mothers arms and then there was one when I graduated, we were all smiling - it was a moment I remembered, tears fell from my eyes. I missed them terribly, but being here gave me some small comfort. My purpose now was growing inside of me and that's what I now needed to concentrate on. Our future.

The week began with grey skies and a damp atmosphere, even the sun room didn't lift my spirits, so I ate in the kitchen and then holed up in the library. I worked hard and kept in contact with my clients, keeping them happy and doing what I enjoyed kept the thoughts of Jacob if not at bay, at least manageable

Wednesday I woke to the sun shining through my window and it drew a smile on my face. After emailing Mr Rogers with a work update, I advised him I would need to take a few days off for some rest as I was feeling unwell. I decided to explore more of my estate.

The previous week while in the gardens I had heard horses so I wanted to see where they were. Dressed in shorts and Tshirt ready for the sun. I put on my trainers and set off for some breakfast before looking for the stables.

'Good morning Riley.' Mrs Chester said. 'Good morning Mrs Chester.'

'Would you like some eggs on toast today?'

'Ooh, yes please. I haven't had egg on toast for years, it used to be my favourite breakfast as a child.'

A smile broke on my face, as well as Mrs Chesters. 'Ok, would you like it in the sun room?'

'Yes please, thank you.'

Mrs Chester handed me a coffee and I went to the sun room to wait. Shortly after Mrs Chester came in with my breakfast.

I smiled as a thank you.

'Mrs Chester, can you tell me where the stables are please, I'd like to go see the horses.'

'Oh, it's out to the right down a little lane past the pool and tennis courts, you can't miss it.

'POOL. I said, my eyes wide. 'Yes, we have it all here' 'Wow, thanks - I'll check itout.

Leaving the house thirty minutes later I followed Mrs Chesters instructions. The walk to the stables was lovely, taking in the trees and lawns wrapped around the main house; it was bliss. I passed the walkway to the pool and courts, but I would explore them later. I heard the horses as I drew near, the sun on my skin was glorious.

I turned the corner and saw the stables. I could see five horses in the paddock at the end of the yard. Just then a gust of wind took me by surprise and blew my hair across my face, as I tried to tame it and pull it into a hair band, I saw a shirtless god come out from one of the stables walking a magnificent horse. It was champagne in colour, with a platinum tail and mane and practically shimmered in the sunlight.

The guy was tall with shoulder length hair loose with curls. He was tanned with a good physique, wore low hung jeans that showed off those muscles and well worn knee boots, Jesus, he was a dish! Heat rose in my cheeks, as I felt my heart beat quicken, his back was now facing me, as he walked the horse into the nearby field. His muscles reacting to his movement moved hypnotically under his skin.

I stood there watching him, enjoying the view, in a little world of my own. I hadn't noticed he'd turned and was watching me, watching him.

'Morning,' He spoke, smiling gently, bringing me back to the here and now. 'Oh, hi.' I replied, raising my hand, looking sheepish.

'Like what you see? He said amusingly.

I blushed a little before answering.'Yes, he's beautiful.' I smiled, my eyes sparkling. He cocked an eyebrow at my riposte, smiling back.

'Yes they are indeed.' he hesitated for a second before continuing. 'You do realise you are on private property.'

'Yes I know.' I smiled back, being deliberately obtuse. 'So, you shouldn't be here,' raising his eyebrows at me.

'It's ok. I'm Riley, I'er, know the owner, pleased to meet you.' I held out my hand and he took it in his.

'I see. I'm Xavier, Xavier Marshall-King. We run the Farm at the edge of the estate, I wasn't aware the owner was here.' He said quizzically, looking for further information from me. He still had my hand in his. I reluctantly pulled mine back.

In close proximity, I could see the deep blue of his eyes, creases in the corners showing he smiled a lot. The scent of the outdoors clung to him, that mixture of horse, hay with his own sweat; it was a heady combination and it drove me a little crazy

'She's been back for a couple of weeks now. So, do the horses belong to you or…?'

'They belong to the estate owner, I have been looking after them for the past couple of years though. From what I have gathered she has only recently become the owner.' He gazed up in the direction of the house. 'Know doubt we'll meet up eventually.'

'Lucky you. I mean, working outdoors, in this beautiful countryside.' I quickly said as he raised that quizzical eyebrow of his.

'Yes I love it.' He smiled again, I felt like a schoolgirl. 'Can I stroke them? I asked.

'Yeah sure, come.'

He led me to the fence and called them over. There was this black horse that tossed its head and trotted up to the fence. Xavier pulled out a pellet from his pocket and gave it to the horse. He was gorgeous and had no qualms letting me stroke him.

'He's beautiful,' I said barely a whisper.

'Yes, this lad is quite a character, his name is Thor. Most think it's after the film character, but he was actually born during a thunderstorm, hence the name.

I laughed at this, my dad always liked comics so it made sense.

'Hello Thor,' I said while stroking him. 'You fit your name beautifully.'

Xavier took me into the field to see the others. He pointed to where his own farm was, and pointed out the estate boundaries, well those that were visible. I wrapped my arms around my body and turned back to look at the stables. It was great to be around horses again, I couldn't remember the last time I had ridden.

Sensing my thoughts Xavier asked. 'So, do you ride?' 'I haven't for a long time,' I replied honestly.

'Maybe we should go for a ride sometime.' He looked me in the eyes. 'Yes, maybe.' I said, meeting his gaze and smiled widely.

I started to make my way back to the gate. 'Thanks for taking time out to show them to me.' I said as I climbed the fence, my shorts riding a little higher, as I cracked my leg over.

'Your welcome anytime, Riley,' he said. He was definitely checking me out. 'So any idea when the owner is gonna come see them?' he called, gesturing to the thoroughbreds in the field.

I couldn't help myself.

"She just did," I called, as I turned and walked back up to the house. I didn't see his face as I had already turned, but I could sense a smile.

⸺◈⸺

Chapter 34

Xavier

Wednesday was glorious, after two days being overcast it was a result to see the sun back and it was getting hotter.

As usual, I tended to the horses on the estate next to our farm Marshall-King Farms - we specialised in training and breeding only the best horses. So when I was asked to take care of the six horses on the adjoining estate, I jumped at the chance. Mr Whitmore was a great man and had only the best horses.

I remember him saying they were for breeding and that their lineage was practically bordering the equivalent of horse royalty. His mares brought in a pretty penny to the estate and I was responsible for ensuring they continued to look their best.

When I heard of the Whitmore's passing I was pretty gutted, especially with the thought of losing my job, however Mr Whitmore had stated I was to tend to them and help to breed them until such time as the new owner would take over.

My morning's work was going well. It was hot in the stables, so off came the shirt, I had forgotten my band for my hair, for a guy to have longish hair it wasn't always appreciated but I didn't care. So the hair did its own thing that morning.

Last of the mares, a champagne palomino, was waiting for me to take her out into her paddock. She was whinnying inside, impatient to get out into the field. She was a beautiful specimen, had a wonderful temperament and was a dream ride.

Safely tucked away in the field I turned to find a young woman staring at me. She was gorgeous, dark hair, dark eyes, luscious lips and long legs in the shortest shorts I've seen in this stable block, that's for sure.

She seemed in her own world when I said hello, she had a bit of a start.

She looked as though she had been caught being naughty. I could do naughty I thought, before talking to her.

'Like what you see, clearly noticing how she was checking me out.

She blushed before she replied to me. 'Yes, he's beautiful.' She had a smirk on her face; this was interesting.

She said it was ok as she knew the owner. Shit I thought better be a gentleman the owner could be watching.

I told her who I was and she told me her name was Riley - she held out her hand and I stepped forward and took it in my own.

She was closer and my body reacted to her closeness, my dick twitching just holding her hand.

An immediate image of fucking her in the stables came to mind, her tight round ass, sitting astride me, her breasts at the perfect angle to suck. I was getting lost in my own lust, with a hard on that was going to be difficult to explain, when I heard her speak.

'So, who do the horses belong to? She asked.

I explained they were the owners of the estate and I was taking care of them. She was stroking Thor's neck and he in turn nuzzled her breasts. Fucking horse was feeling her up!

She told me she rode and I offered to take her out, which she accepted. Shetook off shortly after, choosing to climb over the gate rather than go through it, one lovely, long leg lifted up over the top, closely followed by the other and over she went, her shorts riding up higher, so her ass cheek was on view, fuck! My dick got a littleharder.

'So when is the owner gonna come and see them?' I called out to her.

She paused for a moment, then as she turned she floored me with her next words.

'She just did'

Her back was now to me and I couldn't help but smile. She had got me all worked up, teasing and flirting, then tells me she's the owner.

My day was just a little bit better knowing I was going to see Miss Whitmore more often from now on.

Chapter 35

Riley

I checked out the pool and courts when I left Xavier. I god he was gorgeous I He could unbalance my equilibrium with a look; he was gorgeous AND dangerous. It was too easy to imagine my hands running through that hair of his and down his perfectly tanned, hard, muscly chest. I was horny as fuck now, I groaned aloud; it must be the hormones.

I returned to the house and changed into my bikini and took a towel from my bathroom. Slinging it over my shoulder, I walked back downstairs. Mrs Chester was in the kitchen where she normally hid this time of the day, having a cup of tea and reading the newspaper.

'Hello Mrs Chester,' I said as I walked in.

'Hello Riley dear, are you hungry? Would you like a snack?' She started to get up from her chair.

'I'm good thankyou, relax, enjoy your newspaper. I'll grab a bottle of water, I'm going to sunbathe for a while.'

'Ok, let me know if you're hungry.' 'Thank you, I'll grab some fruit.'

I left the kitchen and made my way back outside and down towards the pool where I was gonna stay pretty much all afternoon soaking up the rays and not think about Xavier's perfect torso!

The pool was heated so getting in every now and then wasn't too much of a shock to the system. You could just about hear the horses in the distance, which then started me thinking about the hot bod not far from where I was.

Going without sex for this amount of time when my sex life had been hot and horny was killing me. I sat in the shallow end resting my elbows on the side of the pool enjoying the sun on my exposed body and the coolness of the water.

I placed my towel behind me and layed down enjoying everything around me.

I must have fallen asleep, because I was unaware of Mrs Chester approaching. She had come out to check on me, bless her! I lifted my head, my eyes sleepy.

'Sorry to have woken you,' she said. 'I have brought you some snacks, we can't have you going hungry now, can we?' She smiled and then returned to the house.

I cleared the plate of food she left me, I layed down on the sun lounger, took off my bikini top and enjoyed the sun on my back.

I felt his rough hands rubbing suncream into my back. Gently rolling over my shoulders and down my spine and over my ass. He moved them seductively back up and grazed the sides of my breasts and then ran his hands down my arms. He repeated this again, his hands getting closer to cupping my breast as my body moved with his hands.

He momentarily stopped and I moaned for him not to stop. He then started on each of my legs, his hands running up one leg and then down the other. As he reached the top of my thigh he gently brushed my pussy, I raised my ass slightly, inviting him to continue in that particular area but he never took up the invitation immediately, just continued massaging my legs. His constant caress across my bikini clad bush had turned it into a hot, wet mess that sooo needed sorting out. I felt Xavier sit himself at the foot of my sunbed, he opened my legs and murmured something. Again his hands worked their way up my thighs, but this time there were no teasing touches. He slipped his fingers straight into my soaking wet pussy, two fingers pumping in and out, whilst his thumb rubbed rhythmically over my clit. I felt my ass rise as I started to feel my climax approaching. I moaned for him and next I felt his mouth sucking one of my breasts, the other being fondled, my nipple rolling between his fingers. I ran my hand through his wild locks. We locked lips and a fiery, passionate kiss, his hands moving to my ass and he held me there whilst grinding against his rock hard cock. My orgasm was seconds away, I groaned into hismouth.

'Riley,' he said gently, in my ear. It sounded like he was urging me to reach my peak.

'Riley,' he said more forcefully.

'Wh-hat…?'

I was drawn from 'what the fuck, I was dreaming of Xavier', to 'who the hell woke me from my dream!'

I lifted my head and turned to find him standing there, my wet dream. His jeans riding real low on his hips, his muscles on show -still no top I noted and he raked his hand through his fucking glorious hair.

'Hi, sorry I was asleep.' Crap! Did I make any noise while he had been standing there because I knew I was fucking wet.

'Nice dream,' he asked, smiling.

He walked closer towards me. Fuck, I thought, caught fantasising about the stable hand.

'I,um,' I put my head back down, my hair hiding my obvious embarrassment. 'So, Xavier, what can I help you with,' I asked, sexual frustration no doubt written across my face, in a great big neon sign!

'Well now,' pausing, he rubbed his hand over his chin and then through his hair, 'there are many things you can help me with Riley but I'm not sure whether you would think them appropriate.' He gave a throaty reply, his eyes dancing, inviting me to all sorts of naughtiness. God! I should just fuck him and release all this tension screaming for release inside me. But, I just stared back at him and his glistening body, before asking his real reason for being here.

Reining in my over fertile imagination. 'Ok, flirting aside, what is it you want?'

I reached behind and tied my bikini top, then sat up to face him. The look in his eyes when I sat up, made my heart beat faster.

'I wondered if you fancied a little ride out tomorrow. Just a couple of hours or so. I can show you around the estate…?' He stood there looping his thumbs into the hooks of his jeans, they moved a little lower, drawing attention and exposing the deep 'V' directing my gaze to his groin.

I couldn't help what my eyes were doing and he caught me oggling; we made eye contact, and the look in them was enough to make me want to fuck him.

'I would like that. I'm a bit out of practice, so be gentle with me.' I pulled at my lower lip with my teeth, looking at him. 'Fancy a swim?'

'Thought you'd never ask,' He kicked off his boots then slowly unbuttoned his jeans, unhurriedly he dropped them to the floor and kicked them off. He stood up, hands on his hips, standing there like the perfectly carved male specimen he was, and he knew it. Raking my eyes down his body, they lingered a little longer than necessary on the nicely filled black jockey shorts, fitted snugly around his hips, thighs and….cock. He laughed again, shook his head, and dived straight into the pool, with barely a splash.

He rose from under the water droplets of water showering over him. 'You coming?' he queried, stroking his hair back, the water holding onto his body while the sun glistened on his tanned skin.

He watched me as I stood and walked to the edge of the pool - I sat down and put my feet in the water hesitating for a moment.

Xavier swam over to me and stood in the water looking me in the eyes. 'You coming in, or do I have to pull you in?' he said with a glint in his eye.

Before I could respond he came up close and reached his hands to my waist pulling me towards him into the water. Goosebumps erupted all over me, whether it was the water or his touch I couldn't be sure, but his calloused hands on my waist stirred an ache in the pit of my stomach. My eyes had closed when he pulled me into the water, I now opened them, Zavier was so close, I could feel his breath.

The water made my nipples hard which he was well aware of as they brushed against his hard chest. We looked into each other's eyes, his hands tightened imperceptibly on my waist. His hair was slicked back, much darker than it had been this afternoon, droplets of water clinging to the ends; it framed his gorgeous face. His eyes were mesmerising, the pupils slightly dilated, a clear

indication he was turned on. The atmosphere between us was intense. I couldn't give myself to him, so in order to break our smouldering look, I did the only thing I could think of; I splashed him. The playful act had the desired effect and he released me and proceeded to splash me back.

The tension between us was only temporary though. The messing around in the water was like foreplay. He grabbed my waist and held me close to him, my back against his chest, his face close to my neck, he held me there, not moving, just holding me. I could feel his hardening cock against my ass.

The feeling inside me was about to explode, if I didn't do something. I put my hands over his and he loosened them just enough for me to turn and face him. He moved in, as did I and we kissed. Xavier's lips like my dream, were soft, plump, gentle against my lips own his hands found my waist again and my hands rested on his shoulders, his tongue delved into my mouth, searching for mine, our tongues met and ignited the fire within me and I pulled him in deeper to the kiss, my hands in his thrust through his hair, moaning into his mouth.

I was being destroyed by my own feelings and desires for this god-like man. Our bodies pressed together in the water, he reached down to my legs drawing them up and around his waist, his dick pressing into me right on my spot.

This felt soo good, he felt soo good.

We had only kissed at this point, thank the lord, because it slowly became obvious that I was the woman I said not too long ago, I wasn't. The kissing was passionate, and would take very little for our hands to start exploring each other's bodies and then...

We pulled apart and stared at each other. I spoke first, realising things should never have got as far as they had..

'Im sorry Xavier, I didn't mean to -'

'Shh, it's ok,' he placed a finger on my lips and smiled.

He kissed me hard and fast one more time, then I released my legs from his waist to stand.

'I have to go Riley,' he said and got out of the pool.

He stole my towel to dry himself off, then pulled on his jeans and boots.

He turned to me before leaving, winked and said, 'thanks for the dip in the pool, more than I bargained for!'

God, I was embarrassed, but admitted to myself, still horny!!!

FUCK MY LIFE! I'm pregnant with another man's child while getting off with someone else.

Why does shit happen to me?

Chapter 36

Xavier

She left me gobsmacked. She drove me wild. I needed her.

'I wondered if you fancied a little ride out tomorrow?' I stood looping my thumbs into the hooks of my jeans, pulling them down a little more exposing my muscle a little more. Her eyes darted to the movement.

I caught her staring which made me even more determined to have her.

'I would like that, I'm rusty so be gentle with me,' she said, sucking on her lower lip then looking at me.

'Fancy a swim?' She said coyly.

'Thought you'd never ask.' I said, then I removed my boots, then slowly, I undone my jeans, dropping them to the floor, just in my boxers to her delight. I'm sure she wanted to see more. Once I was done I dived into the pool.

'You coming?' I asked her, sweeping my hair back.

I watched as she got up her bikini fitting her like a glove exposing her beautiful body for me. She was fit as fuck. She sat down on the edge and dangled her legs into the water.

I swam over to her and stood in the water looking over to her.

'You coming in or do I have to pull you in' I said with a glint in my eye.

Before she responded I couldn't help myself and reached up to her waist pulling her towards me into the water -

She closed her eyes as I drew her near to me, when she opened them we were very close and she was now in the water, her nipples hardened by the sudden impact of the water.

We stood in the water still no movement, I wasn't sure what was going through her mind, in my mind I was fucking her in the water and she was screaming my name, the next thing I knew she splashed me with water making me release my hold on her.

The messing around in the water started to get a little more touchy and I was growing more aroused. God I wanted her so bad.

I grabbed her round the waist and held her close to me, her back pulled against my chest, my face low down to her neck.

I held her there for a while, not moving. I could feel the warmth between us. She then released my hands and turned towards me, looking me right in the face.

At that moment I moved in as did she and we kissed, her lips were soft and juicy, the passion was there. I could feel it, when our tongues touched I could feel the pull between us. She pulled me deeper into the kiss, which is what I wanted, her hands reaching into my hair and moaning in my mouth.

Our bodies pressed together in the water, desire building between us, I reached down to draw her legs up and wrapped them around my waist all the while pressing my cock into her mound.

I wanted to push it further but decided that kissing was a good first move and I wanted to take it slow with her as she was too good to push away.

We pulled apart and stared at each other. she spoke first even though I wanted to keep kissing her, not letting the moment slip away.

'I'm sorry Xavier, I didn't mean to - she started to say. 'Shh, it's ok - I placed a finger on her lips and smiled.

I kissed her again then she released her legs from my waist and stood in the water.

'I have to go Riley.' I said and got out of the pool. If I had stayed any longer I would have fucked her.

I picked up her towel to dry myself then pulled on my jeans and boots. I turned to face her before leaving, winked and said

'Thanks for the dip in the pool, more than I bargained for!'

Walking back down the lane and towards the farm, I was happy as a pig in shit. I would however have to have a wank, I was a little too turned on.

So, I thought the procurement of Riley has begun and she is a very easy target to which I will have her in my bed by the end of the weekend.

Xavier Marshall-King doesn't lose.

Chapter 37

Riley

The remainder of the afternoon into early evening seemed to go by in a blur, the heat and lust I was feeling, topping me off.

When I returned to the house around fiveish, Mrs Chester was busy in the kitchen singing away to the radio. I crept upstairs even though she wouldn't have heard me and got into the shower. The water was like stingers being whipped onto my body. clearly indication that I had had too much sun.

After applying some cream to my body, I put on my comfy trousers and a cami top and headed to the kitchen where the smells had drifted up to me.

'Something smells good.' I said, peering in through the door.

'Oh Riley dear, come in. I'm cooking a nice mexican chilli, tortillas salad and the works. 'Oh do you like mexican? I never thought to ask.

'Omg yes! It's one of my faves, I love it.' We both smiled and she carried on. 'Do you want some help, I'm not used to just watching.'

'Um ok, you can prepare the salad if you like.' So salad duty for me while everything else was prepped and cooked by Mrs Chester.

Later after stuffing my face I went to bed earlier than normal. I was feeling the effects of the sun. Sleep was always a blessing for me, but the little nugget inside of me decided that mexican wasn't for them, and I threw up during the night.

God, I hated morning sickness, afternoon sickness and evening sickness, that was my reality check right there.

Thursday morning I was still feeling rough, so I stayed in bed the whole morning. Mrs Chester came to check on me and decided that she would make soup, as my father always liked soup when he felt under the weather.

She really did take care of me and I was extremely grateful for her and her company.

The day was a combination of sleeping, feeling sick of being sick to sipping water to sleeping again. I wanted to wave a magic wand to make the sickness go away, how long does this go on for my mind was going like a thousand miles at the thought of this the entire time.

Friday morning I felt a little better, still sore from the sunburn but the sickness had for now decided to go away. Mrs Chester had left me a note saying she had gone to the market and would be back in a few hours as she was shopping too. I was so privileged to have her and all that she was doing for me.

I made some tea and went to it in the sun room where thankfully we had sun still and the room was warm. I curled up on one of the sofas and just looked out onto the gardens. I was lost in thought when I heard my phone ping. I haven't even picked my phone up for over twenty four hours which really wasn't like me.

Messages from my friends, some emails - work related. I was hoping that maybe Jacob had messaged, but nothing.

I began replying to my friends, checking messages were easier to deal with than the prying ones. After telling them I was ok and enjoying some me time away they seemed more satisfied.

I did say that soon I would like them to come to the 'retreat I was at', they didn't know about the estate yet, that would blow their mind.

I did however send them another message about an hour later telling them of the hot guy looking after the horses. Horses of which were mine but I wasn't gonna tell them that, not yet anyway.

The phone went mad:

um ok, spill.

So what's he look like then?

Jesus Riley you dont waste time do ya?

uh hum she is a free agent I'm sure or is Jacob with you?

Girls, no Jacob is not here and I haven't heard from him.

Hmmm, he is gorgeous. he has shoulder length hair, blue eyes, fucking hot body and he kisses so goddam well.

That last piece got them good and proper. I smiled when I pressed send on the group chat.

We spent the next half an hour chatting about shit and the hot guy and what they have all been up to, thankfully Jacob wasn't mentioned again as I couldn't deal with him and then telling them I'm pregnant.

I decided to go for a walk to get some fresh air, just through the gardens, as I knew the gardener was due today, so I bet he is already doing his bits around the place.

Dressed in a long skirt and white flowing shirt, I thought I needed to cover up today. I made my way through to the main garden area and walked through the trees enjoying the intermittent shade it brought.

I was lost in my own thoughts as I wandered into the maze, I never saw it before as it was nestled into the trees. The sides were high enough to not see

where you were going. I love a challenge I thought and proceeded to go in.

I was in there for about five minutes when I realsied I had taken a wrong turn and ended up at a dead in, fuck! I am usually good at these things, I muttered out loud.

Need any help?. I heard a voice approaching me. Before I saw him I knew it was Xavier.

'Hi, I guess I'm a little lost, I said, raising my hands in submission.

He looked just as delicious today as he had done on wednesday, low hung jeans, boots, this time his shirt was on but undone a little exposing his chest, his hair

was in a band away from his face, god his face, I was wet for him just by his presence.

'You ok there you seemed to faze out,' he smiled, knowing what he was doing to me.

'Yeah I'm ok, the sun, too much in one go.' I said trying to hide my eagerness to kiss him.

'So do you want to finish the maze? He asked. 'Yes I do.'

'Ok, let's go.'

I followed him through the different avenues and after about fifteen minutes we came to the centre which had a water feature, it was so beautiful.

'Wow this is just lovely, 'I said looking around at all the flowers and the features.

'It is beautiful, 'he said looking at me.

I blushed a little, embarrassed more like, god I wanted him.

He approached me and pulled me hard into an embrace holding onto my arms, I melted into the kiss. It was what I wanted, needed in fact.

He released me then pulled me into his chest and held me there, he smelt so good.

I had no words. I wrapped my arms around him and responded to his touch. He lifted my chin with his hand and gently placed a kiss on my lips. The fire within me was burning higher than before.

Before I knew what I was doing my hands were in his hair pulling it free from the band and his hands were all over my body, we kissed passionately and I was lost. I vaguely felt his hand reached down to my skirt and hitching it up, my heart beating faster at the prospect of fucking him right here right now, Xavier,

Oh my god my words escaped as his hand reached my pussy, he deepened the kiss even more as he navigated through my underwear and found my clit.

'Oh my god,' the words in my head, as his fingers found my wetness.

'I guess you like that he said parting from me briefly with a smile on his face. Before I could respond his mouth was on mine and his fingers were doing all kinds of magic to me.

One finger two fingers in and out making me feel fucking fabulous as he circled my clit driving me wild, I really wanted to fuck him right there and then. He was the master and I was his puppet, his kissing moved from my mouth to my neck and with his free hand he undone my shirt exposing my breasts which he then took into his mouth one after the other, oh this feeling was fantastic, my body craving attention and he was giving it to me.

I could feel my orgasm coming on quicker by his skillful hands and his mouth on my body.

Omg!. I'm coming.' I whispered out.

He went faster and faster and I was lost. I called out not knowing the words that left me as my orgasm took me to a different place.

I laid my head on Xavier's chest, as I got my senses back. The feeling inside was electrifying.

I was met eye to eye by a confused look,

'Not one to ruin a moment but who is Jacob, he asked Shit, what the fuck did I say out loud.

'Oh, he is someone who I recently broke up with, I'm sorry I'm really embarrassed, I think I need to go.

'Oh, um can you show me how to get out of here please, I never made eye contact with him as my face was already red im sure of it.

'Its ok Riley I understand, he seemed not overly bothered however he walked off first so I followed him.

They say silence is golden but there was clearly something in the air and I bloody well put it there, fucksake I seem to ruin everything.

As we approached the entrance Xavier turned towards me.

'So I think we might need a do over don't you?, he smiled a sexy smile at me which helped to lift my spirits a little.

'I think we can arrange that, however there's stuff you don't know about me that might put you off.

'I'll take my chances, 'he said, then turned and walked off through the gardens towards the out edges. I was assuming he was going back to the farm.

I returned to the house and chilled. I didn't want to get myself into any more trouble.

The lounge area had an impressive television and sound system so I made it worthwhile and binged on movies right into the evening. My stomach still wasn't really better so I had a light dinner, Mrs Chester was off for the night so I just made some toast and honey.

I must have fallen asleep during a film snuggled in the blanket I had wrapped around me, it was about three in the morning. I turned the tv off and headed upstairs, it was weird being in this house with so much space, no one here, alone. As I crawled into bed thoughts of my little bean and Jacob filled me as sleep took me to another place.

⊷⊷◖◗⊶⊶

Chapter 38

Jacob

It had been at least eight weeks since I had seen Riley and then there was the email that changed my life forever. I can't believe I said those words to her yet I haven't even contacted her. I was scared she would turn me away. I buried myself in my work and isolated myself from everyone, even my family to a certain extent.

My social time wasn't great either. I made up excuses to my friends that I was busy with work and stuff to go out, drink, hook up with girls, the usual stuff I enjoyed before Riley.

During those weeks we were apart, I wanted to find her and found myself at her apartment building many times. She wasn't there, obviously, she hadn't been there for weeks. I had posted some letters in her box, but I was sure she hadn't seen them otherwise she would have contacted me.

I sat there thinking on sunday afternoon looking out into the world below that she would be around 4 months maybe even pushing 5, she would obviously be showing and fuck! Would she have told anyone?

I had popped into Rowthornes a few times to speak with Rogers and happened to ask where she was on pretty much every occasion, he said she was working from her new home and hadn't really been in only met with clients if she needed to or had meetings remotely, I did ask if he knew where she was, he didnt which only fuelled my anger and frustration.

We were coming up to autumn now and the leaves were changing colour. The nights were a little fresher, which was a nice change from the heat we had experienced, during the summer months.

If Riley had kept the baby, it would be due in the new year. I wasn't sure when, but going by her dates, I was sure it was early January.

It was then I decided I needed to find her, make things right. I made enquiries into a private detective agency to find her. Operation to get Riley back was now a go.

Looking ahead to my future with Riley was going to be a tough one, but I was ready for the fight.

Chapter 39

Xavier

The maze should have been my opportunity to have her except that she called out another guy's name when she came. As much as I wanted her I felt deflated at her outburst. The fact she had called out this Jacob's name was definite proof that, whenever she had broken up with this man, it was clear she wasn't over them. I had to accept she was going to take a little longer to wear down.

I left her when we exited the maze and walked back to the farm. My duties for the day were completed until after dinner when I would put the horses away. Sitting on the front porch outside my home I couldn't help but wonder why anyone would give her up. She was incredibly beautiful, hot, sexy and her body so responsive. Just the thought of her got me aroused.

I knew then I would have to make her mine and even though she had said there were things I didn't know about her, I was certainly up for the challenge. I would give her a few days' space, before I began my fight for her affections. I already knew I could turn her on and after touching her and tasting her I had no intention of letting her go. My cock, already filling with blood, started to twitch again, as I remembered the passion she had shown in the maze. Her response lit her up like a firework, she was all passion, all woman and she was going to be mine.

I began to hatch my plan for Riley. I carried on with my duties over the next five days, purposefully keeping my distance from her. But I watched the house covertly.

It was Wednesday the following week, I decided would be the day I would have her.

The housekeeper, Mrs Chester, had said in passing to me that she would be out for the day on Wednesday with her husband doing 'the rounds', so I knew the

house would be empty for a few hours. Riley would be alone and that would be my opportunity to get her alone.

I watched as the Chester's left the grounds, and I quickly finished up with the horses and made my way to the house. The weather was again glorious, so I was a little sweaty by the time I reached it, with all the rushing around I had done that morning.

I could see that Riley was in the sun room, perfect for me I thought.

I entered the house through the french doors near the sun room. I took the time to stand and watch her for a while. She was lost in her work wearing small shorts and a cami top. The sun glistening on her already tanned body, she looked young and innocent and alluring. While standing there watching her, she got a call on her mobile.

'Hi, Riley speaking.' She was animated for the next few minutes. Although I could only hear one side of the conversation it appeared she had received good news.

'Yes. I can meet you there. Excellent. I can come whenever you like,' she was saying.

'Yes, tomorrow. Thursday, yes. Ok. I'll see you there. Eleven. Yes, that's great,' 'Brilliant see you then.'

She hung up and smiled. That was my cue to let her know I was there. 'Hi,' I said hoping I wouldn't startle her too much.

She twisted round startled, her eyes were as wide as saucers.

'H- Hi' she eventually got out. 'Um, what are you doing here?' She asked quietly.

'I thought I had left you alone long enough, I wanted to see you. I hope you don't mind me popping in - the door was open.' She looked out of the room even though she couldn't see the doors. She believed me.

'Of course, come in, can I get you something to drink?'

'I'm good. I guess the last time we saw each other it was a little awkward, so I didn't want to pressure you with questions, but I thought it was a good time to reacquaint ourselves.'

She smiled at me, I smiled back and sat on one of the sofas.

She got up from her chair and came and sat beside me. I took her hand in mine, rubbing the palm with my thumb, and pulled her gently, but firmly to face me. Her breath caught, her mouth was slightly open, just aching to be kissed and I couldn't help myself. I swooped down, covering her lips with a kiss aimed to destroy any defences she may have built up over the last few days. She never pulled away from me, in fact she leaned into me, kissing me back hard. Still thumbing her palm, my other hand reached up to the back of her head and held her close. We kissed hungrily, exploring each other's mouth, moans escaping from each of us. I was rock hard and just wanted to sink myself into her. She pulled away, breathless, her lips swollen and a juicy pink colour. Eyes full of desire.

'We shouldnt do this,' she said breathlessly.

'I know,' I tucked a tendril of hair behind her ear and she shuddered. 'But we.....*want* to, don't we?' I said back, pulling her back to continue the kiss.

She hesitated, her hand against my chest, then she stood up and held out her hand for me to join her. I stood and pulled her close to my chest, kissing her again, my tongue probing and demanding a response. Her hands went into my hair deepening the kiss and I reached down, and lifted her up, she automatically wrapped her legs around my waist. Her crotch rubbed seductively against my hard cock, making it ache even more. I groaned. Walking out of the glass room, I made my way to the hall. I released her mouth, and continued to trail hot, wet kisses down her neck.

'Where's your room?' I whispered hoarsely.

'Up the stairs, end of the corridor' she whispered back, dropping breathy kisses on my neck. Now it was my turn to shiver.

I walked through the door to a bed that dominated the room. She dropped her legs from my waist and slid her down me, so she was as fully aware of my erection as I was of her wet pussy. She stood in front of me looking adorable. She looked at me a little hesitantly, with a blush across her face.

'Xavier, there are things you need to know about me before we go any further,' Her voice was husky and melodic.

'Shhhh,' I placed a finger on her lips, 'it's ok I want this, you want this, whatever it is it's ok.' I reassured her not knowing what she was going to tell me.

She really looked at me then, I felt like she was looking into my soul. I wanted her, ached for her literally and now I was going to have her. I moved in closer to her, running my hands down her face to her neck and shoulders to her hands. I pulled her towards the bed. I sat on the bed in front of her, my hands ran down her legs then up to her shorts, not breaking eye contact I went to the waistband and undone the button, then took the zip and pulled it down, tugging the material of her shorts just a little so it tightened around her clit, she closed her eyes and a moan escaped her mouth. I cupped her ass and gave it a little squeeze, before lowering her shorts to reveal a wisp of lace. I ran my thumb along her folds, back and forth, her knickers were sopping wet. She grasped my shoulders and threw her head back, pushing into my thumb. I leant in and nuzzled her mound, she smelt so good. She opened her legs slightly giving me better access, but instead of taking her up on the invite, I flipped her onto the bed beside me.

I swiftly moved up the bed and kissed her. Deep, hard; my tongue plunging into her mouth. With my free hand I rubbed her bush, still covered by the lace. Taking her tongue gently in my teeth, I sucked at it, the rhythm matching my strokes against her clit. She started to move as if trying to reach something - I knew she was near orgasm, but I had no intention of letting her peak just yet. She wouldn't be calling out another man's name after I had finished with her.

Pulling my lips from hers. I lifted my hand from her crotch, she cried out 'Nooooo,' she didn't want me to stop. Her eyes open, she watched, as I smeltand licked each of my fingers. Her eyes darkened and pulled me down to continue kissing me. Her body lifted from the bed, encouraging me to continue playing with her pussy. My hand trailed to the bottom of her t-shirt and I pulled it over her head - no bra! Fantastic! My kisses moved to her neck and impatiently sucked on her nipple while my hand massaged her glorious tits. Fuck me, I didn;t know how much longer I could hold on for. Foregoing her hardened nipple I moved down her belly to the juncture of her thighs. Standing again, I bent over her and hooked my fingers into the lace that covered her neatly trimmed bush. Slowly I pulled it down following the path with featherlight kisses, until it reached her ankles. I pulled it off and her shorts that had been dangling from one of her feet came off too.

My gaze roamed over her glorious nakedness possessively. This is what I had wanted from the first moment I saw her.

I opened her legs, making her bend at the knees at the same time. I dipped my head between them and took a long, hard lick of her glistening flesh, like I was an ice-cream. She thrust herself up, pushing further into my face and I, I was more than happy to oblige!

'Fuck!' she called out as my tongue flicked over her clit, first hard then soft.

'You're so wet, I could happily drown in your juices.' I breathed. I looked up at her then, not breaking my tongue's attention on that swollen nub of hers and she met my gaze, her eyes were a mixture of hunger and frustration. Whilst she watched my head bobbing between her legs, I took two fingers and pushed them into her entrance, curling them as I searched for that sweet spot. She bucked and screamed out when my fingers found it. Perfect!

Riley was a quivering mass and so ready to come.

The combination of my tongue on her clit and my fingers rubbing over her sweet spot took her to her peak in seconds. She arched her back like a woman possessed by the devil himself. Her body racked with wave after wave; her climax was hard and loud; this time it was MY NAME she cried out, it drove me wild.

Withdrawing my face and hands, I hastily stripped off everything and stood before her, butt naked. Still coming down from her orgasm, she swept her eyes over me, lingering on my cock, which was aching for release. She licked her lips, and looked right at me with a 'fuck me now' look all over it.

I nudged her legs apart a little more and crawled up over her dropping kisses up her body as I went, until I reached her breast. This time I took the other nipple in my mouth and teased it with my tongue until she was writhing beneath me, but I was getting impatient, I needed to be inside her.

I placed my hands either side of her shoulders, taking my weight and stared into her beautiful eyes. She looked up at me and we stared into each other. A funny feeling came over me that this was the first and last time we were ever going to be together like this.

It felt like we were staring at each other for like forever, I leant down to kiss her. She raised her hands and linked them around my neck drawing me down onto her. Our bodies pressed together, it felt so right. I moved myself until I was safely nestled inbetween her legs my cock resting into her sexy, fucking pussy.

The kissing heated up and I hardened even more, her body responding to my touch. I pulled her hands up over her head and held them there with one hand while the other went to her pussy and I played with her already sensitive clit. She was so wet I lost control and grabbed my cock and placed it at her entrance then I looked at her as I pushed my way in.

Holy fucking shit!, she called out as I pushed deeper into her feeling the stretch as I went, she felt like it was her first time, so tight and so fucking delicious, my thought was then is she a virgin?.

I moaned as I withdrew and pushed into her again, her body rising for each thrust, her moans growing louder.

Oh, yes, '' she said. Saying yes with an elongated moan.

'Yes. Riley.' I thrust deep into her. 'Say my name,' I demanded. 'Xavier please, yes, harder' she begged.

Fuck, she was a witch for sure, she had cast her spell and I was bound to her. I released her hands, lifted one of her legs up over my shoulder and pushed harder and deeper into her.

'Holy fuck!' She wailed out loud. Her sweet spot getting plenty of attention now and she was obviously loving it.

Shit! She was gonna be the end of me for sure.

I stilled for a moment, as I didn't want to come too quickly yet and I was so close. I looked her in the eyes then leant down to kiss her.

'Riley you are so fucking gorgeous, why would anyone ever want to leave you? I couldn't help myself. She was laying there, eyes full of lust and hunger - for me.

She looked a little stunned at my comment and came out from her sexual haze.

'Oh, Xavier not now, just fuck me please!' She dragged my lips to hers and raised her hips, grinding into my cock.

I released my lips and I pulled out of her. Flipping her over, I drew her hips up to meet mine, she flicked her hair to one side and smiled at me. She went down on her elbows, in one thrust I entered her causing her to arch her back and moan out loud.

'Fuck yes!' I said as I pushed harder into her again and again. My hands on her hips as I pumped into her faster and faster. I could feel her orgasm come as her insides clenched around my cock.

'Fuck I'm coming,' she she screamed again and practically convulsed as it took over her, I pushed again and again until I came too.

'Fuck Riley! Yes! oh fuck yes!' I had the best orgasm filling her so deep with my seed. I stilled for a moment, holding on to her hips, as I came back to earth.

Riley had her head down, her face down in the bed covers and I could hear her panting.

I slowly pulled out of her and watched as my cum trickled out from her. I walked to her ensuite and returned with a washcloth and cleaned her, she jolted as I touched her and faced me all confused by the look of her.

'I'm just cleaning you,' I said.

She smiled and then when I was done she laid on the bed ass in the air. I laid beside her and stroked her back. She turned to face me with her hair over her face, so I gently took small strands of hair and tucked it behind her ear.

She closed her eyes, she was flushed and looked fucked, it was a good look.

I kissed her shoulder and then moved to my side so our faces were close.

We lay like that for a little while, no sound made by either of us. I smiled at her and she smiled back.

'So,' I broke the silence first. 'So.' she replied.

'I guess we got reacquainted then,' I smirked. She hid her face in the bed and I laughed at her. 'Don't laugh at me Xavier,' she said.

Oh, babe I'm not - You were amazing, are amazing. She curled her body towards me and gave a little laugh. I liked the sound of her laugh; it was musical, husky and deliciously sexy.

I reached round her waist and pulled her in close to me, our faces so close I could feel her breath as it left her mouth.

She closed her eyes as my lips touched hers ever so gently. I laced gentle kisses across her jaw, back to her mouth.

She momentarily pulled away from me, staring at me with a look on her face I had not seen before, but it worried me.

'You didn't wear a condom?' she asked

To be honest this had been the furthest thing from my mind at the time. 'Um no I just thought you were kinda like on the pill or something,' I could have told her I got too carried away, but that was no excuse. I dragged my hand through my hair and sat up.

'I'm truly sorry Riley,' I said. 'But…'

'It's ok I'm the one who should apologise,' she interrupted. She got up and started to dress. I followed her lead, putting my boxers and jeans on, then I sat at the end of the bed.

'Why are you apologising?' I asked, not understanding her.

'It's just, I tried to tell you about me before,' she gestured to the bed. 'But you kept stopping me,' She fidgeted then walked over to the window.

'Riley, what is it, tell me.' I walked over to her and gently placed my hands on her shoulders, and tried to turn and face me. She resisted.

'I um, the thing is I um, shit' she said. 'Riley, come on.' I was irritated a little.

'There's no easy way to say this Xavier. Fuck this has just made things harder now we have slept together,' she took a deep breathe.' I am pregnant.'

She turned towards me when she spoke the last words, she was pregnant! 'What? I'm confused, you don't look it.' I said. Fuck she didn't, she was so hot.

'I'm about ten weeks now so I won't show for a while.' Again she hesitated. 'This shouldn't have happened, I feel so bad right now, you're a great guy and I really like you, but you don't need this shit in your life.'

She had tears in her eyes as she wrapped her arms protectively around herself. Instinct took over and drew her into my arms and held her tight.

'It's ok, at least I now know I WON'T get you pregnant,' I chuckled nervously and she relaxed a little, even putting her arms around me.

We stood holding each other for a while looking out of the window, I kissed her head and stroked her cheek, hoping it helped. I wanted to comfort her. I tried not to think about the fact she was having another man's baby. It must have been that guy she called out that time before in the maze.

Well, she was mine now and I wasn't going to let her go. I had no idea what the other guy had done, but he wasn't here and I was! On the bright side at least she couldn't get more pregnant AND I'm the one who gets to explore and make love to this beautiful woman. This was going to be ok. I could do this. Or could I?

Chapter 40

Riley

As I woke Thursday morning the full impact of what Xavier and I had done hit me. Trust me to make my life just a little more complicated by starting an affair with Xavier, but god he was just perfect! He made me feel like is was the most desirable woman in the world, sex with him was fantastic and he was such an unselfish lover, everything about him was wonderful, even when I told him about the baby. Oh damn! The baby! The guilt kicked in, what was I thinking, the last thing I should be doing is getting involved with someone else. My baby was the priority not my fucking clitoris!

I messaged my friends and asked them to the house for the weekend. We had things to talk about, I had said in the invite and *I* needed to come clean with them. I hadn't seen them for about 3 weeks and it just wasn't the same without them. Of course, they all said yes and would be here Friday evening. I would have to tell them then, as they would expect drinks, drinks and more drinks.

I missed them so much but when I looked back over the last few weeks, I was honest with myself and knew it needed to be done. I needed to come to terms with my pregnancy on my own. This weekend was going to change us all, hopefully the girls would be on board with the decisions I had made.

Sitting in the sunroom drinking my first coffee of the day, I opened up my laptop and logged into work.

I spent roughly an hour responding to the most important ones, before I trawled through the rest.

I found a message from the superintendent of my apartment building, he said that I had a lot of letters in the post box and that I should come and sort them out. It was a hassle going back to the city just for post, however I knew I should do it.

'Ok, I can do this,' I said out loud and then sent a message to Mr Rogers and told him I would be back in the city today and that I would check in with him.

My mind kept slipping back to yesterday and what I let myself get into with Xavier. My eyes closed and I immediately thought of his touch, the way he kissed me, the way he held me and when I told him about the baby. I thought he would run if I'm honest, but he didn't. He was surprised but not scared, didn't ask what I intended to do, just let me know he was there for me. He was perfect but was he too perfect I wondered.

Pushing Xavier's image to one side, I gave myself a mental shake. I didn't know what I was going to do with my life now the future picture had changed but for now I was going to get my arse in gear and head to the city and hopefully not see Jacob at Rowthornes.

I arrived at my apartment nearly an hour later and pulled out the post and went up to check on things.

It had been a little over three weeks since I'd been here, but everything was more or less the same. The post was mostly junk and some letters from my doctor, which I stuffed in my bag. I'll deal with them later, I thought. Then I saw there were letters from Jacob, I wanted to rip them up instantly, but my conscience got the better of me and I just put them to one side but not opening them. I would look at them another time, I'm not ready for what it might contain, the excuses, the apologies, that's if there were any.

I grabbed some lunch from the cafe near work, then made my way up to see Mr Rogers. He had the biggest smile on his face when he saw me waiting for him outside his office.

"Riley, how are you? I'm so happy to see you.' He was genuinely happy, which made me smile too.

'I'm ok, doing better,' I said, making a note not to rub my tummy. We went into his office and he closed the door.

'So, how are you really?' he said when he sat back down at his desk. I sat opposite him in one of the chairs and sighed.

'I guess in truth, I'm a little lost right now. Things are way beyond what I was expecting, and well there's lots of other things going on besides,' at this point my hand rested on my non-existent bump. 'Things are strange,' I smiled ruefully and tried to laugh it off, but he knew me too well.

'It will get better, you know.' 'I'm hoping so.'

We chatted for a while and I updated him on my clients and what their status was regarding the projects. All was well I told him, and they all felt well informed.

Rogers nodded approval, asked a few questions which I was able to provide responses to and he ended that conversation stating he was more than happy for me to continue working remotely for the time being. Then he happened to say that Jacob had been in and asked after me. My attention sparked at the aside, maybe he was sorry, I thought.

His phone rang and he looked at me apologetically whilst he answered the call. 'Sorry Riley, just one minute.'

'Yes, what is it, oh I see.' He paused and looked at me with a worried look on his face.

'Ok then, I'll come to the meeting room, take him there, I'll be there shortly. Yes, thank you.'

He put the phone down and looked at me. 'Jacob is here in the building to see me.'

'Shit!' the words just came out before I had a chance to censor my language. 'I'm sorry Riley I didn't know, can you stay? I won't be long.'

'I um ok, please don't let him know I'm here though, will you.' I pleaded. 'I'm not ready.'

'Of course, don't worry.' Mr Rogers patted my shoulder in a paternal way, then he left to see Jacob.

I was shaking at the thought that he was so close, but I couldn't face him not yet. It was still too raw. I subconsciously placed my hand to my stomach protectively. How strange that I was changing so drastically in such a short space of time.

Mt Rogers wasn't gone long. He entered his room looking a little shaken but smiled when I looked up at him.

'All good, you can relax.'

'Thank you, I'm sorry to be a burden on you.'

'It's ok,' he said assuringly. 'We do have to discuss your stake in the company at some point. Paperwork needs looking at, meetings arranged etc. but for now it can wait.'

'Yes, I knew I would have to face the companies, but was hoping it could be delayed a little longer.'

'Ok let's give it another month and we can then meet and go through how your involvement with us will look going forward. How does that sound?'

'Sounds good to me." 'Excellent.'

'I guess I'm going to go. I have some other things to do before I head back, and I've arranged to see a client while I'm here to finalise some details. I'll see you soon and thank you again.'

I waved as I left him and took the elevator down. Once exiting the building, I relaxed a little more. I needed some caffeine, I thought and walked to my favourite cafe that wasn't far from work.

As I approached the street where it was located, I caught sight of a familiar figure, fuck! it was Jacob, he was leaving the coffee shop by the look of it.

I ducked into a shop doorway and watched him get into his car and drive off. My heart sank a little as he drove off without seeing me.

'Fuck that was close!' I said out loud. My heart was racing just at the sight of him. I got my coffee and met my client before heading back to the countryside and my safe haven.

I informed Mrs Chester later that day that my friends were coming to stay for the weekend.

'Ok dear. I'll get one of the housekeepers to set up three rooms, right?' she asked. 'Yes please, thank you.'

Off she went, busying herself and I returned to the sunroom and went back to work.

I didn't see Xavier at all Thursday and wondered if he had decided I was too much trouble to bother with, now he had had time to think things through.

It was ok. I thought I could handle this type of rejection.

When Mrs Chester had retired for the evening, I decided a nice hot soak in the bath was what I needed. I had my music on and was enjoying the time when I heard my bedroom door open, then close. I called out to Mrs Chester but there was no answer. A little scared now, I started to get out of the bath when the bathroom door opened and there stood Xavier.

'What the actual fuck are you doing?' I said, in a higher pitch than I would normally use.

Looking a little taken aback by my screeching, he said. 'I wanted to see you; the doors were unlocked. You need to be careful of strangers, you know.' He said with a smirk on his face, as he walked towards me.

My heart was racing as I slipped back in the tub.

'You really should have seen me earlier; it's late you know.' I sounded petulant even to my own ears.

'Yes, that's why I came.' Unabashed, his eyes roamed possessively over my body.

I rolled my eyes, trying to keep the blush from my cheeks and my voice even. 'You are unreal boy!'

He laughed out loud at that. 'Oh I'm not a boy Riley and you know that or shall I show you again?'

His words made me tremble as again my internal movie reel started playing back the images of our love making. I shivered deliciously.

'I -' I started to say something then blushed. He started to undress removing his t-shirt first then his belt. I was mesmerised, he was doing a silent striptease for me, and I couldn't have dragged my eyes away if my life depended on it.

He slowly pulled the zipper down, then removed his jeans all the while watching me, watching him. I licked my lips at his sight penis pushing urgently againsthis jockeys and my pussy was throbbing without being touched.

'Liking what you see then?' He asked.

My eyes caught his and I smiled. He stood for a moment and played with his cock before removing his underwear and letting his cock free.

My eyes were as big as golf balls when he took two steps towards me and stepped into the tub. The water rose as he sat down in front of me cupping his hands in the water and covering himself.

'You have got a cheek,' I said, smiling at him. Trying not to let him see how much he affected her.

'Well, I have two that your hands will be grabbing later,' he replied smiling. 'You are so sure of yourself, Zavi,' I said teasingly.

'Maybe, but maybe it's just that when I see something, I want to reach for it.'

He moved in the water and came up in front of me, opening my legs so he could rest in between them. His hands either side of my body, face so close to mine.

He smiled, his eyes shining down at me like blue sapphires, he was fucking delectable in every way. He moved slowly and began to kiss the side of my neck; I closed my eyes and felt every kiss that he planted. His lips were soft against my skin, his warm breath drew goosebumps over me, and my nipples hardened, aching to be sucked. He continued dropping kisses across my jawline to the other side of my neck.

I moaned as desire coursed through me. My lips sought his but I had to satisfy myself by nibbling, and kissing his neck.

He pulled me towards him and sat in the bath with me on top, legs either side of him, his cock resting at my pussy. I was thankful for the size of the bath at this point.

He ran his hands up my sides and across my breasts squeezing them gently.

'Mmm you're so gorgeous,' he whispered, and then his lips found mine. My hands were in his hair, as our tongues entwined heavy, deep, demanding and I was so very lost.

I could feel his hard length twitching against my opening and I just wanted to feel him inside of me. He must have had the same thought as his hand reached into the water and moved me, so I was just above it before he pulled me down onto him, he went in in one thrust. I threw my head back at the feeling of it stretching me, filling me with so much pleasure. I clenched my pussy around him and deepened our kiss further. Xavier groaned. He liked that!

His hands mapped my body, massaging it, stroking it, I leant back slightly pushing my breasts up towards him and he answered my silent invite, taking first one then the other nipple into his hot, sweet mouth. Pulling him hard against me and anchoring his mouth on my nipple, I began to move up and down on his shaft.

'Fuck that's good' I purred.

'Yes baby,' he said hoarsely again, thrusting into me. He grabbed my arse with both hands and squeezed pulling me into him.

'Ahhh,' I cried out, as he went deeper with each pull.

I looked at him and he looked at me and he slowed the pace down, the desire I felt inside was a hair's breadth from erupting. Frustration gnawed at me; my jaw set - why the hell had he stopped!

Xavier gently extricated our bodies from their position. 'Come let's get out of here,' he held me against his wet, naked body. He sucked on my ear lobe and whispered. 'I'm gonna lick you til you scream.' Then he swept me up into his arms and strode towards the bed.

He dumped me unceremoniously on the bed, I moved back to give him room to join me and he crept towards me like some magnificent panther stalking his prey, but oh god, I wanted to be caught!

On all fours, he bent and gave my clit and exploratory lick and nuzzle with his nose. He let out a small groan, then sank his tongue into my pussy, licking and probing as he urged my body back to the peak of climax. Then as I came, he lifted my body; kneeling he impaled me on his cock and started to thrust into me. The position rubbed against my sweet spot and before my orgasm was over I could feel the waves rising again as I headed for another. This was too addictive, he was too addictive. I could not get enough of him nor the feeling he could draw from my body. As another climax shuddered through me I screamed Xavier's name, my back arched and in seconds I felt him tense and convulse and he spilled into me. I slumped over his shoulder, my chest heaving in tune with his.

I was dazed as my post orgasmic feeling lingered. He lowered me onto the bed and followed me, placing his body over mine, his arms keeping his weight from crushing me. He kissed my breasts and worked up to my face. Finally he planted his lips on mine, sucking gently at my bottom lip as he lifted his head to look at me.

'You are going to send me to an early grave, Miss Whitmore,' he said as his mouth went to my neck, kissing me and biting my flesh.

I reached my hand up and placed it on his head, threading his hair through my fingers as his kisses grew into biting.

I pulled my legs out from under him and wrapped them up around his thighs and managed to push him up and over so I was now on top. He liked that; his smile stretched across his face.

I stroked his chest as my breasts were captured between my arms

'You have beautiful breasts, Riley'. He reached up and cupped both in his hands.

My eyes closed with his touch and I melted into the feeling. I needed to be bold and embrace the new me that I was becoming.

I removed his hands and then lowered myself down his legs and rested in between them.

He lifted himself up onto his elbows, his hair falling a little over his face, his eyes so blue. His normal stubble look was a little more prominent and I felt it when he went down on me. From this angle I seemed to have complete control and he knew it. I grazed the side of his penis with my hand teasing him a

little, he gasped at my touch and closed his eyes. When he opened them I lowered my mouth onto his tip and licked the end. Fuck! he said as I slowly licked it more then I took him slowly into my mouth, watching him, watching me.

His eyes were wide and he throbbed in my hand which was stroking him at the base of his shaft. My mouth lifted and went down on him again, my tongue flicking over the rib of his head, as my lips pulled up, then down again, eliciting a deep groan from Xavier.

I rubbed him hard with my hands as my mouth was working him from the top, he moaned out loud each time I went deeper.

'Jesus Riley, fuck thats so good.' He said, and I made eye contact with him.

I was enjoying being in control and tasting him like he had tasted me. My thoughts were running wild at flashbacks with Jacob and the first time he said he

wanted to taste me. My memories of Jacob were getting confused with Xavier. My emotions were all over the place, I began sucking harder as my thoughts raced between Jacob and Xavier. I even moaned out at one point as I was so turned on by it, god who was I?

I was in my own world when Xavier stopped me, his eyes hooded and so fucking sexy.

'Come here,' he growled.

I did what he asked and moved up to him, he quickly turned me so I was on the bed and he was on top and then he fucked me, nothing gentle about this fuck. It was carnal, brutal, gone was anything soft. There were no words, we were lost in our own emotions the harder he went the more I moaned out the more he moaned the more turned on I got. He was branding me and I welcomed it! I grabbed his arse cheeks like he said I would and with each thrust, I grabbed at him, digging in my fingers. He circled my clit with his finger as he fucked me. I came so quickly my body wrenched up, it felt like electricity was coursing through it, opening every nerve ending, allowing me to feel every single emotion shooting through. My pussy clenched hard on him as he pushed one last time before climaxing himself. He collapsed as spent as I was. Equally moved, equally sated.

For the first time I cried. They trickled down the side of my face, my emotions were sitting so close to the surface I was unable to contain them. I felt so utterly vulnerable, my hand went to my belly, not protectively but by way of acknowledging where I believed all this emotion came from. Pregnancy indeed, messed with your hormones!

Xavier looked at me and gently kissed my tears then he kissed me still inside of me holding on like his life depended on it.

'Ah love, there's no need to cry. You are a truly special woman, do you know that. So generous, so passionate,' kissing me again, he wrapped his arms around my body pulling me close to him.

I was gone. If this was a dream then I never wanted to wake up.

The last thing I remembered before sleep took me was Xavier withdrawing from me and had pulled me into a spoon position nuzzling into my neck and kissing me gently.

I vaguely remember making a sound like a purring cat, before my eyes closed, feeling fabulous and well and truly fucked.

Chapter 41

Xavier

The sun rose early this time of year and it was glorious, its warmth embracing me as I woke. It took me only a few seconds to realise I wasn't at home, the warmth of her should have been enough, but I kinda second guessed myself.

She was laying on her front head to the side facing my direction. She looked so peaceful and I was happy I was here. However, I was a little unsure how Riley would feel waking up to me and realising I had stayed the night. I wasn't so sure we were in a...well it was quite an emotional time last night and I fucking loved it, but I didn't want her looking at me this morning with any regret, so I dressed quickly using the horses as an excuse in the note I left her. I signed it with an 'X' - she could take that as a kiss or just my name. The last thing I left her was my number.

Although I didn't really want to go, I had sprung myself on her last night. I slid out of her room and made my way downstairs only to come face to face with Mrs Chester.

Shit I thought, she looked at me, smiled and then went about her business. Ok then, no trouble from the Housekeeper I thought as I left the house through the back door and went to tend to the horses.

I was happier than I had ever remembered today. My lusty appetite had been well and truly satisfied AND I had woken next to a beautiful woman. I wasn't 100% sure, but things seemed great and I intended to keep it that way too.

Once back at the farm house I tucked into the breakfast my mother had made for me.

'Where were you last night Zavi?' She said she always called me Zavi when she was questioning me.

'I stayed with a friend,' I said. Hoping she wouldn't pry too much. 'A friend eh?' She said.

'Yes a friend, stop questioning me mum, I'm a grown man.' I growled at her. She never could stop poking her nose in.

She threw the towel at me and smiled.

'I heard you were with Miss Whitmore Zavi, is she your new *friend?* 'She raised her eyebrows and chuckled. She was standing at the stove, her second home; her first being the island where she prepared the food she cooked on the stove...

I was a little embarrassed, maybe I didn't get away with it then. Mrs Chester must have told her. Bloody women and their gossiping tongues!

'Don't play with fire and or you'll get burnt Zavi. Remember that. She's a wealthy young woman, I'll give her that, but with that comes the background, namely old lady Whitmore.'

'I understand Mum, but she isn't like that at all.' I tried to reassure her.

We had always worked hard as a family and my fathers hard work paid off big time. We weren't in the same league as the Whitmores, but neither were we piss poor. Dad had made his money breeding our horses, and we had bloodlines that people paid good money for. But despite all that we were a grounded family.

Normal. Whatever normal was these days.

After showering, I wrapped a towel around my waist and threw myself onto my bed. Grabbing my phone I checked to see if Riley had messaged.

She did, I smiled as I opened it.

Good morning, I was a little disappointed you didnt wake me or stay, I wanted to speak to you.

I know I was a little rude last night when you turned up. I'm sorry for that but seriously I had the best night so thankyou.

I have my girlfriends here for the weekend but I would like to see you again in the week if you're free.

Riley x

Shit, I should have stayed! I scraped my hair back and put it in a tie before answering her message.

Hi, I wasn't sure about staying as I kinda interrupted your bath time.

I'm free all week. Why don't you come to the stables? I can show the ropes if you like.

Xavier x

I smiled ruefully. God, I wished I had stayed now, I could have made love to her all morning.

Fuck! Love, now there's a word I don't use very often. Surely this wasn't really love was it?

The afternoon went quickly and I was ready to set the horses down for the evening, when I heard a car pull up to the big house as I was walking through the field.

I couldn't really see but I could hear it, music blaring out loud enough to wake the dead. Must be her friends arriving.

I wondered if she would tell them about me or not. I would like to think she would but I'm happy to be her secret if that's what she wants.

I finished up at around seven and my phone went, my mates were asking me out on the town. We had a place outside of the city where we all went, the music was always great and the beer cheap. I could do with a night out, so I agreed. I texted Riley and told her about the bar if she wanted to hang out with her friends there she would really like it.

The Whistler was a great place and I knew she would like it.

After another shower I changed into a white shirt, jeans and boots, I left my hair down and trimmed up my beard, sprayed some cologne and I was out the door. Ben picked me up on the way as he caught a lift with his sister Michelle.

'Thanks guys,' I said as I jumped in the car. 'Been too long Zav,'Ben said.

'Yeah I know, don't go on, I've been busy.' I said, rolling my eyes at him.

We arrived in no time and it was already alive with a crowd. The music was pumping bodies on the floor, drinks flowing. We found a place to sit and parked ourselves. Deep down inside I was hoping that Riley would come, fuck I really wanted her to come.

The rest of the gang turned up a short while later and we were on the beers and they were going down nicely.

It was around ten when I was checking out the entrance I was a kinda drunk by then and almost didn't see her, fuck she came, I smiled.

Four gorgeous women entered the place. But I only saw one. Riley was dressed in a black dress that clung to her in all the right places, her friends too were dressed up and caught almost every eye, as they made their way through the crowd to the bar.

'Jesus fucking christ!' Markus said, pointing to them. ' Heaven just walked through the doors!' He grabbed at his chest theatrically.

'What a delightful sight' Reign said laughing. 'The girls Markus, not your excuse for a heart attack.'

I studiously looked at my beer. 'Come on Zav, you must have seen them?' Jasper said, prodding me.

'Yes I did and I have my eyes on one only.' I looked over to where Riley was ordering drinks with her pals.

They all looked at me with their brows raised.

'Now brother don't be keeping stuff from us, which one, I like the brunette with an ass I could eat.' Luke said.

'I'm kinda seeing her already so she is taken, the other brunette, her friend. She is all yours. knock em dead lads.'

With that I left them there and made my way to the delightful quartet by the bar. As I got closer I made eye contact with Riley. She looked shocked, but smiled at me.

God, she had a smile that made my stomach somersault. I was falling for her, or was it the drink.

'Ladies,' I said. 'Welcome to the Whistler, you must be new to this place.' Riley laughed at me and her friends looked a little puzzled at her.

'Girls, this is Xavier, please that was so cheesy. Are you drunk?' She said, eyes sparkling.

The girls looked at me like they were checking me out and raised their eyes at Riley, she blushed.

My mates had arrived behind me and the girls were all smiles and then they all got talking which gave me time to speak to Riley.

'I'm glad you came,' I said with a little slur.

'Well Mr Marshall-King I do believe you are drunk. Bad things happen to people when they are drunk,' she said seductively.

'Really,' I said eagerly. 'Are you making a promise?' She giggled delightfully which caused her girlfriends to turn toward us, simultaneously.

'Well you did leave me this morning, so you really do owe me.' She said, pulling on her bottom lip with her teeth.

Fuck! I said out loud and kissed her hard. I didn't care who saw me, I wanted her. She turned me on so badly just by being here. I left her breathless, as I pulled away my head a little fuzzy. I held onto her waist and stared at her.

'I need you.' I said.

'I want you.' she said back.

Fuck, and she was sober I knew this for sure. I had to think fast, I knew this place had a barn for their summer events.

'Come with me,' I said, taking her hand. 'Girls... I'll be back,' she yelled.

'They will be fine,' I said, as we left them all.

The fresh air hit me and I felt the effects of the beer and shots we had done.

We walked out back and the barn was open. I took her in and pushed her against the barn wall and kissed her hard, forcing my tongue into her mouth, she never resisted once, in fact her hands were in my hair pulling me in tighter.

She looked so sexy. I pulled up her dress, she was wearing a lace thong, I leant down and kissed her over her underwear before I removed it exposing her to me.

I took her to my mouth first, my tongue, darting out to stimulate that tiny little pleasure zone that made her come part in my arms. And my god did she!

In seconds, or so it seemed, she had reached the peak of her orgasm, arching her back and pulling at my hair. She was wet, willing and waiting for me. I twisted her around. Kicked her legs out a little and entered her from behind in one hard, frantic moment. She steadied herself against the barn wall as I penetrated her, my hands on her hips were tight and with each powerful thrust I was lifting her from her feet. Any other time I would have taken it easier but this fuck was raw and elemental, there was no time for fondling or caressing. I wanted to shoot my cum right into her, claim her, make her mine for always! She moaned out loud, as she started to edge to another climax.

'Fuck! Omg' she cried out. She spasmed as her body was swept up with another orgasm. Her knees started shaking and then gave way, but I took her weight and thrust into her one last time. I pulled her close to me, my cock still embedded inside her, my arms now round her breasts and tummy, she didn't move. I was gripped by some emotion I couldn't name, but I knew I wanted to stay here, with her, in this position, sunk inside her, the smell of our bodies and sex hanging in the air. But of course that wasn't going to happen...

'Xavier, we need to get back, my friends... ' she tailed off. She was right, but my brain fog was taking a moment to clear.

I pulled out of her and she gasped, I loved it when she did that.

She pulled up her underwear, as I tucked myself away and we left the barn and returned to her friends.

I kissed her hand as we walked back in, her friends were still at the bar with my mates all laughing and drinking.

All eyes were on us when we approached them. 'All good bro?' Jasper said, punching my arm.

'Shut it will ya', I replied thankfully no one really took much notice.

Things came to an end a little while later and we left the girls there. She waved at me as we left and carried on with her friends. The last thing I wanted to do was leave her there in case other vultures started circling, but the alcohol had other intentions.

As I went to bed with the world spinning around me all I could think of was Riley. Then the spinning stopped, and suddenly everything went dark.

Chapter 42

Riley

I woke to the sun in my room, and turned to find that Xavier had left, I was alone. Kinda felt a little used after last night's events, but quickly pushed that aside. I needed to stop these thoughts, they were not good for little bean.

Trouble was, Xavier filled me with such powerful emotions. He was everything I needed at this very moment in my life, he answered a longing I had deep in my soul, one I had hoped Jacob would fill, but he had put paid to that with his email! But Xavier hadn't turned away, had accepted my pregnancy, and the fact it was another man's child I carried. He had filled the void left by Jacob, and if I felt guilt in the very deepest part of me I just buried it deeper, Xavier made me feel…adored, safe and so many other things that were hard to identify. I shook my head, trying to remove the marshmallow feeling that filled my mind so often these days - it was too much thought for such a perfect morning. Looking at the note again I entered his number in my phone and messaged him straight away.

Good morning, I was a little disappointed you didn't wake me or stay, I wanted to speak to you.

I know I was a little rude last night when you turned up. I'm sorry for that but seriously I had the best night of my life so thankyou.

I have my girlfriends here for the weekend but I would like to see you again in the week if you're free.

Riley x

I smiled at the memory of last night, feeling incredibly horny and again pushed away the guilt gripped me because of Jacob and the baby. Xavier messaged me straight back.

Hi, I wasn't sure about staying as I kinda interrupted your bath time.

I would like to see you, yes. I'm free all week. Why don't you come to the stables? I can show the ropes if you like.

Xavier x

He was sweet and sexy and god I loved what he did to me; what we did to each other, but today my friends were coming, and I had to get organised. What to tell them, how to tell them. How they would react to it all was the biggest worry at this moment.

Later that evening I heard the car pull up music blaring from it and instantly knew my girls were here.

I stood at the doorway and greeted them, the looks on their faces told me they were beyond words right now.

'Oh my god, is this place yours Riley?' Robin said first. Eyes agog at my new home.

'Yes it is girls so welcome to the retreat,' I waved my arms to my surroundings with a big smile on my face.

'Oh my god!' Emma and Hannah said in unison.

Mrs Chester's husband was on hand to help with their luggage, good job too as they looked like they had packed for a fortnight, rather than a long weekend. I smiled at them as they looked around in awe at the hallway, my girls were here and I couldn't be happier. It would all work out, I could feel it in my bones.

I led them out to the sunroom. Mrs Chester had put on a buffet style dinner for us and some chicken which I plated up while they got comfy. It was still early and the gardens were awash with colour as the sun dropped lower in the sky. It was peaceful and serene and I needed to take the initiative.

'So, girls, there are some developments in my life that I need to update you of before our weekend starts.'

I was shifting my eyesight to all three of them.

'So I guess you have gathered things have not worked out with Jacob and I'm sorry I bolted rather than telling you at the time but truly I was dealing with so much I wouldn't have known where to start. But being here and having time to sort through everything I am so much more together, anyway so here goes.I'm pregnant…'

The girls all gasped. Whatever they were expecting it definitely wasn't that I was! 'Now before you say anything, I did tell Jacob and he well, didn't take it very well and asked whether I was going to get rid of it.' My voice cracked at the last few words, but I recovered quickly. 'I have no intention of having an, an abortion.' I clarified quickly. 'I've no problem being a single mum as I'm lucky enough that this little one is going to have three of the greatest aunties alive.' I patted my tummy as I looked at the girls.

They jumped on me then with hugs and cries and congratulations.

'We are here for you Riley don't you worry about that hun,' Robin said as the other two nodded. I looked at them, how blessed was I to have these awesome women in my life!

'Thanks girls, I really am grateful to each of you.' Group hugs sealed my gratitude.

Dinner was a mixture of questions and screams of delight, to worry a few tears by me of course and then lots more hugging.

We all held hands before Hannah then broke the serene moment with a clanger. 'So who's this hot guy from the stables then Ry, have you um made contact?' she said, wiggling her brows and giving us all that cheeky smile she was always doing when things got a little sexy.

'Yeeees, you could say that' I said blushing and trying to hide it.

More screams erupted and hugs and laughter. God I loved laughter. I then had to give them an account of mine and Zaviers trysts - abridged of course…

Once dinner was over I showed the girls around the house and to the rooms in which they were staying. They loved it.

'So what do you want to do tonight?' Hannah said.

'I'm game for anything really apart from alcohol,' I laughed, placing a hand on my tummy where the little bean was growing.

My phone pinged just as Robin was about to speak.

It was a message from Xavier telling me about this place called the Whistler. I placed the phone down and faced my friends.

'So I have it on good authority there's a place you guys would love, not far from here, you wanna go out, out?' I said.

The reply was in unison and very loud, 'YES'.

We got ready and went to town with dresses, hair and makeup, the full on works it was great to dress up and feel a little more like my old self.

The girls were on the fizz and me on the water. It was fun watching them get that buzz before we decided to set off for the place Xavier had told me about.

We arrived shortly after ten, the atmosphere in the place was buzzing, it was fantastic the girls loved it.

We made our way to the bar and felt incredibly carefree. We were out and ready to party. Out of the corner of my eyes I could see the impact we had on the crowd, then I saw him there in all his gorgeousness. White shirt, jeans and I'm sure he was wearing his trademark boots, just getting up from a table full of lads. He seemed to sway a little as he came over to us and was followed by a few lads behind him.

My girls were wide eyed and mouths were a little oh shaped, it was funny. 'Ladies,' he said, 'Welcome to the Whistler, you must be new to this place.' I had to laugh at him and my friends looked at me a little puzzled..

'Girls this is Xavier, Please,' I said to him. 'That was so cheesy. Are you drunk?' I laughed again, I had never seen Xavier drink anything more than a single drink.

The girls looked at him checking him out and raised their eyes at me, I blushed a little.

Xaviers friends appeared behind him and the girls were all smiles as their flirt mode kicked in.

'I'm glad you came,' he whispered to me with a distinct slur in his voice.

'Well Mr Marshall-King I do believe you are drunk, bad things happen to people when they are drunk,' I said with a more seductive voice than I had meant for it to be.

'Are you making a promise?' He said to me with a glint in his eye.

'Well you did leave me this morning so you really do owe me'. I said, trapping my bottom lip in between my teeth, so hungry for him right now.

'Fuck!' He said out loud and then kissed me hard in front of my friends. He left me breathless as he pulled away. He held onto my waist and looked me in the eye.

'I need you,' he said.

'I want you.' I said back.

I was rampant with desire, my bloody hormones making me crazily horny. 'Come with me,' He said, taking my hand in his and leading me out of the bar. 'Girls, I'll be back,' I yelled.

They seemed to be in good hands and I knew they could handle themselves very well.

We walked out back to a barn it was open Xavier seemed pleased at that and we went in. No sooner had he closed the door he pushed me up against it and kissed me hard pushing his way into my mouth with his tongue. I reached and raked my hands into his hair and pulled him in tighter to me.

What happened then was beyond my imagination. We fucked, Oh boy did we fuck. He behaved like this was his last moments with me, He took me quick, hard and with a raw abandonment that he had not shown before. To say this turned me on was an understatement. My body bent to his will, took everything he gave with its own lustful wants and when I for the second time, my body could not hold me up, but he did. Tight, possessive and reluctant to let me go.

'Xavier, we need to get back, my friends,' I said, bringing Xavier back to the here and now even though I knew he was drunk.

As he pulled out of me I gasped it was like being empty and lost. We got sorted and returned to the bar where my friends were waiting for me.

He kissed my hand as we walked back in, my friends were still at the bar with his friends all laughing and drinking.

Covert eyes darted towards us when we approached.

'All good bro?' Jasper said to Xavier and punched his arm. 'Shut it will ya,' he replied. I smiled at the exchange.

Xavier left us not long after, as they were all very drunk and I'm guessing they had other places to go.

I waved at him as he left and turned back to the girls. It was a great place and thankfully the girls didn't bring up my disappearance even though I looked like I had had sex.

We had a fabulous time and got home a little after one am, which was an early night for us usually, but with the music, the vibe and the drinking it was a good time to call it quits.

A few coffees later, some snacks and water we all headed off to bed, it was so good having them here and I was hoping that the weekend would last forever.

I was first up Saturday and got myself sorted and had breakfast. I had given Mrs Chester the weekend off, she didn't have to wait on everyone, even though she said she didn't mind and that having more people to fuss over would be a lovely

change. She did however prepare lots of yummy food for me to cook. She was an absolute peach and I loved her and her kindness.

I sat in the sunroom enjoying the warmth through the glass when I heard the stumbling of feet, along with a few groans and knew someone was up, it was almost eleven so it was a good time to be awake.

'Good morning pudding,' I said to Robin as she came into view. 'Uh oh my head,' she grumbled. Pushing sunglasses up her nose.

'Ahhh, that would be the alcohol consumption, my lovely,' I laughed at her. 'Yeah, no shit Sherlock,' she said. I, on the other hand, chuckled.

I got her some coffee and we went to the sunroom and she lay on the sofa enjoying the warmth too.

A little while later the other two surfaced and we all ended up in the sunroom just lazing around, this was perfect. My friends in my new place, just being us.

Time like these your friends were the rock you always wanted and needed and I loved them to bits.

The weekend was a collection of walks around the grounds, a few dips in the pool because the weather was great, more drinks and more food, oh some takeaway food as all of Mrs Chesters yummy food was consumed all tooquickly. I didn't want the weekend to end and neither did they so they stayed Sunday night as well, leaving early on Monday morning to go back into thecity.

We had some great times and the memories we made were priceless.

The week ahead was intense with work and I had a few messages from my Grandmother, asking to see me and inviting me to the estate for dinner.

I had put her off for like five weeks now so I said I would go, albeit rather reluctantly. She offered to send a car for me and I was in two minds to decline, but thought better of it as I wanted her to know I was now in my fathers old home. Petty I know.

I had messaged Xavier to say that my schedule was super busy this week and I would catch up with him when time allowed. I was hoping he would understand as life gets in the way with everything. He seemed ok and said he would speak to me at some point.

My grandmother and I had agreed to dinner on Thursday and at six pm the car pulled up outside and a lovely guy opened the door for me as I left the house.

'Thank you,' I said as I got in. 'My pleasure ma'am,' he said.

Ma'am, I thought, I'm still a bloody miss!

The ride was like three quarters of an hour away from me. I was a little thankful that it was a fair distance and that she wouldn't just turn up out of the blue, we didn't have that kind of relationship, so there was no point in thinking that far ahead.

The Whitmore Estate was far greater in size than I had ever thought, not that I had a vision about it. It must have been at least four or five times the size of mine and I wouldn't even dare to think how many acres of land there was with it.

We drove along a great road filled with lawns and trees. It was a good while before we pulled up outside the house. There was a butler waiting for the car to stop and he let me out.

'Thank you,' I said, stepping out onto the stone driveway. Yes it was a little intimidating.

'Mrs Whitmore will entertain you in the drawing room please follow me'. He said in a very posh voice. Maybe I should have worn the pearls, I thought sarcastically, really do people still live like it was the Victorian era. I looked pointedly down at my casual attire I had chosen to wear. Oh bollocks! Who cared, not me!

The entrance hall was vast, set in dark wood, marbled floors and a sweeping staircase. The butler or whoever he was led me through some double doors, into what I assumed to be the drawing room. This was a huge room too, it smelt of old leather and a hint of some other kind of aroma, I think disinfectant but whatever it was it was making me feel a little nauseous. But we didn't stop (thank goodness) and I was shown into a lovely light room filled with windows to let in the maximum of light. Decorated in muted tones of blue, it was a very feminine room, without the 'frillies'.

'Please take a seat, Mrs Whitmore won't keep you long.' He promptly left and closed the door.

I took a good look at my surroundings; it was like something out of those period films you watch, ladies with their empire lines and heaving breasts and the men in long coats and tight breeches. I giggled to myself.

True to his word my Grandmother came in a short while later followed by a maid with tea on a tray. I stood to acknowledge her.

'Set it down here please Rachel,' she said in a kind manner, the woman smiled toward her.

'Riley dear, I'm so glad you're here,' she said, moving to hug me.

'Hi, sorry it's taken a while. There have been things going on that needed settling before I do anything else,' I said trying to be calm and at ease.

'It's no trouble, it must be hard adapting to a new way of life,' she said as she poured the tea.

'I'm getting there,' I replied. 'Tea?'

'Yes please,' I seemed to like tea more in the evenings and so did the baby.

'So, I'm guessing you have some questions for me,' she got straight to the point.

'To be honest I am trying to put aside the why and what went on with my parents, but I will in time like for you to tell me how things were from your perspective, if that's ok. Just now, I am looking towards the future and more importantly my future.'

Pain crossed her eyes very briefly, she nodded and accepted at face value what I said. I smiled back as I drank the tea, she didn't press me anymore and the evening went very well.

We had dinner together and she talked about the house and gardens. She was particularly proud of her orchid house which she promised to show me on another visit. With dinner staying firmly in my tummy, it was looking like the evening was a big success.

'So,' I began. 'How did all this wealth get made?' I was genuinely curious. I was thankful for whoever had made and then maintained this vast empire enough for my father, and then me, to inherit.

She had then started to explain the generations back invested in land in the 1700s, oil, real estate and that it just grew. The businesses were part of a conglomerate, which would oversee and protect the Whitmore estate.

They also owned, or were involved in, quite a few developments all over the world.

Business had changed dramatically over the last 50 years, she said, more homes were required, and the companies were investing heavily in sustainability and ensuring they were environmentally friendly, future proofing she called it.

I was curious as to why my dad had stepped away from the family. I couldn't see anything untoward with my grandmother that would have made him stay away. When she was talking about the business I could tell there were huge chunks of information she had left out, possibly because they were areas my father had been involved in, but who knows, there was plenty of time to find out, I thought tiredly.

Shortly after, the evening came to an end and the car returned me home. I was thankful as I was so tired. Jammies on, sleep came easy that night. But that night the dreams began and interrupted the bliss I had been living in since leaving the city.

Dreams can feel real and this one wasn't a nice one. I dreamt I was on a boat, it was early evening and the sky was a stormy purple, the wind whipped my hair around my face and created huge rolling waves which pummelled the boat.

During a particularly violent lurch, I was thrown into the sea; the waves kept

crashing down on me, the undercurrent dragging me out into the deeper, darker water, away from shore, away from safety. The harder I tried to keep my head

349

above water and swim to shore the further it seemed. The feeling of loss overwhelmed me, and the futility of trying to reach the shore. I could feel myself giving into the cold and sinking into the depths, my lungs were bursting for air as I tried in vain to kick to the surface. The last of my air left my mouth, just a tiny bubble…

Sweat poured from my body as I jolted right up, reaching for the light. Tears had wet my pillow and were still on my cheeks. I drew in my breath and shuddered at how vivid my dream had been, my hand went to my tummy, touching my non-existent bump protectively.

Weeks passed in what can only be described as a blur. The dream returned intermittently, leaving me shaken and on edge. My initial euphoria and 'pregnancy bloom' had faded a little *and* I hadn't seen much of Xavier due to some issues with one of the stallions they sold earlier in the spring, who had decided he didn't like the mare he had been bought to cover. He didn't know when he was likely to return. He did call occasionally but Xavier was not a telephone guy, so they were very infrequent.

I went to my appointment with Dr Abrahams. He scanned me and I saw my child developing inside me, hands, legs, feet and nose the works. Wriggling around and making it difficult for him to do his measuring. It was a true miracle, to know I had a life inside me.

'So Riley, do you want to know what you're having?' he asked.

'I, I'm not sure, I do and I don't.' I was for the first time not really sure of anything after looking at my unborn child on the screen.

'I'll tell you what, I'll write it down and put it in an envelope and you can look at it when you are ready,' he said with a warm smile.

I left his office in a daze holding my growing belly, which was protruding nicely from my tight top I wore, just to show it off.

I went to a local cafe and had a hot chocolate as it was a special occasion. Looking at my scan picture again while waiting for my drink to cool down I couldn't help smiling, lost in my own world unaware of someone watching me.

'Only three and a half months to go baby and I will meet you face to face,' I whispered while holding my bump.

I messaged the girls and sent them the scan picture letting them know I was in the city and did they want to meet up before I went back.

They had been a constant in my life and came to visit as much as they could. 'Yes I'm free,' Robin said.

'Can't hun sorry I'm swamped,' Hannah said. 'Sorry Ry, meetings all day,' said Emma.

'So I guess it's just you and me then Robin,' I replied to the group chat. We met at a baby store and went shopping for some clothes and stuff. 'So what are you having?' Robin asked.

'I don't know,' I replied. ' I mean, the Doctor gave me this envelope - the answers inside,' I wafted the envelope under her nose. 'But I haven't opened it. I'm not sure I want to know, I'm nervous' I said.

She smiled at me and held my hand, I knew she wanted to know and in a way I did too.

We spent a few hours just looking around and I bought some neutral items. I kept feeling as though I was being watched. It was a strange feeling. It reminded me of my dream or should I say the nightmare. Protectively I placed my hand on my bump and frowned.

'Are you ok?' Robin asked, looking a little worried.

'Um yeah I think so, I just got a weird feeling you know, can't seem to shake it off.'

I kept looking behind me but it was pointless. There wasn't anyone following me, it was in my head for sure.

Later that night when I had taken myself to bed I decided I might spend a few weeks back at my apartment. It was coming up to my busy period at work and I could do with a little more human contact. I hadn't heard from Xavier either. It seemed a little weird, he had been away for so long and contact had dropped off to almost nothing and no mention of when he was going to come back.

I wanted to message him to ask, but I didn't want to be seen as needy.

The following week, I moved back into my apartment. It felt a little weird at first and if I'm honest it was also a little small, it takes a surprisingly short time to get used to a little luxury.

I had brought some shopping with me as I didn't have anyone to cook for me here. Mrs Chester was happy to reduce her duties for a little while. She was always amazing and I knew a little free time would be good for her and her husband.

A few weeks here would be good for me and bring me back down to earth where I really needed to be right now with my emotions all over the place.

Chapter 43

Jacob

My investigator gave me all the information I needed. All Riley's comings and goings, timetables, photos, names and vignettes of those she had met, along with photos of them too. For all it's content, she had actually done very little. Although, one piece of information brought a wide smile to my face, she was back in the city and back at her apartment! I behaved like a jerk and still couldn't believe I had actually emailed her that crap. My defence albeit somewhat pathetic was I wasn't clearly thinking straight and had lashed out, most likely through fear. The last thing I had expected with my time with Riley was a baby, my god I had only just got to the point of admitting to loving her, then I get hit with that. I mean any man in my position would have freaked! Shaking my head at my own train of thought, who was I kidding. I fucked up and fucked up big time and now I had to make amends. It had been a while since I saw her and I planned to accidentally bump into her this weekend. I knew I would have to pull out all the stops to get her to even talk to me.

Thursday morning, I knew she was at the office. I could have gone there and try to arrange a meeting with her but if it was anything like the last time, they will shield her. My man on the scene had watched her recently buying baby stuff with one of her friends. I smiled, warming to the fact she was carrying my child.

Thursday afternoon, she had a late lunch with what I'm assuming were clients. She stayed in the restaurant for a couple of hours and came out looking a little tired. She didn't see me as I approached her. She was hailing down a cab. When I was close enough and her frustration was clear I made her aware of my presence.

'Riley, hi.'

She turned towards me and her eyes were wide like a trapped kitten. She froze on the spot and then put a hand over her stomach. I immediately felt wretched, just thinking back to when I asked if she was going to get rid of it. I gestured with an open hand, as if silently telling her I meant no harm to her or the baby.

Our eyes met then and I could feel that powerful gravitational pull between us. That feeling I had lost, had not felt for so long, was there, invisibly binding us together.

'Jacob, what are you doing here?' She said softly.

'I was walking past, sorry I didn't mean to interrupt you, do you need some help with a cab, or I could drop you where you need to be if you like.' It was a kind of olive branch which would at least give me some idea whether she minded breathing the same air as me!

She seemed undecided whether to accept, but to my surprise and delight she agreed.'I um, ok that would be great.'

I pulled out my phone to call my driver, quickly before she changed her mind 'He's on his way,' I said, smiling at her.

She smiled back, but it was a little strained. She looked great but I could see she was tired around the eyes. I then wondered if she had moved on without me, and got herself a boyfriend. The dossier I had mentioned a man but not whether they were romantically involved. The silence between us started to grow a little uncomfortable, so I made a judgement call.

'Riley, I have so much I need, want to say to you right now. Could we, I don't know, go somewhere to talk. Please?' My voice held a pleading note but I didn't care.

'I'm not ready to discuss things yet Jacob, there has been too much hurt for me to even consider it. I think I should just get a cab, it's for the best.' She started to walk anyway.

'No Riley please, I won't pressure you, but I want to see you home safe.'

She looked at me in puzzlement and just a hint of disgust - no doubt due to my belated display of chivalry - but she never said a word, just nodded. My driver arrived and then we were making our way to her apartment building, it wasn't far so not really long enough for things to get too icy. I wanted to hold her hand, kiss her, hug her bump where my child growing inside her was. But my hands stayed firmly on my lap. Only touching her to help her out of the car.

I walked her to the security door and lingered for a while hoping she would invite me up. As she turned to walk through the doors, I grabbed her hand feeling the electricity pulse between us. It was so strong, I swear I saw blue sparks; she couldn't deny the feeling and her eyes lifted to meet mine, she looked at our hands then back at me.

'I *am* truly sorry Riley.' I said fervently. 'I know I have a lot to do to make up for what I said but I'm willing to do whatever it takes, just give me hope.'

I could see the tears well in her eyes. It broke me and I leaned into her and kissed her eyes and kissed away the tears that began to fall. She didn't move, just looked into my eyes, I hoped she could see the sincerity in them. She glimpsed at my mouth and this time I placed a gentle kiss on her soft pink mouth. I felt her relax and a small whimper escaped her and I immediately pulled away.

'I'm here when you're ready to talk,' I touched her cheek before turning and walking back down to the car. I was just about to get in when I heard her call to me.

'Jacob, I just, give me some time, yeah, I'm gonna be here, at the apartment for a while.' This time she smiled at me with a real Riley smile, and I smiled back.

I went home a little happier than I had been for a long while.

Friday morning and today was going to be a good day. Riley was at home this morning so I had a dozen red roses sent to her apartment. Cliched maybe, but Riley *loved* roses, that I knew for sure. I allowed myself a little hope to seep into my heart. Whatever the situation, Riley was back in my life and I wouldn't let her go.

It was lunchtime and I got an email from Riley thanking me for the flowers and that I shouldn't have. Yes, I fucking should I've been a bastard to her. I emailed her back telling her I was going to win her back no matter what and she should get used to the flowers, as I would send them every day.

The following day, I sent a hamper with some baby items in it. I didn't know what she was having. I mean what we were having, god that threw me again knowing that this was my baby too. She messaged me as soon as she received the hamper again thanking me. This time she left her number for me to text her which I did.

I'm glad you liked the hamper, Riley, I want to be there for you both I truly do. I hope we can find what we had.

J x

I need time Jacob, I'm far too emotional to deal with this all right now. Im sorry

Riley

I had to understand where she was coming from. I was being too intense. I left her be for the rest of the weekend and began my offensive again on Monday.

I sent her flowers and treats all week. I found myself shopping in baby shops, an incongruous picture, me suited and booted, handling booties smaller than my thumb! But there I was picking out items that I thought a baby would need, thankfully, the women in the shop were all very helpful, telling me what sizes to look at for each of the baby's stages.

I had settled on a few items that Riley could comfortably store in her apartment and then I had some items delivered to my apartment. I was hopeful that we could be together but I needed to be realistic just in case, so I had a few items in case I had the chance of an overnight visit.

My investigator messaged me on Friday to update me on the latest. He had looked closer into this man linked to Riley. Jealousy rose up inside me as I read his report, it stopped short of identifying any relationship. Was he her boyfriend though? Were they together? The report stated he had been away for a couple of months on business. I wondered whether that was why she had moved back to the city. I needed to get her to open up to me, she knew we still had that connection, surely I could get her to talk, and I had to do it sooner rather than later, before I lost her again.

I decided I needed to make the next move. I knew she was at home so I went to her apartment. I buzzed and after a few seconds she answered.

'Hey it's me, I was passing by and thought you might like to go for a walk or have a coffee or something.'

The door released and I went in, the ride to her floor felt like forever, but then I was outside her door, I hesitated before knocking, no idea why, maybe subconsciously I realised how much depended on this first proper meeting.

When she opened the door she looked breathtaking, even in comfy clothes; she was glowing.

'Hi,' I said.

'Hi back,' she replied with a smile. 'Come in.'

I walked into her apartment and was hit by the memories as I relived our time there. God, I felt so connected to her right then, why did I fucking ruin what there had been between us.

'Would you like a drink? she asked.

'Yeah sure, whatever you're having will be good.' She busied herself in the kitchen then called out. 'So just passing where you?' She came back into the main room carrying two mugs with a smile on her face. I had the grace to look sheepish.

She handed me a coffee, I took a sip wishing it was a whiskey or something alcoholic, I needed some dutch courage.

She was sitting on the arm of her sofa, swinging a leg and sipping from her mug. I started to say something then stopped, then started again but nothing came out. The atmosphere was beginning to thicken, but then she sat down next to me on the couch and I quietly relaxed. Her scent was as delicious as she was. I was instantly aroused by it and her nearness.

She looked at me and I looked at her. It was like we were having a conversation with just our eyes. It was our connection. I had never had this with any other

woman in my life. Right then I knew I had to make this right because I never wanted to be away from her again, ever. I placed my hand over hers and felt that all too familiar spark of electricity flow through us, she was home for me.

Very slowly I placed my other hand up to her face and gently caressed her cheek. She closed her eyes and leant into my touch. It was just a moment but it felt like a thousand years had passed between us in that one gesture.

'Riley, I have missed you so goddamn much and there isn't enough time in the world to begin to make up for my behaviour. But please let me try.'

She looked at me with her beautiful eyes and I felt lost in them, her eyes began to glass over as the tears forced their way out, I wiped them away with my thumb before caressing her lips.

'Jacob, I don't know what to say right now'.

'Don't say anything Riley you have done nothing wrong it's been me, I want to kiss you so badly. Can I?'

She looked at me with such vulnerability, I was expecting her to say no but she nodded and my lips met hers as my hands held her face.

She felt so fucking good like I was home right there with her like this. I deepened the kiss and her hands were now in my hair pulling into her. We kissed and held each other like we were teenagers in love.

My hands moved across her body to where our baby was growing. I placed my hands on either side of her waist and held them there. While she held onto me, kissing me like it was her last dying wish.

She pulled away breathless and looked down at my hands on her bump. When our eyes met it was me who had tears in their eyes. I wasn't ashamed of them, and let them fall, I wanted her forgiveness and if it meant me being equally vulnerable then I would give her that to her gladly. This time she wiped my tears away and held me. I wrapped my arms around her and we stayed like that for a while.

'Are you hungry, we should eat, don't you think?' I said releasing her from my arms.

'Yeah, I'm quite hungry, what would you like? I can cook something if you like.' She was so beautiful, I instinctively knew she would make a fantastic mother.

'Let me order, my treat.'

We settled on Thai, apparently, her tummy was sensitive to too much spice, but she said she could cope with the milder spice of Thai food. We sat together on the sofa and put the television on and for a short time it seemed like a normal relationship, just sitting, snuggling and being together. It got to about nine thirty and I thought I best get going. I didn't want to push it as I had now spent the whole day with her.

'I um gonna get going Riley, it's getting late.'

She looked at me with longing in her eyes, and I could easily have taken her up on the silent invitation, but it was too soon, even if she didn't recognise it herself, I knew.

'Yes, sorry I shouldn't have made you stay this long, I understand, thankyou for being here today.'

She was genuinely surprised I was going. 'I can always come back tomorrow if you like,' I said smiling.

'I would like that Jacob, really I would.'

I went home that night with so much hope in my heart, that little spark I had let in earlier was growing.

Chapter 44

Riley

Things with Jacob seemed to be going well. He was attentive, kind, generous, but except for a few kisses, he hadn't tried to go any further. In fact, it felt like he was deliberately avoiding any intimate contact, or conversation, with me now we were trying to build bridges. I started wondering if it was because of the pregnancy, that he didn't find me attractive anymore or was it something worse and he was only being friendly so he could be involved with the baby. I was also experiencing moments when I felt I was being watched, so my paranoia was in overdrive. I tried telling myself it was my hormones, but it didn't help panic settling in my mind. I was getting stressed, I could feel it. I had to try and relax for the baby's sake, this wasn't doing little bean any good at all.

Because of how things were going with Jacob, I had stayed longer in the city than I had initially planned, but I had to decide what I was going to do, or rather where I would be, by the time the birth came around - did I intend to stay around here and continue to see Jacob? Should I broach the subject of our 'relationship' with him, so I would know once and for all whether there was a future for us?

Panic and paranoia aside, in my heart I wanted to be with Jacob. He was the father of my child, our child, and wasn't it better for both parents to be together? My brain fogged over again, it was obviously just too much to think about and decide and my mind was trying to reduce the stress I was feeling. Sighing

I had been into the office and sorted some stuff with Mr Rogers about my shares and my position in the company if I ever chose to take it, I liked what I did there and it was easy for me I didn't want to rock the boat by putting my feet in another persons shoes, I had clout and that was all that was needed. The same feeling for the Sylvester Group wasn't the same. They continued to be nervous about me and my stake. With the help of Mr Quinn, I was well aware of what was going on and again how I stood if I wanted to, things with Jacob were good so I didn't feel threatened at all.

December came round all too quickly and I was just off for my last appointment with my doctor, I haven't messaged Jacob as I was used to going to these appointments on my own. I seemed to be on my own alot since I found out I was pregnant, even though my short term fling with Xavier went south it seemed he was staying out for at least a year as they needed him. I was happy for him and sad for me.

I decided when I came out for the appointment I would go and see Jacob at his office and give him the picture I had done of the baby. I wouldn't tell him what we were having as I didn't want to know, even though that little piece of paper was burning a hole in my purse.

It was a relatively short journey and I was glad of the fresh air. I approached his building along with other passers by when a black limo pulled up outside.

I stopped in my tracks when I saw Jacob get out, adjust his coat and then hold his hand out to the woman easing her way out of the limo, a woman! What the actual fuck. She stood in front of Jacob and placed her arms around his neck and kissed his cheek. It was then I saw the enormous engagement ring she was wearing.

My mind exploded in that second, he was fucking engaged, what! what is happening right now. I couldn't seem to think straight, my hand went to my bump and the tears fell. I felt as though all the air had been scuked out of my lungs and I staggered to the wall trying to keep myself from falling.

'Are you ok miss,?' a voice came from nowhere.

'I'm not sure, I think I need to sit down.' I was almost gasping for air.

The next thing I knew a chair was placed under me and I was being lowered carefully down.

'Um get some water please,' the voice said again.

A bottle of water was placed in my hand and for the first time, I was able to breathe.

'Thankyou' I called out.

I sat for about five minutes before I felt as though I could move.

At this point, there were a few people around me and I looked up to the person who had helped me. I was greeted by a smile from a lovely man. He had greying hair but such kind eyes.

'Thankyou for helping me,' I said.

'You are most welcome. How are you feeling do you need to go to the hospital?.' 'No, I'm good, I think.'

I smiled back and he helped me up to stand.

'How long do you have to go?' he gestured to my bump. 'Four weeks baby is due early January,' again I smiled. 'Right let's get you a cab, get you home.'

Small gestures meant the most to me. Before I left in my cab I took the man's details and I vowed to return the favour to him.

It took me two hours to pack up my stuff and call for a driver to take me back to my sanctuary. I was done, done with Jacob and his lying. Now I knew why he didn't want to be intimate with me; he just wanted me on his side for the baby. Well, fuck him this baby was mine and mine only.

We pulled up to the house at around four. It felt so calming as we rode the long road up to the front. Mrs Chester was waiting for me alongside her husband Mr Chester. As I walked up to them she opened her arms and hugged me so tight, the tears fell again I just wanted to be loved.

Mrs Chester knew I was low and made me comfort food. I sat in the sun room and ate while staring out at the gardens. This was my life now and I had to adjust to it properly. I didn't need a man to do well. I was rich and powerful if I wanted to be, and right now he has pissed off the wrong woman. When I was strong enough I would be back and I would fuck him over.

Messages came from Jacob asking where I was as he came to see me. Then there was the text messages:

what's up?
Then there was the are you ok?
Is the baby ok?

God, he was just pissing me off.

I replied back to him that I no longer wanted to have anything to do with him and his fiance. That he made me feel so fucking cheap as though he saw me as a mistress.

He called me straight away, I hesitated to answer the call, I just wanted to scream at him.

'What do you want Jacob,' I said in a curt tone.

'Where are you? I thought we were seeing each other today', he said, confused. 'Well let's see I thought I would come and surprise you today with a picture of our child. I stopped by your office and well let's just say, I now know the reason you didn't want to be intimate with me.'

'What do you mean you came by today I didn't see you'

'No you were preoccupied by the blond on your arm your fiance I should say. I couldn't help the venom tone in my words.

'Riley I don't know what you mean'.

'Cut the bullshit Jacob I saw you ok, I saw you, she kissed you and draped her arms around you, you are a fucking shit. Don't call me or try to contact me, we're done, ok we're done.' The tears rolled down my cheeks.

'Riley please listen it's not what you think she's not my fiance' 'I don't want to hear it Jacob, goodbye'.

I ended the call before he could say another word could come from his lying mouth.

I placed the phone on silent before I put it on the table, walked to the window and placed my hands on my baby bump. 'It's just you and me little bean you and me'. I whispered.

For the next two weeks, Jacob continued to text me explaining the woman wasn't his fiance and that she was a friend only. That she was his best friend's girl and that he had picked her up from the airport that morning and she was just happy to be there.

I couldn't believe him, it was just too convenient for him to say that to me. I didn't reply, there were no words I could reply to.

I then realised that I wasn't in love with him even though I thought I was how could I love a man that did this to me, lust it was just lust and the love thing well I had a baby coming that was my love. Or did I really love him and felt betrayed?God I wasn't making sense. The only thing that made sense right now was my unborn child.

I'd been having braxton hicks for a while now but nothing indicating an early birth which I thought was good as I still had at least two weeks to go. A hot bath would do the trick, I thought.

My Christmas in my new home with my new family and a baby imminent, I had just finished wrapping my friends gifts and put them under the tree ready.

I held my bump through my pyjamas and gazed at the tree.

'Mum, dad I am going to be having your first grandchild any time soon. I love you guys so much and wish you were here with me. I hope I make you proud.' Baby must have heard as my tummy went so hard I had to hold onto the side for stability.

Fuck, shit! I groaned.

Wow, that was intense as it subsided, 'ok baby I was just saying ok'. I rubbed my tummy hoping that would help to calm the pea down.

I left the lounge and went to go upstairs when it hit me again, fuck! I held the banister this time as the pain ripped through me.

Shit, oh no shit. I curse so loudly when things aren't right.

'MRS CHESTER,' I called out, fuck this was not right. Then I felt it, warm fluid running down my leg.

'Oh no, I called out, baby is coming, holy shit baby is coming, this time the pain was worse. I fell to my knees holding onto the stairs as the pain again ripped through me'.

Mrs Chester came running and immediately froze. 'oh no it's too early.' She seemed somewhat dazed.

'I don't know what to do Mrs Chester, it hurts, it really hurts.'

'Ok, Jeffrey,' she called out, 'Phone for an ambulance. We need to get to the hospital now.'

The next twenty minutes were hell, contraction after contraction came. We were too far away from the hospital and I knew the baby was coming.

Mrs Chester moved me to the lounge and Mr Chester got blankets and stuff to make me comfortable I'm sure.

He made a makeshift bed on the floor and I was reluctant at first to get down there but really I had no choice.

By the time the ambulance arrived I wanted to push. After a quick check they looked at each other and agreed that the baby was coming and that I would be delivering very soon. Radios were going, conversations were had while I was sucking on the gas and air, it felt good to have something to ease the pain.

Shit, this was painful beyond my wildest dreams.

December the 24th at 2:30am baby Amelia-Jade Whitmore was born, she weighed in at 6lb 3oz and was beautiful, she had jet black hair and eyes like her dad. She was perfect.

We were wrapped up and then travelled to the hospital Mr & Mrs Chester followed us in their truck. It was a long journey but made all the more better by holding my baby daughter in my arms.

I was on a cloud and never wanted to come down. I was a freaking mother, I had to make sure my cursing wasn't as frequent as before.

A journey had begun tonight, a journey with my daughter just the two of us.

Chapter 45

Jacob

Things between Riley and myself had been going great until she completely misread something she had seen and went off at the deep end. That woman was so frustrating! If I could have got hold of her at that moment she called me a fucking liar, I think I would have strangled her!

I had got a call to collect my best friend's girl from the airport the day I was going to see Riley, he was caught up in a meeting and couldn't get away. It was no biggy for me, I had time to kill before meeting up with Riley and I knew my pals fiancee. She was a bubbly character, very tactile and friendly. She was always hugging people. That's just what she did! It wasn't something I was particularly comfortable with, but when I dropped her off at her little office after collecting her from the airport, that's exactly what she did, and gave me a kiss on the lips too. I felt completely weird about it and pulled quickly away trying not to offend her. It then completely vanished from my mind as a non occurrence and I droveoff.

Riley wasn't at home when I turned up later. I sent her a text, then another and another. I banged on the door and shouted at the door, but nothing, no answer to my knocking and no answer to my texts. I called her then, and got hit by her verbal onslaught. It was quick, venomous and final.

'I don't want to hear it Jacob, goodbye.'

She had refused to listen to anything I said, once I remembered what it was she was referring to. She just hung up and I was left standing there, looking at my phone bemused.

The first thing I did when I had calmed down was to find out her address in the country; this madness had to stop now. I wanted her and I wanted our child, she must know that really. She was, is, my everything and I need to make sure I let her know before that crazy mind of hers started thinking in overdrive. I was a dick before, I admitted, but I wasn't about to make the same mistake again.

I had had the address for the last two weeks but despite my best intentions I had done nothing to follow up. I had hoped Riley would have come to her senses and called me back, telling me she trusted me and believed me. But no, nothing. So I kicked myself up the arse and got to work. I had decided to write a letter to her, rather than try and say the words, to tell her how much she meant to me and what my hopes and dreams were for the future. I had bought her a christmas gift and a small one for the baby even though it isn't due until early January. I wanted to beg her forgiveness. I wanted…

I exited my building on the morning of the 24th December. It was fresh out but the sun shone. I breathed and watched my breath as my exhale caught the frigid air. My phone beeped in my pocket and I pulled it out, unknown number, it said.

'Hello? Sylvester here.' I went from nonchalant to full on panic in a microsecond.

'What happened? Where is she? Is she ok? Ok. Yes. Yes, I'm leaving immediately, thanks.'

Shit, Riley had gone into labour last night and gave birth this morning, fuck I needed to get there to see her and fast.

The walk to the maternity unit was interminable, with each step my nerves stretched to almost breaking point. I was a dad, I had a baby. I could feel the tears welling in my eyes, my hands shook, my body numb.

I stood outside Rileys door for a few minutes trying to gather the courage to go inside. I was scared, really scared for the first time in my life. This was bigger and scarier than being the CEO of a company, and had so much more responsibility attached to it. I took a deep breath, I'm a dad now, I can do this!

I gently tapped the door and turned the handle to go inside. As my eyes scanned the room, Riley was sleeping, a t-shirt emblazoned with 'Just the two of us' covering her ample bosom and there just the other side of the bed, in touching

distance of Riley's hand, lay our baby. I closed the door gently and walked over to meet my child. It was a little girl. She was swaddled in a soft pink blanket and wore a pink bonnet. She was beautiful, like her mother and from what I could see poking out of her bonnet a tuft of black hair, just like me. I was mesmerised by her at once. I reached into the crib and lifted my daughter and held her in my arms. She smelt so good, I kissed her forehead and just gazed down at her in wonder. Then my eyes blurred and the tears fell. I sat with her for a while and was in a little bubble of my own making, just the two of us. I wasn't aware that we were being watched.

'Hi,' a soft voice pulled me from my thoughts.

I looked up to Rileys face with the biggest smile on mine. I wasn't sure if she was going to shout at me, so I stayed quiet and just stared at her.

'She's just like you,' Riley said with tears in her eyes.

'No, she is just like you, beautiful' I replied. 'Have you named her yet?' She half smiled at me, as she told me her name 'Amelia-Jade'

'That's a great name, Amelia was my grandmothers name', I told her 'Jacob -'

'Riley please listen. With all that I hold dear you got this all wrong. I am and will always be yours. Everything that is important to me is in this room and I will never do anything ever to jeopardise that, please believe me.'

I reached out my hand to hold hers and she never pulled it away. It was a sign that maybe this would work out, we could do this for us and Amelia.

'Riley, I want her to be a Sylvester.' I said holding her hand and giving it a little squeeze. I asked and didn't demand.

'Jacob, she is your daughter. I won't deny you this, even if we aren't together, I would never come between you and our daughter.'

'I love you, Riley. I really do. I will do whatever it takes to win you back and for us to have a future, together, as a family.'

The tears flowed from her eyes.

Life was going to be complicated, however right now, at this moment, this is all that I wanted and needed.

⚜

Chapter 46

Epilogue
6 months later

Riley

The last six months have been a roller coaster of emotions, being a mother to the most beautiful little girl I could ever have imagined and getting to know her father all over again.

My home was now in the country and I loved the seasons changing from one to the other, as I watched my daughter flourish. I was blissfully happy, Jacob and I were not together as a couple, but we were kinda dating and that for the time being, was great. We walked together and held hands and we kissed a lot, the touch of his lips on mine stirring up those early feelings of when we first met and sent the most electrifying pulse through me.

I had to admit it, I wanted him so badly, but he was doing everything he could to prevent our new relationship from crumbling. In the early days after Amelia's birth, remaining chaste was easy enough but now as the memory of her birth began to fade and my body healed, it was getting harder keeping my libido in check.

My Grandmother had even come to visit and held her great-granddaughter. She was smitten with her at first sight and has visited as often as her schedule allowed. Jacob's mum and dad were born to be grandparents and completely doted on her. Bethany too had taken to visiting and taking Amelia out for walks around the grounds. And my girls, well, who would have thought that my crazy, potty-mouthed, clubbers would become the biggest softees when faced with a chubby-cheeked baby, until of course, she started crying and then they ran for the hills. I smiled inwardly, these wonderful people meant the world to me, they were my family. I never realised how much family meant to me but I hugged myself, knowing how lucky I was that I had them.

Mrs Chester was my main source of support; she was a mother and nanna figure rolled into one much loved lady. I always referred to her as Nanna

Tonight, Jacob had organised a meal out for us and I was getting dressed up for it. It had been the first time we had left Amelia for any longer than it takes to walk around the gardens, but I was ok with it, Mrs Chester had it covered. I told Jacob it would be better for him to stay here, instead of driving back to the city, he agreed with alacrity. He was aware this was a huge step and for me, the butterflies began to tumble around my insides at the thought of being alone with him.

At 7pm he arrived in a limo and I was coming down the stairs to meet him when I caught him holding Amelia in his arms. He looked so handsome and was everything I had hoped for in a father. He smiled at me with his megawatt smile and my insides flipped over, god I just wanted to have him right here in front of everyone.

'You look breathtaking Riley,' he said, gazing over my body. The baby had caused a lot of change in my body, my breasts fuller, hips wider, but Jacob's slow perusal of it, filled me with confidence; he still wanted me, his face said.

'Thanks, you look very handsome yourself, I blushed trying out a seductive tone. I was so out of practice.

He kissed my lips as Amelia tried to grab at me laughing. I caught our reflection in the mirror over the fireplace. It showed a happy, beautiful family, the backdrop of the Christmas tree and the twinkling lights, giving us an ethereal glow; it was a serene moment. I would cherish the picture forever in my heart.

Jacob took me back to the restaurant we first went to when I discovered I had a Grandmother. Those memories seemed so long ago. The questions as to why I was hidden away from her for so long and the stories about her being 'evil' still lay there unanswered but she had never given me cause to distrust her, maybe it was my parents who were the ones who were the evil ones? Whatever the story was, it was not uppermost in my thoughts at present, I would get to it eventually, I told myself.

We ate steak, no points for guessing that, and we drank fine wine. We laughed as we told each other stories, staying away from anything slightly contentious but silent mutual agreement. It was a lovely, relaxed evening, until we made our way to the car. My insides started churning with the anticipation we might actually have sex tonight, just the thought of it got me wet. I remembered back to the times he touched me and took me to sexual heights I had never experienced before. With Xavier, it had been raw, lustful sex, but my heart had been in no danger of being hurt but Jacob was different, my feelings had been involved. My heart, as before, was in danger of being hurt. As each day passed those feelings deepened and I was already halfway in love with him.

The Wine had gone to my head a little and I randomly started to giggle. Jacob looked at me puzzled.

'What's so funny Riley?'

'Oh I was just thinking, sorry I got lost in my thoughts.' I looked at him through my lashes.

'Well, now you need to spill.'

'Well I was thinking back to all the times well, you know, we had sex. We did some crazy shit.' I was laughing now.

He eyed me seductively, liking the train of my thoughts. His expression was lustful; he was a man in need of sexual release.

'Shall we go then and remind you of all the ways we fucked'. He said seductively and got the waiter's attention to pay the bill.

I almost choked, but I was now ravenous for something completely different than food.

The ride back to my place was fueled by touching and kissing, his hand stroking along my thigh sending shivers through my body and electric shocks straight to my core. He kissed my neck and jawline, soft breathy kisses which had me moaning. He lifted his head and looked deep into my eyes, looking for something, I don't know what. The alcohol mixed with the weight of my desire for him was palpable and I was fast losing control.

His lips returned to mine crushing them with his, his tongue sliding across my lips until I opened my mouth and gave him access, which he took full advantage of. His hands moved to either side of my hips and he lifted me across his lap, my knees either side of his hips. I could feel his erection pressing urgently against my core and I ground down into his cock. I had not been touched by Jacob for so long. I writhed against him, desperate to feel the quickening of my clit again.

Oh my how I missed this!

I felt him shift and his hand moved along to the front of my lacy thong, shit! The nerves and butterflies and heat were all whirling like a tornado in my head.

'Fuck, I want you so bad Riley,'

His words were my undoing, I wanted him too. The next thing I felt his fingers trailed over my hot, wet clit down to my opening. He teased along the line of my panties, whipping me up to a frenzy of need, before pulling back and trailing those same fingers over the insides of my thighs. I was so fucking wet for him.

'Fuck Riley your so ready for me. I want you now, right now.' He groaned into my mouth as he crushed my lips again.

He sank his finger deep inside me, making me gasp. It felt like heaven! It was so fucking good, his fingers skillfully found my sweet spot and my body remembered! I could feel my climax building inside of me. My eyes closed concentrating on his ministrations, fingers inside me and his thumb brushing my clit and god I didn't want him to stop.

Thankfully the glass panel between us and the driver was up and blacked out. To be honest right now I wouldn't have worried at all. As I reached my climax I called his name; he rocked my world and my body shook as wave after wave of a delicious, mind blowing orgasm took me over.

Wasting no time he unbuckled his pants, whilst I sorted his shirt dragging it off over his head as my hands shook so much I couldn't manage the buttons. I raised myself slightly as he pulled his boxers down, his magnificent cock standing proud just waiting for me to sit on top. I almost had forgotten how big he was and how good it felt inside me. Guiding his tip to my entrance I lowered myself down on him, making his breath catch in his throat; a deep groan escaped him as I went down to his hilt. Fuck he felt so good! I took a moment to get used to him inside me - we stared at each other, not moving, just letting the moment take us. His eyes shone like the diamonds I knew and I could have sworn he had tears in his eyes. I had remembered that very first night when I bumped into him, all those months ago and now we had a daughter. Life! 18 months ago I wouldnever envision myself like this. I brushed my hand lovingly over Jacob's head, then threaded my finger through his thick hair, I tugged his head back and kissed him with all the passion I felt for him. His hands traced lines up my thighs and grabbed hold of my hips and then he started to buck his hips up, pounding into me and I gladly met him thrust for thrust.

His lips did not leave mine as both of us felt our orgasm rise. 'Don't come til I tell you to.' He leant me back slightly so his cocked hit my sweet spot, he removed his hand from my hip and his fingers found my nub and he rubbed until I could barely breathe.

'Pleeeease,' I begged him. My knees shook, I was so near to climax. I rode him harder, he too was near. It was the best feeling.

'Come now!' he demanded, and I did. My body jerked then shuddered and I let out an earth shattering scream; I could feel him spilling into me as his face contorted into that pleasure/pain look. I was fucked!

I had bit into his shoulder so as not to alert the driver we were making out in the back seat, thankfully his jacket had padding, otherwise, he would have had a bruise there for sure. This was what I missed so much. The intimacy between us, his touch, his smell.

After adjusting our clothing he drew me onto his lap and held me, until we got home. His hold make me feel protected….and loved.

We entered the house and went straight to my room. I knew Amelia was taken care of, Mrs Chester was the best.

We stood in my room close to each other just staring into each other's eyes. Questions swirled around in their depths, both of us wanting answers but neither prepared at this moment to say anything out loud. It was intense. I made the first move by removing my dress to reveal my lace underwear, his eyes roamed possessively over my body. He removed his jacket and shirt revealing his muscular physique, which was just as I remembered. I reached out and touched him ever so gently, trailing my fingertips across his chest, then down towards his waistband of his trousers.

I made easy work of them and he stepped out leaving him in his boxers which showed that he was more than ready for round two. Hunger and desire flickered in his eyes. My bra dropped to the floor, he removed his shorts to reveal his length, oh my how I wanted this man!

His hands trailed the outside of my thighs up towards my panties which he looped them with his thumb before drawing them down to the floor. I stepped out of them as his mouth went to my sex, I groaned in pleasure as his tongue licked over my sensitive clit.

We moved to the bed and he made love to me, taking me over the edge time and time again. We took our time getting to know each other again. I don't know what the reason was, whether it was the amount of time that had passed, or the fact we had a baby together strengthening our emotional connection, but this was the best night of my life. With our bodies spent, we lay in bed, holding each other. I rested my head on his chest and he stroked my hair. Shifting slightly to look into his face, I whispered the words I had been scared to say and he had been dying to hear.

'I love you, Jacob.'

I fell to sleep moments later with a smile on my face. This was my happy life forever.

I drifted awake from my sleep by a persistent beeping. It sounded like it was far away, I tried shaking my head to clear it; it felt woollie, the thoughts in my head unclear.

I slowly opened my eyes and tried to adjust to my surroundings, expecting to see my bedroom and Jacob beside me, but instead, the room was small, white and sterile and I was on a hospital bed.

'Well good morning to you lovely,' a voice said gently, she had got up from a chair and pressed a button at the end of a lead.

'Um, good morning,' was my reply. I tried to search my memory to determine why I was in the hospital. I could barely raise myself from the bed. I was as weak as a kitten. Confused, I asked the woman what was wrong with me. She said for me to wait just a moment and then disappeared from the room.

I was left alone looking around to see where I was. I touched my arms and tried moving my legs again. It was a struggle, but they moved a little. I felt exhausted and lay back down on my pillow.

The door to my room opened and a man in a white coat came in with a big smile on his face. He had a handsome face and friendly eyes. He came close to me and sat on the side of my bed. Taking a penlight from his top pocket he looked into my eyes, then hmphed, with a satisfied gesture.

'So young lady, welcome back, I'm Dr Matthew Grayson,' he began. 'We've been wondering when you would wake up, we have been waiting for this day for a long time. Are you able to answer some questions for me?'

He looked at me with gentle eyes and a quizzical lift of a brow. 'I, um, I can try,' I said, still unaware of what was going on. 'So can you tell me your name?''

'My name is Riley Shure. No Whitmore.'I said matter of factly.

'And what year is it?' I looked at him strangely and told him. He had taken my hand and patted it. 'Good, good.' He said.

'Ok, so can you tell me about yourself?'

'I have a daughter, omg where is she? Who has her?' Again I tried to raise myself up but it was just too exhausting.

'It's ok, just relax, it's going to be alright,' he squeezed my hand and I felt a warmth go through me. I calmed down and tried slowing my breathing down.

'So what I'm about to tell you is going to be a little strange for you to understand, but just know that we are here for you, no matter what.

My eyes were huge pools, tears threatened and a sense of dread filled my being. I was scared.

'You have been here for nearly four years, asleep, in a coma. You had no ID on you, when you were brought in and despite attempts, the police have been unable to locate your family - if in fact, you have any.' Each word was delivered in his deep baritone voice; every word felt like they were being delivered with a sledge hammer.

'Clinically,' he continued. 'There is nothing wrong with you, we just could not wake you up. Nurse Rosa has been reading to you for the last 18 months or so, there are reports that reading to coma patients can help stimulate their brain, bringing them around. It's possible that it has worked, she finished the book she had been reading this morning and look, here you are.'

He smiled at me again and I was numb with shock. There were no words I could say right now, no words at all. Was my life with Jacob and Amelia just a dream? Had I dreamt my whole existence?

I closed my eyes, confusion and fear clouded my already fogged mind. I tried willing myself back into Jacob's arms. This was all just a silly joke, telling myself when I opened my eyes, Jacob would be lying there next to me and all would be well. But when I finally did open my eyes, there was no Jacob, just the smiling face of Dr Grayson.

'So what was the book the nurse read to me then?' I asked.

'An adult romance I believe, I really didn't think it would work but I was willing to give anything a go. Nurse Rosa said it didn't matter what book she read to you it was a form of communication on a subconscious level. She read a few books over the past few years but this one you became responsive to - particularly recently - so she carried on.'

'So my name isn't Riley then?'

'We don't know your name. We were hoping that you knew it but as you show signs of a type of retrograde amnesia, this is where you are unable to recall past memories. We will undertake more tests as it is still early days, so give yourself time. As you can recall details from the book we know you are able to form new memories which is a good sign but, we have no starting point at the moment.'

He scribbled some more notes onto the paperwork attached to a clipboard the nurse gave him, then he placed it onto the chair next to the bed. He turned his attention back to me again and smiled, he reached down to my hand and held it with both this time and that warm feeling spread through my hand and up my arm. My eyes met his and I smiled for the first time since I awoke.

'I will help you to remember, ok, I promise.'
'Thankyou, Dr Grayson'

'Matthew please, call me Matthew.' His smile broadened.

'I'll leave you for now and we'll get some food organised for you and some fluids. I'll also arrange for the physical therapist to visit, so we can start your exercise therapy.'

I nodded and clasped my hands together. I felt so tired and weak and all of a sudden lonely.

Who am I and what the fuck happened to me?

That question swirled around my head as sleep took me and it was dark again…..

Note from the Author

What is going on in her mind right now is anyone's guess, a lie all along.

A world, a life taken from you and fed back in the form of a story, however, some stories are real and our story isn't over just yet.

Will she ever recover who she is for real, will the truth finally reveal itself?

Will the skeletons come out from the closet and will she finally find love that is lost?

Find out in unravelled.

Thankyou for reading. I hope you enjoyed it as much as I did writing it.

Until next time

Xxx

To Caz thank you for all you have done to support this book. You have been so helpful with your guidance and time spent on it.

About the Author

I am a 47-year-old contemporary romance author living in Buckinghamshire with my husband, two children and my beloved border collies.

I started writing short stories from a very young age but it took many years and quite a few false starts before I finished my first book, Too Good To Be True.

It has been a long road too but one I have learnt so much from. It taught me to bring my characters to life by developing their personalities, their backgrounds, this in turn saw my writing style emerge.

I spend many days getting involved with the plots of my characters and their stories; they inspire me to write.

I hope you enjoyed the book as much as I enjoyed writing it and become engrossed in each of their stories as their lives unfold.

With Love
Patricia Jelbert